'S'

Also by John Fraser
and published by
AESOP Modern Fiction:

'S'

John Fraser

AESOP Modern Fiction
Oxford

AESOP Modern Fiction
An imprint of AESOP Publications
Martin Noble Editorial / AESOP
28 Abberbury Road, Oxford OX4 4ES, UK
www.aesopbooks.com

First paperback edition published by AESOP Publications
Copyright (c) 2018 John Fraser

www.johnfraserfiction.com

A catalogue record of this book is
available from the British Library.

First paperback edition 2018

ISBN: 978-1-910301-47-0

Printed and bound in Great Britain by
Lightning Source UK Ltd,
Chapter House, Pitfield, Kiln Farm,
Milton Keynes MK11 3LW

CONTENTS

1

'S'

'I HAD WAITED all my life to visit the town of S, where my parents had abandoned me. There were no cobbled streets, no church, no mosque. Nothing I'd imagined. A half-track loaded with cabbages came smoking up the street, and that was all the movement ... low houses without stucco, an open lockup full of rusty fruit machines.'

'I know those places – there's always people looking out, that you can't see.'

'The name had changed. It had no mayor, no governor – it was swallowed by an abandoned larger city, in a district with a new name, new people.'

'They'd have to do that.'

'Young kids like me – they wanted us so young we'd have no memory, and grow up grateful, swallowed in a new society. We were given refuge, but we'd always look like aliens. And I wandered, naturally. We were invisibly badged. Everyone knew we were under surveillance, watched to see if we had caught the sickness, the vendetta. The killing urge.'

Nothing more to say. A life history set out, a leitmotif, at least.

*

The two naked men stare at each other – the tribal penises, the guts – not unalike, despite the different dietary rules. Some laid down by God, and others by the doctors. The sweat bath – the only place in this big city males can be unclothed together and not gay. It's effortful.

It would be easy, thinks the younger man – an outstretched hand, offhand – a tweak, a twiddle – it would be a lark. The kraken wakes, the member stirs... Death in this world, punishment for ever in the ones to come. What a joke! What fun! And yet – the older guy ... nearer to extinction: the appetite is lacking – the skin – a pale, pale omelette, bread pudding colour, those crumbly bakelite buttons of oxidised fat on chest and neck, the muslin bags of borrowed suet underneath the arms...

The older guy, his friend, acquaintance, says, 'It's better to forget, forget about it all. I'd hoped to get a post with Marvel comics. Deadpool – it fell through. Like you.'

'We were babies, Claude,' the young guy says. 'It was a war that everyone joined in.'

'At that age, Gary,' Claude says, 'you have no memories.'

Claude examines him. 'You're not appetising, Gary: my dear,' he says. 'You're spavined. A broken umbrella. You can see your wiring, the blues ascending, reds descend. Your last two shaky legs! The final stretch! We could get drunk, Gary. See how sallow you've become – face tight as a shaman's drum...'

'Wanting to be drunk – that lasts,' says Gary, 'But being it – does not.'

They turn towards their different paths. 'Are you colours or outlines, Claude?' asks Gary.

'I buy space. It wasn't needed,' says Claude, tartly. 'That business – it used to be fun, grotesques. Then it was magic and shooting. Making fairs of it, and sects.'

'Desire! Art is desire – desire is empty, Claude,' Gary shouts after him. 'You wanted to join a team ... there's nothing there, no one at all. Best to be me – thin and faithless ... people don't attach, it's better so...' Claude doesn't hear him, maybe it's better so.

*

'I don't have a biography, Nadine,' says Gary. 'It's all scenery around.'

'Don't fool about,' Nadine says. 'I don't care about you, Gary – it's you in the pack, the clan – you and your peers. Ideal types – now, those are interesting.'

'People don't come from anywhere,' says Gary. 'All that matters is what you're given, after the start. Then, what you take.'

'A random past?' asks Nadine. 'Taking whatever from something that might please?'

'It doesn't please,' says Gary. 'The sacred books, the holy rules – it's threats and promises. I can't be bothered with all that. If I was back where I was taken from, I'd have the fears and hostility built in. That's the faith. Outside – you make your list yourself, of where you stand, what side. The rules are yours – you're free, you're watched.'

Nadine taps it all down.

'You plan to make a career, spread light with all these webs and shadows?' Gary asks.

'People relax,' says Nadine. 'Then they want to hear about guys like you. What are you, Gary?'

'I'm a drunk,' says Gary.

'For the money?' Nadine asks.

'I send acts all over, all over the world. Bands, dancers, speakers. I watch them in the clubs. They pay me to send them off,' Gary says.

'You make it sound crooked,' Nadine says, digiting it all.

'No, Nadine,' says Gary. 'You don't get paid for being bent. They love me. I fulfil them. They get cash, and throw it all away. I give out praise. They must keep on – or someone else will steal their thing...'

The town of 'S'. The grey-green mosque, pegged out like a turtle in the sand. 'Worth the visit', says the old book.

'I send acts everywhere,' Gary goes on. 'When there's peace – there's my group; and people waving arms, dancing in sheds, believing they are weightless, free, thistle-down, blowing to the flattened sea.'

'There's war, and then there's postwar,' Nadine says: 'If there was peace, they wouldn't need an agent.'

'I must have come from somewhere,' Gary says. 'Most everybody does. It's a literary thing. You get the script – then, it's up to you: – to sing the songs, wear the masks, avenge your sister... Or you can drift. Drift's best.' He thinks of Claude. 'I sell space,' says Gary.

'You seem quite full of it,' Nadine says.

'Oh, we're all packed full,' says Gary. 'Our inside's all insides. Space is inexhaustible. You've got things wrong.'

'We could lie together on the bed,' says Nadine, 'and see what we believe.'

*

'*Turkey? Syria?*' *Gary says.* '*There's peaceful bits all over. Just watch yourselves. They're crazy for your classic stuff. Pick up a drummer when you're there. Run if threatened.*'

'*There's my woman – she does readings too,*' *says Phil, who sings.* '*Balzac. The human condition – you must keep it short, it calms them down...*'

'Ah – if you had seen my year, my month, my day,' says Gary. 'You'd know all you'd want to know, all anybody knows, about the species. Keep it all short, you're right.'

*

'Enough!' says Gary. 'Nadine – this music, the clang and bash! Music! The greats! It makes a sound like war, the fight: parades and drill. Well-tempered, it starts off – yes; it's fencing, and the duel. Gents with their lead balls, arithmetic ballistic. It swells and swells – there's peasants with scythes and hammers, piping up their courage, *a cappella* in the pub. Then – there's cavalry, moustaches, boasting: guys in white trousers, drawn up in squares like toffee. With Wagner – you listen in ... the chatter of the generals. Then comes the artillery, the bombs – deserters, cowards woken at first light, guts ripped out and laughing gas. Guys in flat caps, wooden rifles, tramping lopfooted to the front with Mahler. When that's done – listen to the beat! – "I love you", pissing on the floor, yumyum, taste that pistol in your rusted mouth ... beat out the rhythm on those black skins, those hollow femors tock out more resonance than boxwood – louder and louder – every note scraps for itself...

'It's not for me, Nadine. You know – that serpent: there was no apple. There was a picture – a caricature, a fruit-face in the likeness of a god. There was no hiss, no word, no warning light. Just an image, made in another image. Listen to the lady, try your luck! Where is the lucky bean, my friend, where's the right shell, the third card, righteous king, loving queen – where's the good life hidden, where the bad? You innocent! The snake – he came out of a tube of paint, his bright greasy coils, and tumbled on a canvas orchard – in his hand, a fruit, a chubby red-cheeked apple, a still life. That's what everybody wants. Stillness and life. Ah – the silence of paint, the blessed silence of the painter.

Up on his ladder, paints the ceiling – heaven without snakes. Everybody's framed – all guilty, ignorant of what. Those galleries, shelves stacked with inedible stuff, the naked saints, desirable epiphanies – the functionary asleep, all night there's quiet, and then the kids come, hushed into a burble... "Oh look at her, the painted hussy – I want her"... "The gods a-gambol ... fucking each other, then they come down and do the same to us...'"

'The evil, Nadine – it needs silence. It's my birth fluid, I have swum in it ... all my life, the dead photographs, the stills of skeletons scrabbling at the wire, the charcoal cities, the etchings with the padlocked mouths. Quiet! Not a squeak. It's over, everything just happened. That is my element, Nadine – not the noisy types, jumping around like Cerberus, barking. Enough of music, and her sister muses – the actors shouting, readers pausing for effect, and then they trill, they shriek like elephants, a trumpeting glissando... Those concerts – the people, narcissus in a flowerbed, the applause ... it's folly, Nadine, explosions, forts bombarded, love letters lanced, transfixed and penetrated... courage and sacrifice, suffering with a grin – I hate it, Nadine. Bring me my evil, silent let it be; my slug, voiceless, poison, my miniature reptile, personal to me, curled on a leaf of arsenic green: let me not see the plane too high to make its sound – and then the rays, behold the light, the radiation – not a whisper ... ghosts fossilised upon the tarmac...'

'It isn't so, Gary,' says Nadine. 'You're offered a fruit – eat it, or not. There's good in abstinence.'

'There is no choice,' says Gary. 'The story requires there's also good. It isn't so. You're hungry, so you eat. Or else you die. Quiet or noisy – that's the choice. Not guys with guns and coloured hats – not stumbling over furrows, into mines, and into trenches... You've done that. Follow the story! You must do what comes next: I mean the storming of the walls ... nine metres

tall and razor wire – no weapons, but you shout, someone to
heave you up, and when you fall down the other side – you've
won, you shout some more ... and then the battle starts again, but
you've no officers behind, no baggage train, no war chest, no
war bonds – just bondage round your hands and feet, hooked up
on the wire – and over, over again, drop down and down, into
the paradise... Then, make war to escape the war, a very civil
war, with regular hours, a pension at the end... A permit to work,
maybe, a passport so's you can return to where you were not
born...'

*

'That Gary,' Nadine says, 'You might think he's just a slob.
Escaped to make you pity him...'

'Oh no, Nadine,' Chloe says – her friend – 'I'm sure he's
ardent when it counts.'

'I study him, of course,' Nadine says. 'His story's fluid –
sometimes he was adopted, sometimes he just ran – an *ado*,
escaping military service, fleeing devastation – a jackal, thief, a
hitman – maybe everything's involved in him... Or just like us,
he's following the cash, and making it a story when it doesn't
fruit and multiply...'

'He rants,' says Chloe, 'but it's all conventional, I'm sure.
And, dare I say, Nadine – so are you. Your studies, your
interests... Anglo Saxon, dear.'

Nadine ignores her. 'Gary hates music. He'll turn to selling
paintings. He thinks music starts – then ends. First slender, then
obese and loud. The history of music – that starts too, slim and
economical – and then it's over. Into craquelure, than dropped,
final, on the floor. I expect he thinks – "painting starts with
God's first outline – then it's storms. It ends in scribbles."'

'That's what I mean,' says Chloe. 'That view's quite infantile. Music's all simultaneous. It all goes on, on all the time. The scribbles – it's like God, making the universe from clouds.'

Neither of them has much thought about all that.

Chloe goes on, 'Happiness. Acceptance. You must have a space for that, Nadine. Gary's not into it.'

'Those aren't part of history,' says Nadine. 'History's my country. There, the nearest thing to lasting happiness is making structures: a tax, an army, draining a marsh. Pony express. Chasing a people from its fields. Things that endure, the real accomplishments. The rest's unhappy families. Culling and parades. Those pyramids of skulls.'

'It's words, Nadine,' says Chloe. 'Words is what impacts and remains. Words is the power I have, the spoken ones: your power, the little that you manage: written. You're safe, a mouse, a scholar, under the floorboards, nibble nibble at the insulation of the wires. You produce a study – maybe it will spark. One day – perhaps, there'll be a bang and fire. Up you'll go! Me – I'm in there all the time – politics, Nadine. Helmsman and lookout. Captain for the trip... Mine is the eternal flame, you twist in it and scream – and never are consumed. You couldn't stand it, my dear friend. Of course, I love you, like you were my little daughter, a mousey, all pink and curly by my side... But words, Nadine! They can dynamite the ruins, what remains, is somewhere in a book. The power is chiselled there as well, my dear. The book for you. The pyre for me.'

*

'No pictures,' Gary says. 'And, it's the noise music makes that I can't tolerate. Pictures – multiplying realities? I don't go with that. Nor if they try to show what goes on in your head. Mine's full enough of prancing images to last my time. I need never

open up my eyes. To live – I could sell bricks. They're real and
silent. Pile them up – and there! They are transformed – a
temple, or a pighouse. Silent too, and real.'

*

'The city of S? Where can it have ended up? Like the magic
floating Russian city ... in its magic Russian country. A place of
pilgrimage where you can drop unwanted kids. A Suzdal?'

Claude says, 'There's cities disappeared and cities under
siege. And those transformed. You can't be Jewish, Gary...'

'I know,' he says. 'Not speaking Hebrew. What might my
first words have been? "A document"? "Don't shoot"?'

'There's Samarkand – the golden road. Or Salt Flats – when
the lake dries up. Sahara – a city without buildings. Scythia, a
cemetery – the golden tombs for houses...Syria, cities once
abundant, Seleukis: there were eight of those. Close by, there's
Smyrna, birthplace of Homer. Are you a poet, Gary?'

'Who knows? I might have poetry inside, "the silent worm
that burrows 'neath the bark". Cerberus again... Most life is
automatic, Claude, in everyone there's everything, a thousand
eggs – only the miraculous butterfly gets hatched and wavers
down the twisty path, and disappears. It's Nadine, Claude – she
wants to study me,' says Gary. 'So I need have an origin. My
end's the common one, no problem there. The city must have
disappeared – there's no use listing ones that's known...'

'Nadine will study you as long as you are in her sight,'
Claude says. 'That is her tic. You are her unicorn. Your horn
attracts, even if it's hidden underneath, between your legs...'

'Maybe I'm a miracle – a mystery, inventing everything,'
says Gary. 'Parentless, birthless. Not recorded, ever. As if in my
wonderful beginning is an unheard of end. I'm sent here as an
obsession – the hit that's lodged inside your head, your personal

monkey on a squeaking stick – then, oh no! – its group turns up and beats those drums, the sax bleats ever louder, guitars thrum on ... and I must send them off to gigs so far away I cannot hear their sound, their beating hearts, the shouting out about their love, their self-destruct ... the demons stamping, the electric heat, the crimson lights... The music biz is that, dear Claude.'

Well, it's turned out a bad choice. Claude's heard it all before. 'Where are you from, Claude?' Gary asks.

Claude turns angry on him. 'The place? That's your mantra, Gary the un-Indian from Indiana, a foundling, wrapped in a scroll, a Musical Express, sliding along the tracks, guided by a shift chart, towards its destination? What's place to do with truth, the orderly, the just? You don't live well, Gary. You've slumped, you're an illusion. When you become a Teresias like me – your breasts grow out and sag, your cock won't work, you're de-sexed but you're not holy, you're not wise. You're in-between the father and the mother, in-between the death, the life. It's a message, Gary – the message, the warning – first, it's all you, all yours, you flesh it out! Then, the flesh starts to pour and melt down, down it goes – towards the sinkhole. So – where next...?'

'But Claude,' says Gary, 'your story is absurd. You're a pro in kiddyland, in the comix – Korky the Kat; of wonderwomen, supermen. That's why place doesn't matter. It's Valhallah, and you're a dwarf. Your end is trivial, like your start.'

'How you deceive yourself, dear Gary,' rages Claude. 'You're a reluctant agent. Me – I have a multitude of agents, everywhere. A web, a net. When they do their terrible acts – I weep and I despair. And yet, the horror and the cleansing must be done – import and export, suck and blow, decay – rebirth. Without the destruction – we'd be stuck in our imperfection, our bullying, our daily mediocrity. Those comics set it out: explosions and plots, armed guys abseiling down the buildings, killing the managers. That's the truth – your kids buy the book, and frown. They recognise it's true, it happens all around...'

'Is that your empty secret, Claude?' asks Gary: 'There's thousands of them, everywhere – secrets: they run around us, like the lines round paving slabs and cobblestones.'

'Exactly so,' says Claude. 'You're not surprised. The networks: like clubs with no armchairs, no pool tables, no bar. You sign up – nothing's required: there's sites, and nothing's built. There's some for anarchy, for religion, give a hand to your state or some other state – a state quite inexistent, faiths with no buildings, an order in the past, the future ... nothing can surprise... You're a sleeper. A citizen, mail-ordering your arms. Cities disappeared: Gary, those all look alike. It can't amaze you that I have one too – a cause, an impulse, or a need, fatality... There are many cities, waiting to be born. This is how the change is brought. The rest is tinkering. You need the cause – it's quite irrelevant. Big, or tiny. On it drives, the juggernaut. Those cloudy bodies – they're consumed, or else they're lying trapped, underground, the brains are rot, dear Gary, but the memory lingers voiceless in the bones... Oh, how they matter, those poor soulless souls! They looked like us, they cuddled us in bed... they're quite irrelevant, they're pieces off the board...'

'Yes!' Gary says, enthusiastic for a new idea. 'Everyone can have their network, net, web – they're caught in it. It's home. It's their brigade. Comrades. Us kittens drowning in our sack – a world of us. This is the way the world will bend – utterly transformed. The strip – it's comic, or it's sad and sexy – here it is! The strip. You can walk on it, drive your van up it: encrypt it, frighten with it... You, Claude, you're a genius. You do like everybody else, and everybody's sure they have their unique strategy. All together, hugger-mugger – it's a revolution of everything and its converse – freedom and slavery, obedience and transgression, massacre and reproduction. The text and its travesty, its faithless mirror.'

'No doubt, you're in some nets as well,' says Claude. 'There's songs, subversion, keeping fit... Variety that eats your time. Forget the labels: they are all the same, part of the same plan. The problem, Gary, is – you have no problem: you don't know where you come from. It's not important, not the history you don't know about, religion you've not studied, your colour that could come from East or West of continents afar. Yet you insist. It's a mistake. It's not consistent either – your mind swings round with every breeze like all the rest.'

'I don't trust where you're pushing me,' says Gary.

'Take your city, Gary – S,' says Claude, pushing Gary against the wall. 'Who governs it? What do you get given from it? Maybe you're the inconvenient son, the brother; rolled in a carpet, trampled by white asses... Your parents: priests? or governors? Dalits without a ghost to render up? The city goddess – do you need believe in her, or simply pay the tax? Who was supposed to shore the walls and stole the cash?'

'Claude,' says Gary. 'Don't overplay your hand. You, the great conspirator – you know I can't respond to you. I want to know the origin so I can work out the end. The middle too – how they treat me, what I must do... You know I want to let it out – mistrust and anger. Curiosity. I have my network – there's bands and gangs and guys who rap and some who read some stuff all over everywhere – what should they do? Fire on the public? Run for councillor?'

'Those are just grains, dear Gary, grains in the ferment,' Claude says. 'Listen, for once – listen! What I've been telling you. Not this side or that, not any more. It's process, not agency, my friend. It's not the play of ideas, not who you are, are looking for – that's all done.'

'I just want to see the place – S,' Gary says. 'Nothing more. I know who I am. Don't bully, Claude.'

'Follow the trail, Gary, don't fool around,' says Claude. 'Once you see the track – you follow it, between those high smooth walls. The track will take you where there's no way back, to where you don't want to go. You leave a trace – it's quite indelible, imprinted on your skin. That's why you must leave a space blank – a back, an arm: some living room. That way your life can be written down in ink. The book is dead – you have become the book.'

*

'It's hard to follow Claude,' says Gary to Nadine. 'He makes me feel I am the idiot, unholy and unheard – while all the rest are making friends and joining up and waiting for the call. He thinks he's the global one. But Nadine – those bands, those rappers – I send them out all over. Once, the world had ends – now it's gone slick, and people skim around it like they skate on grease or oil. Those guys, my guys – they don't come back. Do they find space in a favela, in a city that's so big the elephants have nowhere else to go, and wander down Main Street?'

'Why not?' asks Nadine, not much interested in groups – they multiply like cells, although the beat's got softer now, is powering down: 'You know, what interests me is how a guy like you inserts himself, when there's no crust to stand on, everything is on the move, you're everywhere anonymous and yet – behind your eyes, high in your skull, there is that hiss, the S, a tinnitus from nowhere – walls around, a call to prayer or profit, black birds above – or are they paper kites? that whistle – birdcatchers? wind towers? I think it's in the past, poor Gary. Your future's embalmed. Dead or under siege.'

'No!' Gary says. 'It's somewhere I might want to live. Maybe they'll let me in. A city, walled, awaits. I see it clear, its daily toil. I can't see its clock, its time: that anyway goes on for ever. It's just a detail that I miss – I don't know where it is.'

'If you're not an agent now,' says Nadine, 'maybe I can take it on, your job.'

'And I'll do what you do,' Gary says, 'asking people, reading the lives that they discard. Easy.'

'So many people,' Nadine says. 'To investigate. It's wearying, my studying. The insignificant – they lie in wait and snap you, if you don't do their portrait.'

'My work,' Gary says, 'requires the clients trust you totally. A faith without a doubt. Everything gets folded in, a true theology: the nonsense and the menus. For them – the pilgrimage, self-reform, and punishment. *You* are without fault: they bear all faults. *You* know: they're blind. You mustn't listen to them – however loud they shout, or what's their suffering. Your omnipotence – rusts in the barrel of your blunderbuss, omniscience makes you sad, so sad. Don't do it, Nadine, don't do what I did, not if you love yourself.'

'It's just a job,' Nadine says. 'Work's nearly all the same – except, in factories you get to package up some shiny stuff. That's satisfying. People, though – they don't have lustre. Nor does cash, the pay is bad. I do it for the influence...'

'Listen,' says Gary. 'You mustn't listen. Remember – smuggling your girlfriend out of hell. If you hear the music – it's all over. However crass it is, and buried under sound and noise – the music puts its fingers round your heart, squeezes, in marchtime, ragtime, waltztime. Relax; and she, the mistress music, makes herself one with you. She'll climb into your blood. I've never listened – you must do the same if we swap lives, Nadine.' He hesitates. 'We could take a trip, of course ... a group of two, on the road and in the bus...'

'Oh no,' Nadine says, 'I have a boyfriend – it's just sex with you. Then there's my writing – you're the star – "Experimental Lives". Or "Lives of Passage". There's Chloe too. Power: down to her shoes – an exemplar. Besides – Gary, you're violent, in a wordy kind of way.'

*

This is not the place.

But it's so similar to other places that aren't the place, it eliminates them – hundreds at a blow.

'This place – it's like Spain used to be – when it was coking in the pan and then the gas went out,' says Gary.

Nadine wants to go outside – there's a demo going on, quite inventive, the young people, well qualified for other things, mostly.

Nadine and Gary – reluctantly, trying something out, no idea what it might turn out to be.

'Don't go out, Nadine,' shouts Gary. 'There's that awful smell of rancid olive oil. They don't notice – they go to bed so late. You don't belong.'

'I'm not too old like you, Gary,' Nadine says,

'I told you, like I told Claude – I know exactly who I am,' says Gary. 'It's the places here, all over. They're not so sure.'

On the table by the bed, there's a brown bat, folded like a leather purse. Neither wants to pick it up, and throw it out. 'The funny thing,' says Gary. 'Is they had the sloppy kind of fascism here. Killing and tradition. When it was swept away – socialism too had disappeared. They'd left the churches black, to scare, or else they didn't care. No cash. There's still parades of penitents – how do they know what's for the tourists, what's for them? You have to grow up in a place to know who is to blame.'

Nadine doesn't listen: he goes on, 'I was on a train once – it broke down, everyone ran off into the meadow, played guitars and sang. Their train might have been struck there on the track, by some other train... They were all partying, not going where they might have needed to. A guy there told me all about the government. Armed struggle, he said, but not yet.'

'You and the stereotypes,' Nadine says. 'They keep trying new things here – you should latch on.'

'I'm not reactionary,' says Gary. 'It's just I'm waiting for the right loco to come along, and pick me up. History – it runs right through you, like the squits, and leaves you weak, without the appetite.'

'Well, Gary,' Nadine says. 'Don't put a brake on me and call it your conscience, or your hope.'

'I was enthusiastic for things inexcusable,' says Gary. 'Many things. There was reason for them – or necessity. It's easy to invent excuse. I feel bad. Maybe I'm not bad. Everyone's forgotten.'

'Everyone's been wrong. Everyone forgets. True, Gary – I don't. But – you're everybody – you're not Everyman,' says Nadine. 'The meadow, where you all ran for safety – where you lost your innocence – no snakes. Just information. Points of view.'

'A revelation, Nadine,' says Gary. 'But I chose ignoring it.'

'You lack the substance, Gary. You choose to be an orphan everywhere,' says Nadine. 'You're not the digging kind. You wait for poison fruit to drop.'

'My friend Claude, your friend Chloe – they plough. But first, they use the scythe,' says Gary.

'You won't outdo Claude,' says Nadine. 'He's a hard old pike. But Chloe – to reach the top, you must be naive in everything. She's naturally so. I'm trying, and I'll do her down, you'll see. Life. What the spy sees. I'm not interested in living it, just in seeing how it's done. My existence – let the crumbs fall where gravity tells them. And then... The time will come. I'll rise, extend my wings of black and gold – and sing my song...'

'You can't bring fear,' says Gary. 'We're already stuffed with that. Nor transformation – the design is fixed, there's parts that fail in everyone. Maybe – a laugh that sweeps it all away, a squawk that burns the clouds?'

'Wait and see,' says Nadine. 'Find your place, Gary. What awaits? That wooden structure – a lectern? Gallows? Your tree?'

'The place – that's the key,' says Gary. 'It's not the person, it's the collective they have made, inhabited – I know. It's their furbelow – the picture hanging, the stoatskin transfixed upon the door: – not the big stuff, not the execution or the prayer. It's what you'd call the furniture, Nadine.'

'It's oddments, Gary,' Nadine says. 'It's true for you. You're just a simple soldier, tramping where you're told, and skyving when you can. I'm drawn to people here – as they were, their love of death, of making others suffer, then gladly going underneath the axe. I'm their kin. I need my death – that's the way you get a judgment, a resolution, a certificate. Just think – your last day – you win the lottery! Disaster! Your coffin's lined with banknotes. Has your life been happy, sad – or just quite random, lucky, as they say? Look at the penitents, the procession in the street here, Gary, moaning as if they're in the Klan and sorry for it, dressed like candles with the snuffer already on their heads: more minimal than skulls – no nosehole, no drooping jaw ... just eyes that only see the ill within... Not luck, treading the line: it's punishment, finality – that's what sets the seal.'

'They don't repent,' says Gary. 'They're planning riper orgies. They want us to roll about in things we think they did. They're all in real estate – built houses for no people, Nadine – no people, with no lives.'

'The manif outside,' Nadine says: 'The young guys, the hopeless ones. They want it all to change so they can get their salaries, a set of walls to nail diplomas on... It's wonderful, it's pitiful. I love it here... They seek their early death, the marble plot, a choice of songlets, secular popes – success! I don't want that – success is what the others give, not what you are. I want to win, set terms for all the rest: they're shamed, left far behind...'

'That's solitude, Nadine. You need a floor to bounce your ball,' says Gary.

'You, Gary, are a void,' says Nadine, flaring out. 'Your silence! A void. It doesn't mute those music guys! They hammer on. The music in its turn – a cover for the real. What we start from, must not forget, is monkey rage. We need to connect with that – that is our root, and not some ruined fantasy, primal abandonment, a happy end ... All the invention, the beat – it overlays, obscures, what we should really be... Forget the sentiment, the strutting and the rhymes – try, just once, dear Gary – to be a person! Think snake! – shake those rattles, rear and hiss. Flaunt to the world your scarlet bottom, drum your chest!'

She peers forward, into the rest of her life. 'Of course, I could be wrong,' she says. 'Not about you, Gary – but about the rest.'

She picks up the brown bat, the worn-out purse, throws it out. It hesitates on the sill – anybody would. And disappears.

Nadine climbs up, stands over the crowd, arms extended like Athene's. There's noise rising; Gary backs off.

'Just a push,' says Nadine. 'I'll push Chloe higher so she'll fall. Then it's my turn.'

The crowds below applaud. 'Nadine,' Gary shouts. 'You'll fall!'

'I'm sure they saw me,' Nadine says, back in the room, and packing. 'These waves of irritable people, having a good time –

they're part of my design,' she says. 'Maybe it's not death they
see – maybe it's a blank.'

She leaves, leaves Gary. There'll be a bus... Gary wanders
round. He sees Franco: Franco's always around, not seeking
work, but curious about those who've looked and found some.
He cloys. It's his simplicity, not striven for, just dropped on him
like a cloak. 'The women never really leave,' Franco says.
'Whether you wish they would, or not, before you've decided if
that's good or bad. There's purpose under why they come, then
why they go. Don't fret. The thing is – if you have cash, spend it
all at once. It clears your head, then fills it straight away,
thinking how you can get some more.'

'She took my place – I thought I had one, a place along with
all the people,' Gary says. 'She stole my part.'

'You must make peace,' Franco says. 'Not worry about these
guys... Penitents, demonstrators all. You have to listen in another
way. There's music... If you're careful, it comes free.'

'Oh,' Gary says. 'I've many things to be repentant over. This
is not the place, but penitence – here is its home.'

'All civilisations bring the freedom, and new ways of
enslaving you. Measles and dynamite,' Franco says. 'Wage
slavery.'

'I might have a group performing round about...' Gary says –
not explaining.

'I'd forgive you, Gary, even punish you,' says Franco. 'But
I'm not from here.'

There's a bar, some guy with a guitar: there's no train, no
meadow, obviously. 'Buy me a drink,' says Franco. 'Let's move
on, quick.'

'Nadine, who I was with,' says Gary, 'It didn't work. She was
studying me, always. As a subject. Both of us as subjects! She
knew she was different, wanted to end up somewhere different

too. It gets too complicated, when there's not much liking either. I guess it's normal.'

'I'm not as old as you, Gary,' Franco says. 'But I tell you, Gary, you're fine, you're going to be just fine.'

'Listen, Franco,' Gary says. 'I'll take you to the bus station – then I must leave you, be about my own stuff.'

'You may need me, Gary,' Franco says.

*

Maybe this city, this stage – maybe it was Nadine's 'S'? Lives are wish and shudder – hers is all wish. 'I might go to Senegal,' Gary thinks. 'See Khady. New ways of singing. Seeing and listening – the paint, the beat – there, you find a scheme, a depth. But life stories – they don't change. You get used to being left, that is the lesson. You use it, the experience, to wander off... Everybody sings in Senegal, takes lessons on the *oud*. The stories – they don't change. I could warn Chloe about Nadine, I guess: after all, Nadine abandoned me. But Chloe knows about the plots, and wouldn't care. She's already where we're all supposed to want to go...'

'Khady!' Gary shouts down the line to Senegal. 'I'll come and see you.'

'Oh, Gary,' Khady says. 'You are much missed. It's all you wanted here – the colours, silent. Then there's all the rest, of course.'

'The rest,' says Gary. 'It's doing well for you.'

'Don't you have television, Gary?' Khady asks. 'You'd see it's difficult for music here, mine too. Then, there's the roads and all the bother.'

'Maybe I should let it settle, Khady,' Gary says.

'There's money owing, Gary,' Khady says. 'You could stay there where you are, and send the cash you owe instead.'

'Oh, everyone says that about their agent,' Gary says. 'There's what you keep when I'm not there to check... I give you guys a destiny. I inspire. Strategy and fantasy. I'm Lenin pissed and rollicking in the Cabaret Voltaire. Money, Khady? Everybody expects more than they're worth. And when there's trouble – well, you know – I don't know which side I'm on. That goes way back, allegiances, loyalties – it's not straightforward, Khady, it's my biography.'

'That's you alone, Gary, not knowing about the side. You should be on *our* side,' Khady says.

'It's not a question it's worth heating up about,' says Gary. 'Remember – the music lasts until they take the chairs.'

Maybe Senegal is not the place.

*

'In Africa, Claude,' says Gary, 'I'm a sneak thief. A wooden figure, roughcast, with a wallet and a death's head. They strive – I thrive. Is that how it is?'

'That world is over, Gary. See – this new war, last of the series – with all the sad old guys, the stupid crowds, reaction with new guns ... when it's finished, they will all be gone,' Claude says. 'A new map will be drawn. As for me, now – I renounce my body: I'm a presence, disembodied, bold, opinionated. It's my voice – it resonates, like the cockerel's at dawn. But – I'm not there. Not in the body, on the desk, the screen. If you don't follow me and let me be your thought – you'll slog it out: a lump, in your dusty hut, in the holding pen, oldtimer! ... Gary – I expect you'll always be a scrabbler. I'm the voice of God.'

'How can I match you, Claude?' Gary asks. 'I'm not one for wires and screens, bringing the news. Maybe I could be a *salaf*, an original, an ancestor, a whirling Amish. I'd do everything I could repent for. Then – it would be finished. I can deflate anything, Claude, come out lean and flat. Wasn't I a communist? See where that went. If I were a believer – I'd love those processions, with full flagellation. I'd invest my soul in it. Then – the fashion dies. Doesn't make the chart. So – silence. Twenty-four notes can make you every tune there's ever been – anyone can learn them. The combination's infinite – the process, though, degenerates.'

'You're too generous, Gary,' says Claude. 'Twelve notes is all it takes.'

'Twelve going up, twelve going down,' says Gary. 'I knew my business. But what you know, Claude, is dust, stardust. If you're the voice of God, you must remember what will happen. It needs a memory bigger than your head.'

'It's already happened, Gary – the path,' says Claude, 'is paved. We, or someone else, just have to walk it.'

'Let it be me, then, Claude,' says Gary. 'I've had no stricken relatives. Suffered no discriminations, no history, no faith to wrestle with, no kinship with a refugee, an emigrant, a nomad. Yet, I'm all of these.'

'Those of us who count,' says Claude, 'we're all of everything.'

'Now's your time, Claude, you must enjoy it,' Gary says.

'Chloe is far along,' says Claude. 'I don't blame you for dumping Nadine – she enjoyed dawns. No sunsets and no dusks. Chloe basks all day, grows to the light. She knows – if you risk, there's trouble in the future. The foot put in the wrong continent, a giggle behind the wrong back – you're done! Very prudent be, and stay in tune. Wings furled close to the ribs.'

'Cloudy chapters, Claude,' says Gary, remembering Nadine, finicking in bed. 'Chloe's used to conquests – she doesn't trill about them, no conquistadoring, no jails, no walls. She'll scoop your eyes out with a spoon, and next day – sends a sweet parcel with your white stick in. Even a kennel for your seeing dog.'

Claude concludes: 'Chloe says, 'Be very careful. Follow the truth. I do. The truth is me.'

'It's style,' says Gary. 'There's nothing else – the rest is coloured berries on a stalk. Style is how you understand the stuff, see what is new, what's been around.'

'That's true,' says Claude. 'But you have to put it on, the style. Not just understand it, friend.'

*

'Sometimes a war will sort things out,' says Chloe. 'We always choose the winning side, so nothing lands on us.'

Gary says, 'My friend thinks, when it's over, you will all be swept away.'

'Oh no,' says Chloe, 'it's complicated, naturally – but me, my lot – we're not involved.'

'All the same,' says Gary. 'Another lot. New countries. New ruins. New tall buildings full of bankers...'

'That's crap,' says Chloe. 'I'm on the crest. I can do anything I want. My dreams – are quite conventional. Bling! And when I wake, I'm nobody again. Call me the emperor's horse – and look at all the hay I've got! Power, Gary – it's all fun! When they get tired of you, and when you hear the clogs, the bast shoes, shuffling up the stairs – you close your eyes, fill your pockets and your boots with gold – eat some if you can, and, yes, you're swept away. Except – we've made the calculation. It won't happen here.'

'I've never calculated anything,' says Gary. 'People cheat. There's bad karma, too.'

'These wars – it's your conventional hate,' says Chloe, holding Gary's leg quite tight, under the table, with both of hers, wide-eyeing him. 'Of course – there is the noise, the rhetoric. And in the end – you're persuaded it was good – inevitable. You see – we have to whip it up! Both sides, all sides. If we don't manage everybody from the start – who knows where it might end? You must avoid accidents. That's our intelligence. It's like that Chinese guy – no warrior he – who says, you plan from well before the start, and don't stop when it ends. It isn't secret, Gary. Read a book. Those painters – on our side – they invented a perspective. Background and distance – disposed the gods around the stage, some pushed off for good... It was a revelation, Gary. Me – I'm a primitive. I have no depth – it's good. Paint me in gold and silver. The scenery, though – it must be movable, the dancers always land on those chalked dots ... the music, down in its black pit – it drives the scene along...'

'I must be wrong,' says Gary. 'About the movement, the percussion. Silence: that's the aim of music. The heart of it – is nothing. People do epics, conquer the grasslands, kill the beasts – it's all been done. You see it dwindling down, going tiny – the haiku, the spray, wall-coloured, on the wall. You write your thoughts – a wandering thumb, invisible ink – they've disappeared. It's good, Chloe. It's the peak; you're up – but how the air is thin! You work – the papers slide and fade and shred. You're someone unemployed, like me – it's liberation, Chloe. You do not steal, nor add to junk that ends up in the dump... The goal is essence: invisible, inaudible and odourless. The essence, Chloe – contains everything, but has no sound, no smell, no outline, no thickness...'

'That's poetry, dear Gary,' Chloe says. 'But even you wise owls must eat.'

'We improvise,' says Gary, losing patience.

'Can you run, Gary?' Chloe asks, legs pressing harder. 'Forward and back? If there's a fight, running forward gets you in a hole.'

'No, Chloe,' Gary says. 'A family trait – back, or round, that's how we ran, that must be why I'm here. I survive. They say that love too survives ... but, Chloe, you would know – what does it eat?'

She moves her legs away.

'I know about the fights, and love,' says Gary. 'Nadine was a pro in that. But about the silence – libraries with no books, the war and peace without a sequel, an envoi – I know about all that. I sent musicians out. None came back. They didn't send a note...'

*

Again, they're together in the steam, the sweat, only the heads are visible, like first reptiles just created with a bang: Claude says, 'You've made mistakes, Gary, with Chloe and Nadine.'

'Nadine left,' says Gary. 'That's geography.'

'No, Gary,' says Claude. 'It's casuistry. And Chloe – that was sex. You turned her down – she's in your field, enraged. A beast with horns. She'll join up with friend Nadine, avenging her – and hell will come.'

'No, Claude,' says Gary. 'What others see – it isn't you. That's philosophy – you are an image, from outside – a cut-out: what you are is viewed only by you, you in your castle, your eye-holes looking in and out. You and your place, your habitat, that's you...'

'You don't convince, poor Gary. You've been found lacking – what you are, and what they think of you,' says Claude. 'Chloe spoke to me about that guy – the story went, he lost his girl, had nothing but his pocket harp to soothe him down, went down to hell and found her... Then, he ended bad. That's you, Gary, your search for love. Drink, Gary, the grape, the god incapable – that's always been your jug, your mug – your handle to reality, your corkless bottle with the full-rigged schooner glued inside: your prisoners' jail.'

'Oh Claude,' says Gary, much alarmed – 'Orpheus-Morpheus – I don't even know the tale, nor can I play a note. I told you, my destiny's to be invisible, inaudible...'

'The thought is right,' says Claude, 'but – you can't trade silence for your girlfriend's fate. When she comes up from hell, that's where you'll go, down in her place. Chloe's a minister – she can chase you to world's end. Eyes in the sky, poor Gary – every five minutes, they peer, they pin you down. Don't go outside, not ever. Ignore the eagles, circling high. Find a warm niche in Hades. Strum your reflections, not too loud...'

'It's a nonsense,' Gary says.

'You can't choose what you'll be persecuted for,' says Claude. 'You might prefer it's faith or politics – you've neither of them, Gary. Chloe is sport and culture – the sport is you. And the culture isn't your essentialist reduction, a zero, contemplation: – she likes to hear the beat, she wears it in her ears, she jiggles to it, bangs the table with it when she's bored.'

'I played more than fair with Nadine,' Gary says, starting to cry. 'You say she'll blame me for whatever she has not become? And Chloe will pursue me...? Is this the fruit of love? I never mentioned it, not love, nor even liking much...'

'You're not an innocent,' says Claude. 'And nor am I – but I live in the air. You, Gary – you're a target, what every good or evil guy is looking for. It makes you feel important – but take care! The eagles now don't drop their tortoises on bald philosophers' heads. Not any more – there aren't philosophers a-wandering in the fields. It's guys like you, that gyre all round, and pick a flower, and whistle Götterdämmerung – those are the ones that show up on the warriors' screen... Those armed and flying things – watch out! The eagle with the tortoise – that's all gone! It's the machines: they're armed, they fly all day...'

'But sex, Claude. Chloe...' Gary says.

'Sex, when you're up that high, a politico like her – it's just a currency. No fun in having coins – it's what they buy. Acquisitions, Gary,' Claude says. 'Stuff to show off.'

'Nadine?' asks Gary.

'You're her raw material, her pyrites. She thought you were her gold. You're clinker, Gary. You should know about this, being another parasite ... facilitator, as they're known. You were part of Nadine's strategy. After analysing you, a lost boy – comes the fame. No fortune, no one waits for it, that's all gone. Then, she saw the thousands, demonstrating. That's where fame lies... You wasted time. Gave nothing in return,' says Claude. 'You failed her.'

The steam – like pot-smoke in the sibyll's cave, it billows round. Gary's hair rises above – a saurian crest, Claude's grey pate floats disembodied, an upturned drinking bowl.

'You'll need some weapons, Gary – I'll ask low friends...' says Claude.

'Yes, Claude,' says Gary. 'I must have the best. I'm young – that way it's easier to hide. They're – we're – all indistinguishable... The music – that's what differentiates us all. Our taste. Like dipping for jujubes in a jar.'

'But Gary – were you in a noble trade?' asks Claude. 'Did you examine lyrics, prise apart chord sequences...? As a player on this stage – were you quite serious?'

'Oh no,' says Gary. 'I just sent guys out. They work the crowds – no one can leave, the doors are locked, the sound – it stuns...'

'Your silent music – it's suspect,' says Claude. 'There's lots who think it leads to evil thoughts...'

'I'm sure they're right,' says Gary. 'But once I tried promoting – not silence, but the sound of life. *Sons trouvés:* no pursing up the lips, no fiddling harmonics, the parade of love quite excluded from the everything, the all around ... an unintended world of noise. Hark! The birds, the breakers' yards, the background brouhaha. Life sounds. So, Claude – what can I have to fear?'

'Fear is like dust, Gary. It falls from everything. Your origins. Opinions. Indifference – and recruiting all those guys to spread out tumbled messages to everywhere...' says Claude. 'Your search for S. S is for State. Sublime. And Sacred, not to mention Socialist. You pass it off, my friend, as your obsession. It's not so. It's a new origin you want. An educated guy like me – I know the truth.'

They sweat together. Mists dissipate.

They reappear entire, two stooping monkeys. Claude says, 'Do you want to start again, the cycle? The ice room; then whipped with grasses? The hot rocks?'

'I'm done,' says Gary. 'Cooked and ready for the eating.'

'You should do sport,' says Claude, bounding up, upside down to the high roof and kicking off and whirling round and off again – 'With Chloe, doing sport before the culture, it might ingratiate.'

'Sport is the training that you do so you're rapid when your culture makes you run,' says Gary. 'Paddling the Mediterranean, walking the Sahara, through Hungary – that is when it serves. I'm innocent of everything – it's only you, Claude, has pushed me into clandestinity.'

'I'll put you on to Lucas. He can kit you out,' says Claude. 'And – my children can tell each music group apart. I'm proud of them. You're philistine, Gary. It means your trade's debased.'

'Children!' thinks Gary, remembering Claude's drizzle-spout, the pizzle, origin of the world.

*

Lucas lives high up. What does he expect to see, so high, far above the street?

'Suppose I tell you,' Lucas says, 'I don't do retail. Claude reads his comics, where the hero carries heavy guns, and guys come on to him, full frontal, so he can pretend to aim and take them out... It's not like that at all. Besides, me and my fellows – we're a band of types: – assorted and demanding. We'd want to know – what you defend yourself against, what you attack. We're like the gang that founded Rome. Each had his aim, but they agreed: the thing is – get other guys to fight for you. You can't go wrong. It's leadership – that's the bind. You have to follow some big crazy boss. Some mad guy floats up, or maybe there's a family thing. We don't want that. Maybe you should have words with Lily... Pass through here.'

'Music?' says Lily. 'A dangerous biz. That guy who lost his girl, and then his head. So much for going down to hell. You're dead – it's best be left alone. The guy – must have strummed out of tune. No one gets offed for looking back. That's a thing we all must do...'

What can Lily give? Sex? Training in weapons? Lying low...?

'Don't I look like Romy Schneider?' Lily asks.

'Why no!' says Gary. 'She'd be nearly eighty now. I'd give you fifty-five, no more.'

'Even if Claude fantasticates,' she says, 'and sets you up, and frightens you – you must have an aim. It's what drives you that might be interesting...'

'A tiny thing,' says Gary, 'a city – I only know one letter...'

Lily pins him down, knees on his shoulders, he's immobilised. It's weapons training, sex and lying low, all in the single pose, the hold...

'Yes!' she shouts. 'That's the vision! A band of guys, they come ashore, all kinds of primitives around, gods in the woods and in the cellars... Coming from a place destroyed, and maybe mythical – they make a city, ochre and blood-brown... Circuses and sacrifice...then there's the empire, stuck together like a rocky pot. Mad guys and drunks – they run the show, they bring in gods of every kind – there's animals and ginger clouds and dead guys too, you have to worship with no wink – but the *clou*...' and she pauses: 'Soldiers. That's the cement, and the electricity. Its name is Rome. Of course, it can't be done again, and it was done quite bad. It didn't last, and what remains is cloud... But you're the harbinger, dear Gary. The city. Yes! The one that doesn't yet exist...'

'Oh,' says Gary, 'mine – it must exist...' But Lily isn't listening.

'I would be ... what, terrified? Struck mad? Even by the thought of starting Rome again,' says Gary. 'It would be petrifying. Awe, horror, and disgust.'

'You're right, says Lily. 'There is no one word, no sequence of them adequate, if you undertook that. It would be a terrible task – you'd need all the weapons you could find, they wouldn't be enough.'

'The enterprise,' says Gary. 'You wouldn't want it. It's not me, nor anyone. And there's the whiff of kitsch...'

'Whatever happens in the world,' says Lily. 'It doesn't happen to be liked. Or to be just, or anything like that.'

'It's elephants, each holding on a tail and lurching down the mountain path,' says Gary. 'And when they reach the plain – maybe they'll trample you. All together.'

'You must be with them, all along the track,' says Lily. 'Those elephants – it's a circus trick, but they're not in a circus. That Claude – he has kids. That means he's not serious: – you have to do everything yourself.'

'I'd thought we were to have sex, instead of giving me a gun,' says Gary.

She stares at him. 'What can you be thinking of?' she asks. 'No dynasties, no fooling round. No procreation, meant or not. No happy families. Don't tell Lucas about the city that you want to found. Not yet... Maybe I'm more a Vitti, do you think? If only Italians were like that really...You're not so young, Gary. It's late. Now, you'll never have your *grand amour*. You've done half the trip already.'

Gary says, 'You cast a great sadness, Lily. Like having Vitti only on the screen, then leaving the cinema, in the rain.'

*

'What did you do with Lily?' Lucas asks. 'She can be most things – the difficult ones, you can be sure she's done. She finds you soft, Gary. A little wet. Maybe you don't like cinema. Maybe you don't like games. You know the rule, as they say – if you've a stick, you come up against a guy who's got a knife. You've a knife – he has a gun. Whatever happens – you must be convinced, to use your thing and maybe lose... Lily thinks you won't. You want a gun – these people have one too, and more. Or maybe you want something extra – what? A bomb?'

'Well, Lucas,' Gary says. 'Maybe I got your organisation wrong, this import export stuff. I guess that's what we all do now. I don't want to end zipped in a bag. It's nothing, it's just personal, my scare...'

'We can't help,' says Lucas. 'Our business reaches everywhere, but not to you. If you have enemies – talk to them and make your peace – they like that, even if things stay the same.'

*

'You wander into myth,' says Nadine. 'But your problem is your character. Too little of it, like your personality – and opinions much too strong.'

'That's why you're hostile, Nadine?' Gary asks: 'I don't have opinions...'

'No,' says Nadine. 'You don't express them. They're imprinted. Chloe calls that culture. You don't look me in the eye. If you do, it seems you don't trust me, expect me to be deceiving you. The straight gaze, though – it's aggressive. Without it – you're a shifty type. You don't look at me. You don't hold my hand to make a bargain. For you, the hand, and holding one, it's sentiment or symbol – but honest guys use it to seal a contract. Your customs, Gary – they're not casual. It isn't just an eating with your hands or sitting on the floor. It's far, far deeper than opinions.'

'Maybe it's so,' says Gary: 'It's true, perhaps. Say – I don't want a coffin, and being carried down the street, lying down, as if I'm sleeping. I should be buried sitting, even standing. Is that opinion too?'

'They're all clues, Gary,' says Nadine. 'That may explain where you come from. It's not about the singing or not singing...'

'Are you sure, Nadine?' Gary asks. 'Where do you look for origins, for me? Maybe we've always been like that, maybe we dance, don't vocalise ... or maybe we just drum.'

'Where you live now,' Nadine says. 'Whoever can – they run away. They come because they're broke or broken. Those who mend – they fly. The rest remain – it's you, and those alike. Your primal city – you did well. You left, or someone threw you out. Don't look back – you'll lose the gains. Maybe that S was Srbrenica ... or Soweto, Sobibor. Maybe a place that doesn't sound like it once was – a Stettin or a Stalingrad.'

'It can't be those,' says Gary, 'I'm way too young...'

'Maybe then you are a perpetrator,' Nadine says. 'Dark things surround you, perch beside your bed. You purify yourself – still you smell of plague pits. You know that – and so, the stink seeps out … climbs into your pants like extra legs… You stand against us, you look back to things we shouldn't want to penetrate, those places where the ghosts assemble, shake their wings, black feathers falling on the ground; their flightless shadows march before them… What destiny, poor Gary? Denying intellect, denying any classifying… a silent culture, a mourning for what was not, and what we hope won't be…'

'I understand all that,' says Gary, 'but it's not me!'

'I'd hoped you might be found,' says Nadine. 'But there you lay – the crowds outside, a multi-coloured organism – while you were stranded, black on white, inert, arms and legs a broken cross, blurred x-ray marking out your spot. Like a nodule on the bed, a shadow on the negative, a mortal blob, medallion of toxicity, malign and shady there…'

'I don't deserve all this,' says Gary. 'Maybe I get no prize – but I've earned no punishment. A weapon, maybe, to defend myself…'

'Negating Chloe's mission,' Nadine says. 'With a silence that runs you through, your blood replaced with quicksilver … your song quite imperceptible, a humming as you kneel to summon up the nothing you believe in. For the wrong you might do Chloe – not to mention me – some reparation is required.'

'I accept the punishment,' says Gary. 'For what I haven't done. But – forget the persecution. One lashing is enough. Do it, just once, and then be gone…'

'Don't be pitiful,' says Nadine. 'Pity for victims is for when they're dead, and not before. You're here, alive and wavering before me. You're recuperable. That is life – you need educating for it. Our enmity can change, because we're strong – not because we come to like you, Gary.'

'I haven't understood, then,' Gary says. 'Not anything.'

'Exactly so,' says Nadine. 'That's what needs explaining to you.'

'You're collectors,' Gary says. 'People. You offer jewels, and we, the sons and daughters of Orlamonde – we pick them up, then we get locked for ever in a closet. What for? They never tell you. It all happens according to some plan – "*la fée noire est morte*", and on we go. No – don't tell me you've a plan, Nadine. I'm sure it's quite coherent. But it's not you and Chloe set it up. It's all on automatic. Once it brought snakes, and now – it's bigger snakes...'

'Being Chloe's vice,' says Nadine, 'I've learnt that everyone who asks – gets something. But – you have to ask. Be humble. You, Gary – just sent people out. Now, you must plead your cause. We all look for ways of not dying, at least not disappearing. Claude won't die – he's disappeared. Chloe and me – our parts are written in. We're in the original, guaranteed. We're history. You had a good idea – the search eternal. That hasn't lasted: – you've been everywhere, seen every city, every place where people congregate. It's all meant nothing, Gary.'

'I have a thought about those little camels,' Gary says. 'They started large, then shrank. I see myself ... the herds: alpaca, llama, and vicuna. Their fleece is gold, Nadine! Then – look! the guanaco ... the platinum of all the beasts! Thereabouts, I'd have respect. I do best with people who don't know me. Then, over in the mist – there's for ever Brasil, a place where everyone belongs, and everything is found: people with nothing but themselves...'

'You'd be a gaucho, Gary, riding the range: out of our grasp,' says Nadine.

'Oh no,' says Gary. 'Those little camels are delicate, too small to ride, those are derivatives of larger beasts. They'll never grow, never be the real thing you'd expect; what they once were.'

'Wherever you end up, remember, Gary, remember me – how once you were important,' Nadine says. 'Me and Chloe – we'll know exactly where you are.'

'Go see Lily,' Claude tells Gary. 'And don't wash so much – it wastes too many cells.'

'Go on, Lily,' Gary says. 'Everyone advises. If it's not with camels – where do you see me next?'

'Sex is out for you,' says Lily, putting down a magazine. 'The divas are pomped up. They'd eat you, Gary. Nadine nearly did. Sex turns on biology – you guys are mainly ornaments. As for hostility – the powerful will do you down, but if you show you love them, you'll get the chrism: the uniform, the gun. If they'll let you, stay clear, don't trust them, Nadine, Chloe. That leaves the camels. Exotic wools, Gary? Tall mountains, llama crottes? It's hardly you at all.'

'No, Lily,' Gary says: 'You're right.'

Over there, the door says 'Armoury': 'Yes,' Lily says. 'There is "*amour*" in there – but not for you. The locution's quite archaic – think salamanders on a cloth of gold and poison in the wedding ring. Besides – it's Lucas has the key.'

'To me,' says Gary. 'It looks unlocked.'

'Quite so,' says Lily. 'But you keep out!'

'Lily – let's talk about my sufferings,' says Gary, relaxing at her feet. 'My family... the duplicity of those in power: my quantity of reconsidered things, of conquests at the last frustrated, conversions interrupted – dalliances turned to lead and roaring brass... The suffering, Lily – it's a small thing. It doesn't move me. I don't suffer a sufficiency... I never hoped to find a hope – for what? More lives? More work? More women, men, a cat?'

'What they say,' says Lily. 'Is that the important thing – is love. I never tried it. *"Amour"* – it's too much like what lies inside that store, the armoury – the tiny flasks of oil, the pull-throughs, dubbin, blanco – that is just the start. Out on parade! – here comes the chaplain, there's the imam – see them kiss the flag, the regimental goat trots by, but mustn't butt the queen... Oh Gary! Don't get me wrong! I love the sentiment. I'm wild for justice and for self-defence... I love pragmatism too – I'm not a visionary, I love war and peace, it sits there on my shelf and when I'm old, I'll take it down, and learn the French to read at least the start...'

'Lily,' says Gary. 'Forget the poetry. Wind me up, and set me off...'

'There is a place,' Lily starts. 'That only I and Lucas know. There's acres green and fruiting trees, a seminary where you can ponder anything and look for what you please... Laboratories where you do the same, but dressed in white, as pure and starchy as you want... A paddock where your little camels graze, buildings for every fantasy and use – there's every style, and candy floss and photographs with Mickey Mouse: a colosseum and a cinder track, with trotters and some greyhounds too, and shooting booths and supreme courts, stalls for your nougat and a prisoners' jail...'

'It sounds quite awful, Lily,' Gary says. 'But maybe I should try it out...'

'It beats a bath with Claude,' she says. 'And Nadine studying how to do you down, and Chloe scheming... Our rehab province – no one will bother what you think or do, no one will join with you – and so it's safe. You're on your own, your thoughts and problems can't diffuse. You're not contagious, Gary: that's the thing. You can't do good or ill...'

'That was my job before,' Gary objects. 'The music! And the recitation! The guys – they set the sound stage, ticketed the crowd, they played, they stimulated, sold the discs ... and then...'

'Yes,' says Lily. 'That's the way it goes. It all deflates. Another group sets up its stage... But, Gary, you must persevere.'

'And I'll still see Nadine and Chloe?' Gary asks.

'Visiting,' says Lily. 'Like Claude. They don't believe in rehab yet.'

'And Khady from Senegal? That boring Franco,' Gary asks. 'Who put me on the train, and went by bus?'

'People you owe money to,' says Lily. 'Those you did not respect – yes, they will always be around. Remember – the music's regulated: you must pay to hear it; that way the guys can eat. Respect? That Franco's accustomed to derision. May he prospers on it...'

'I'm not sure I'll prosper in that place,' says Gary. 'It sounds anarchic, arbitrary.'

Lily smiles: 'Your adventure with Nadine? That doesn't sound too orderly.'

'I don't want meaning for my suffering,' Gary says. 'That's already there, and in abundance. Just the timing – the past, the future, how and why they have their weight... Though – Lily, what you offer sounds like a theme installation...'

'No Gary, there's no theme,' says Lily. 'We've had a problem with finance – but that can be resolved.'

'I'd still feel better – better armed,' says Gary. 'A gun...'

'Don't worry, Gary,' Lily says. 'Most everybody there is – as they say, "tooled up".'

'A minor thing,' says Gary – 'The city, S?'

'If you don't find it, I'm sure they'll change a name to suit,' says Lily, pushing Gary out. Lucas is standing in the corridor – he has a bunch of keys – enormous, like you need when stealing cars, not wanting to use force... 'And purify yourself,' shouts Lily. 'In those hot baths!'

*

Gary and Claude arrive together. Claude unstraps his left arm, and in the cool fingers leaves his glass right eye. 'The left hand won't know what the right eye sees,' he jokes. 'A last, a real hot one, Gary? A sizzler?' he says. 'Before you go? A sauna? Old time's sake: you run off, and back to me come Nadine, Chloe... I shall start again.'

'Of course!' says Gary. 'I knew them through you. Maybe you were the lustrous one, and me the fake, laid out as a comparison...'

'Dear Gary – you had a history,' says Claude. 'The town of S. It's fascinating. Then the music: you're not a vulgar guy, promoting tyros – but seeking *Aufhebung*. The transcendence. The silence that's enfolded every noise, the nothing that holds every cadence – past, and to come. The end of it, also the start. You couldn't sell yourself, poor Gary, with your genius. That was silence too! Nadine – she saw you were a giant – a size there couldn't be, a tall tall tale. To Chloe – you're a rival – but you don't wish to be ... and so – you rival and despise her, all in one. No surprise – you've earned their enmity...'

The stones are crimson with the heat, Claude pours from a jug – 'Let's call it Krug,' he says. 'A celebration, a libation,' and the yellow mist creeps round their ankles, there's a hissing as he pours on more and more, the vault they're in smells of brandy mixed with piss... 'It's all the badness smoking off,' says Claude. 'Our uric acid, our aggression ... and soon the picture show will start...'

Claude offers some limes: 'Bite on these, Gary,' he says. 'They'll screw your face up, like you really were in pain. Cure scurvy, scrofula, scabies – all that stuff. You're doing fine, going into rehab when you're well. Lots leave it late, until they're hooked...'

The fog is thick, like bathing in a souring wine – a retsina, possibly, left out in the midday sun.

'And will you say farewell?' asks Claude. 'You were close once to Nadine...'

'No,' Gary says. 'It was too effortful. The sex was always hit or miss. I tried to work things out ... the lesson is – if it takes so much sweat, the results won't justify the hoist.'

Sweat. The booze goes in their eyes, their pores. Claude gathers the robe around what's left of him. He and Gary, side by side, lie: cods upon the slab, their hearts go tickytock, a three against a two, then five with seven, then it's one to one. 'You did well with Lily. She always says what's best for you. Those limes – it makes you think of *limes* – like we were conspiring Romans – frontiers: keeping the limeys out. Walls, frontiers – those are sour as well, sour faces standing guard, a border: if you cross, you'll not come back...' says Claude.

'I wouldn't cross you,' Gary says. 'If we were really Romans, the frontier – it would be a liquid. A river. Maybe the Rubicon. There's other two, that's wide and black – the Tiber and the Styx... But let us liven up! The pictures that you promised me – projected on the wall...'

'Yes, yes,' says Claude. 'They're fleshing out; the fleshy tones, the chemistry is right... And, Gary, you are clean, your parents – cowardly officials, murderers and sneaking thieves – it's all eradicated. You're all new...'

The pictures...

'It's your treat,' says Claude.

The camels...

Massive, wild, the savage and the Bactrian, the dromedaries – delightful white, the common brown, aggressive black – behind barbed wire, in sandy wastes, crossing borders, deserts, mountains, pert with long lashes, trotting, padding, drugged, exhausted ... racing and running, sporting and military...

'They're my dream,' says Gary. 'The road, the caravans, the camels – always on the move, a shuttle lurching on the loom, weaving the precious invisible cloth. Lily convinced me, Claude. Along that road – maybe there's my city, S. No more the abstract, Claude. It's sick.'

'Right,' says Claude. 'Remember, Lily lets no one off her hook. It's back into the concrete, Gary. You start again. Redemption, if you're lucky, and if you can avoid what sent you into rehab.'

'I'm not sure what that was,' says Gary. 'Remind me, Claude. Essence was unattainable – camels seemed a second best. The best compromise, that is.'

'Lily explained it all,' says Claude, irritable. 'Going from something into nothing – it's denial, Gary. The concrete – is your future. Think of splicing cables, Gary – all those strands, the telephones – some get connected, others are forever dumb. You can't outsmart the dialectic. Whatever you forget or can't join up – it's always there. Lots of us – you'll never see again. It doesn't mean a thing. We're here. We're always here.'

'I don't see the harm I did,' says Gary. 'I had one aspiration – it wasn't realised. Others naturally would follow on. My wish – to organise the train, all tracking on – follow my leader. A caravan, a carousel of enterprise. Start one thing, a thought, a yak – it follows, there's a chain, a helix going up the hill... I'm not a clown, Claude: I sought perfection, not pratfalls constant and without a bruise...'

'Grasp this,' says Claude. 'Everybody needs surprises, a shock, a turnaround. What's courage, love and loyalty? Being conscripted: learning to love your comrades, as they shoot the prisoners. There's a life for you – it could be yours, and you'll do nothing, nothing at all, that changes things.'

'Look!' says Gary. 'The llamas. The delicate beauties – how those who tend them depend on them, surround them with their love...'

'That's not at all what I had in mind,' says Claude. 'Your face, poor Gary! What a fright! Any dilemma skewers you on its horns! I helped set up the rehab scene. It isn't rough and tough at all. There, they practise moral philosophy. That's what I am. Morality plus a philosopher. I pose the questions, the dilemmas, paradoxes. You have a shot at answering – but there's no consequence – it all goes on. It's hypothetical... Be reassured. There's no conscription, no prisoners are held. You and the rest – must seek a steady state – not hot or cold, not finite, with "best consume before" – but nothing infinite... Living long, but not till it becomes a bore...'

They hold each other, try to stand... Claude snaps in his eye, they hear the socket – "snick" – welcoming it back. Gary helps to buckle on Claude's arm...

'You're ready now?' Claude asks. They totter out. Nothing to pay. 'When you are dried out like a *baccalà*,' says Claude, 'maybe you'll want visitors. But...'

'I understand,' says Gary. 'The camels. They put people off. Maybe I descended from a line of drivers, masters of caravans ... that's why the affinity's so strong...'

'There!' Claude says. 'There's your hypothesis. I told you – work it out! Sing the song of caravaners – it never ends, it has a thousand verses – going, coming back, a palindrome... No wonder silence is welcome to you. The song, or, rather, chant – it means you have arrived – or else you're ready to depart. Philosophy, dear Gary! Remember, that way you're safe, protected...'

2

REHAB

THERE'S THE QUAY – there's no other way you can enter. Enter rehab.

'You remember Franco?' asks the guy, 'Albi' on his dungarees. 'He befriended me. He's a sticky type – he knows how to crop up everywhere. Here, people don't give confidences. It's best to stick to moral philosophy, like they've telling you. No *bismillah* on the walls, no virgin mother at your breast, no Marx beside your pillow. You're a scholar, naturally – it means naught, of course, but ... take care! ... it's the neighbours, how they snoop!...'

'Thanks, Albi,' Gary says. 'The dilemmas of philosophy – I'm not ready to confront. I guess I'm not a citizen yet, so I'll keep schtum. My interest is quite neutral: nature. I guess you have that here.'

'Oh absolutely so,' says Albi. 'And it's the best. You can't go wrong.'

'And in particular,' says Gary, nervously. 'It's camels. All the races.'

'Hmmmm,' Albi says. 'Racing can attract the eager types.'

'It's types I mean,' says Gary.

'That's fine,' says Albi. 'We tend here to neurology – it's a neutral kind of thought. We stay clear of the post-Freud stuff, unconscious urges, or the Tories here, "survival of the best, the

humpiest..." That would put your llamas down, I guess. Stick to
what's not visible, a theory stashed in safety, underneath your
hair. Stick to brain sciences, my friend.'

'I'm not clued on those,' Gary says. 'I know the llamas – the
higher up the mountains, the smaller they became. Enough with
heavy loads: – a blanket, a bowler hat, like they wear there – that
was the limit. Did they prosper? Well, the suffering was less...'

'The point about rehab, the whole setup here,' says Albi, not
interested in loads or animals, 'is there's no treatment and no
cure. No "condition" in a morbid sense. You're here to see that
what has happened earlier does not repeat. The temptation and
the fall: they're both to be avoided.'

'Oh, yes!' says Gary vehemently, 'I know that when I'm
finished here – there's a conclusion. Conclusions mean all kinds
of enterprises can't be followed up. Distance, echo, letters,
instruments – the musical, the paper ones, mechanical – all these
escape conclusion, so it's hard for me to fit them in. You finish –
but they don't, they linger – you are indifferent to them, and they
to you. It's fortunate that we conclude, we humans – what's left
a-dangle has no sense...'

'But, Gary,' Albi says. 'You must try all that, see what
concludes and what drags on. Though – it's true – if you
concentrated on one family – in your case, the camel – all kinds
of other species get left out. The poor people that rely on
animals, the women, and the children, and the men that carry
loads, and trade their stuff – the silk, the aspirins, the opium, the
bullets – all this and more ... you'll maybe find no room for. Dun
villages in the snow, insistent mullahs, everybody stuck indoors,
the stink of crottes, nothing to read, and childbirth everywhere...
And it probably would make no difference if you did, did write
the chronicle. You wouldn't be remembered for it, if you set out
all the sufferings that strike a note in you, and then – Gary!
Would you wish remembrance for it all, that you have set it

down, and maybe kept a file, or notes stood vertical, on margins, in green ink...?'

'There's room,' says Gary. 'To try. Maybe there isn't time – although – they say space and time are the both the same. Maybe I could convert my space to time – live smaller, but for longer. Already, Albi, I see how incomplete it was, my sending out the music, and it never coming back. That was a tiny part of something too large yet to be taken in, or make a sensible shape...'

'You cut out the people, Gary,' Albi says. 'The public. The fiddlers and the ticketed.'

'Oh, I'm sure they're part of everything,' says Gary. 'They sure insist they are. To me – it's like the mist. Is that all there is, when it's all over? – mist leaves some beetle-tracks on glass, and tiny beetle husks, condensed... And yet – when it's a mix of urine and of alcohol, it enters in, becomes you. It's gone to nowhere, Albi – nothing to worry over – quite disappeared, you think you're full of it – the next day you are pure again, the music's somewhere else. Yes, Albi – the mist is music, if you train your ears...'

'Somewhere else?' asks Albi, pushing Gary on.

'Well,' Gary says. 'Not on a map. Where does *pi* go?'

'Exactly, Gary, that's my point,' says Albi. 'What you don't see – it doesn't bother you. And what you see – maybe it bothers you. And you are not the type to dwell on anything... See – if the scene disturbs you – move your head... Your brain will follow, like a well-loved dog. The pain in what's outside – it disappears. But – we'll come back to this. Meanwhile – you must find your place.'

'Yes,' Gary says. 'My cash is low.'

'Follow the noise,' says Albi. 'When it's the loudest – there you are: City Noir. They'll fix you up. You're well, you won't stay long. You'll want to start some caravans...'

'How'll I know when the noise is loudest?' Gary asks, but Albi's gone.

*

It's noisy here. Maybe not enough. People gather round Gary, finger his clothes. There's giggling. If they're all in rehab, Gary thinks, useless to play that card and say I'm different. If they're not in rehab – maybe better leave it till there's a crisis, and a threat.

'Fetch Daphne,' someone says.

'I'm a councillor,' says Daphne. 'I'm responsible for you. There's no room here.'

'I can pay,' says Gary.

'Of course you can,' Daphne says. 'What you think this place is? Or don't you pay where you've come from? Skyving off, from some conflict, a war maybe, bringing it here, along with panic...?'

'No, none of that,' Gary says. 'I don't even like the noise here, the charcoal buildings, standing saggy tall like refuse sacks, the stalls with brown and dingy vegetables, twisted like iris roots...'

'I'll rent you space,' says Fancy. 'I expect someone is crying for you even now.'

Daphne bustles with her large body. Fancy is thin, as if she's not ready to leave her times behind, waiting to be plumped up before a venture into later years.

'No,' says Gary. 'I'm lucky. No one cries for me. I expect, your place, Fancy, there'll be a lot of sharing.'

'You needn't be afraid of me,' she says. 'I'm abandoned here – everyone I know's a soldier off somewhere.'

'That's why there's unused electrics all around?' says Gary. 'That's what they've brought back, nicked, when they volunteered?'

'It's no use to me,' says Fancy. 'I'm waiting for an excuse to leave this place.'

'Daphne's a mastiff,' Gary says. 'Will she let you go? – you're keeping these rooms for guys who're off ... you are their guarantee...'

'Daphne doesn't like you, Gary,' Fancy says, 'because you're neither weak nor strong. You're no use to her.'

'I can't respond to that, Fancy,' Gary says.

'I like you, Gary,' Fancy says. 'You lack the common touch. Or any touch at all. I like it.'

'I'm here to deepen my character, Fancy,' Gary says. 'I've only known tough ladies, and a conjurer with words – Claude... I guess it was conjuring more with spelling... Now, what side are your soldiers on?'

'That means you've never been a warrior,' she says. 'Or you wouldn't need to ask. Cities generally – they're a place for bourgeoisie and servants. If you don't fit with that – you have to leave,' she says. She wipes a window pane, not looking out.

'Your music, all night,' says Gary. 'It's a difficulty I'd not anticipated.'

'Oh,' says Fancy, 'the traffic all night, then the market – I can't sleep without my music. I'm a punk inside, but not to look at, not at all.'

'I can hear you, Fancy,' Gary says. 'Through the wall. You're safe here.'

'This kind of place – it gets bombarded first,' she says.

'It won't ever happen, Fancy,' Gary says. 'And if it did, having me here won't change a thing.'

'You should listen to what people say,' Fancy says: 'It helps you fix the odds.'

'I'm glad to be your comrade, Fancy,' Gary says. 'You picked me out – there's few who have. I'll stay here if you turn it down – the sound, the music... But – when my time comes – I'll be off! That is the point of being here. I won't change your life, or tell you tales. You'll stay just as you are.'

'That would be good,' says Fancy. 'You're wrong, though – there's many better places, even if you don't get to them. I find that things I think are right, that bring real change, or even justice – they end up costing far too much, far too many people pay ... the plans end up being dropped, reversed and criticised, derided. Do I convince too easy? Or do I want what can't be got? That would be sad, if it's all inevitable, and some guys plan it so.'

Gary thinks how this must be true rehab reflection. 'I spend a lot of time just thinking,' Gary says. 'I even end up doing nothing. But nothing's not the conclusion you're supposed to reach. You might as well not start.'

'If the soldiers come back here,' says Fancy. 'You'll have left. It's like violence, them returning, there's the smell... Did you kill, Gary? Before you came, hiding out here?'

'Not directly, anyway,' says Gary. 'Not so's to know.'

'You could be Russian, Gary,' Fancy says. 'That putty nose, squashed on your face.'

'The women here – just twenty years ago – they all wore headscarves, and the widows went into the black. And when you prayed, you had to cover up. Now, they have all forgot,' says Gary. 'You see them – photos – on the barrows here.'

'As you're my friend,' says Fancy. 'When you go, Daphne could take you in. You'd have to work for her, of course...'

'Oh, I can get by with something at the baths,' says Gary. 'They want me to find some stones – not round or flat, but roundish, flattish. I'll get by, Fancy – it's more direct than when

I was in the biz. When the soldiers come back here, you'll have
to end the music anyway.'

'Maybe,' she says. 'Though they'll be used to noise.'

'Well,' says Gary. 'The fighting will be done. Everybody will
be pleased.'

'That depends,' she says. 'On what you want and what you
get.'

'I hadn't thought,' says Gary, 'not that way.'

'Beneath your gloss, Gary, you're quite a simple soul,' she
says. 'You've heard of everywhere, so it all seems quite the
same.'

'The stones, Fancy,' Gary says.

'There's some here left on tombs,' she says. 'Maybe those
aren't big enough, or smooth.'

'Let's go to the beach,' says Gary. 'It's always being washed,
there are no edges left.'

'That's you!' says Fancy. 'You say you come from nowhere,
from the sea, a round pebble washed up, and then you've
concealed it all. What you did, what happened to that place, why
you came and why you covered everything. Your groups sang
songs from everywhere. All jumbled up. Lies! Only punk is
true...'

'Maybe so,' says Gary. 'But you must let me sleep.'

'Sleep in the day,' Fancy says. 'You've nothing else to do.'

'There's nothing authentic, original, unadorned, like what you
want, Fancy,' Gary says. 'Nothing is unequivocal. I know – I've
tried.'

'There's more, and there is less,' Fancy says, piling smooth
stones into a sack between them they can't lift – 'In everything.
And you're less, Gary.'

*

Daphne says, 'When the soldiers come home, Gary – you have to protect Fancy, you should know. I don't think you're the type, but there you were...'

'It's not my thing,' says Gary, 'but of course – one tries.'

'You don't take initiative,' Daphne says.

'I made the contact,' Gary says, 'to get a pistol.'

'Whatever use is that?' asks Daphne. 'It's not self-defence you'd need. No one wants to punish you – you survive because you don't get in the way. But – if Fancy needs it, when the soldiers come – you improvise. There's always scaffolding outside, with poles and platforms...She's blocked off the stairs – you have to climb from the outside – then there's the music all the night... The temptation – and the fall... That's imminent, the way she's set things up. You must avoid them at all costs.'

'The soldier returns, more or less whole, purblind with the heightened reality he's been through,' says Gary. 'He – or she – beats up on Fancy for some peccadillo, some unfinished spat before she – or he – left, or was conscripted... Maybe 'don't go' or 'don't come back' was said, and then ... they're off!... a hostile place, some revelation sought: the true cross, the cross truth ... the state founded, or dismembered ... an intimate wound is undergone, an atrocity – witnessed or committed, even an onrush of humanity skitters past... And now – the moment comes, you're back! Then, there's to be the hand-to-hand, the struggle on the scaffolding, the fall, maybe the bludgeoning... Then – I'm stuck with Fancy all my life. Or else – renunciation, and off I go...! A stasis! No, Daphne, it's not working, not at all.'

'That's what it was leading to – your conclusion, the choice of how it ends...' says Daphne.

'I thought I'd leave rehab, put a caravan together, and make the trek,' says Gary.

'Nonsense!' says Daphne. 'No one master has ever put the goods together, coralled the animals, and been leader of the whole – a navigator, mediator, boss, responsible for everything – the passage and the discipline. It can't be done. It ought not be done. There's no certitude you, Gary, are, have ever been, the principal, three masters in one head.'

'There's my affinity with animals. Adventure,' Gary says. 'I know the songs, I used to choose the groups, I sent them out, I took my cut. That is the nature of the trade, dear Daphne.'

'We here,' says Daphne, 'sympathise with every side. It's important, though, for you – you need to choose the right. I know there's sex and money into everything as well – but when those soldiers climb the stairs – remember: first, the right answer. Then – the decisive blow.'

*

'Hey, Albi,' Gary says, 'have you seen camels hereabouts, a-gambolling round, and looking for some work?'

'Gary!' says Albi. 'Rehab must have worked its magic! I see you ready for the race again – and, yes: there's camels, pacing on the sand. They look quite bored, though I try to avoid an anthropomorphic take...'

'And are they white?' asks Gary. 'Fleet and eager too?'

'White as the cresting waves,' says Albi. 'Maybe you'll take Fancy when you go?'

'Fancy's difficult,' Gary says. 'Her soldiers threaten her. Again – she's quiet. Her music, though, is very loud. Maybe I should finish up my time here, pair up with Khady, go to her home...'

'She'd be on another block,' says Albi. 'From Senegal – they all lodge there ... the music's different. But then again – you're not celebrity – she is. Besides, you owe her cash. So, in the end – you're nothing. You're private, Gary, no public face. Again – she's black, Or brown, And you...'

'I'm going in and out of being white,' says Gary. 'Besides –
she isn't here. I owe her cash, for sure. But she'd have paired
with me...'

'Maybe you're not so white,' says Albi.

'A colour isn't fixed,' says Gary. 'Maybe if it's in a tube,
coiled and waiting. Otherwise...'

'Gary,' says Albi, 'you're kitsch – right through. You're so
modern! If I put my finger in you, you will crumble, like a
chocolate cake.'

'If those guys come back,' says Gary, untroubled, 'Daphne
knows how to handle them. The jihadis – they'll have failed. I
guess they'll be quite angry. If it's the fascist lot – well, they'll
have to fit back in. The problem is with Fancy... There's no
mediation there... They'll take it out on her...'

'Her area,' Albi says, 'it's always been quite mixed. Each to
his own – none of that liberal tolerance. Are you quite sure
you're not a Kurd? That would be why Fancy took you in.'

'Albi,' Gary says. 'Help me load up the animals. I'm back –
into the concrete. Abstraction's gone.

Back to Nadine and Lily, all those guys, their schemes. And
Claude...'

'I can't come with you,' Albi says, alarmed and backing off.
'I have to take a bus. You can't protect the people here – the
soldiers, they will come and kick down doors, make sure the
residents believe in truth and parsimony... Soldiers don't win or
lose – that's for the generals...' On he talks, and Gary shouts,

'You never helped me with the stones!' And Albi's gone.

To organise a caravan – takes lots of guys: a destination too,
some cash, some food. Gary thinks twice, or more, lets fall the
sack, the camels run along the shore, their big feet turn the
wavelets into spray and mist...

*

'Fancy chose me, Claude,' says Gary, back: dried out, his eyes are white like pearls or shining onions – 'I did not choose her. Protection's not my strongest point. Things as they are – that's what I recognise...'

'You are not cured, dear Gary – you were never sick,' says Claude. 'Just, you were misguided, wrong. We're all incurable – we die. Thoughts don't. They wander round, they maybe kick in doors, and dangle Fancy from the scaffolding. But – things go on and on, it's like the caravaners' song. You're quite enlightened, Gary – all the mysteries have been unveiled...Dialectics requires the abstract and concrete. If you try to end in abstract – it's not pure and final. You will just have failed.'

'I feel the same,' says Gary. 'As what I always do. Did I do well?'

'It's possible Dark City is your S,' says Claude. 'And – no! You did quite bad. You're in the concrete, Gary, now – but you left your Fancy, you didn't take a side ... you didn't lift the stones, nor load the camels... Soldiers will come, like they always have, they wouldn't ask about your origins... You've no nation, and no state. That's good. Religion's fading, quite discredited. So, are you just you, and you alone? No, Gary, you are not a 'you'. You're still a feeble 'I', not binding in. You'll never earn much cash. You must find a place, a niche to fit. Dark City – the scrabble to keep fed, pay off the cops, the crooks... Could you manage that?'

'What should I do, dear Claude?' asks Gary, quite cast down. 'You block off every path...'

'You could go back to Dark City: bring the light. We all want nothing to be wrong with us,' says Claude. 'In full control, and powerful. It's true philosophy we have to master, Gary...'

'No, Claude,' Gary says. 'I know I'm fine. It's money that I need.'

'Dark City has it – cash,' says Claude. 'It's risky getting it, is all.'

'For me,' says Gary. 'It's not an ethical thing, existence. It requires a getting more intense, closer to the marrow, to the hand outstretched. Accepting the sound... Being an agent – that was empty...'

'Now, Gary,' Claude says laughing. 'Emptiness. That's touching on the ethical. Though – it may be something Nadine and Chloe should want to think about.'

'I mean,' says Gary. 'As an agent – you left the people who did anything, created stuff – you left them quite alone, you sent them off, as far as they could go. The content – didn't bother me – I had the nose. I didn't analyse. I knew who's serious, who's honest, who'll go far, where they are booked... Their medleys, their ingratiating: their journeys to the stars ... to be – stars, up there and indistinguishable, each one a-twinkle.'

3

DARK CITY

GARY RETURNS – he's not sick. Maybe he was cured. Samir loves to watch the camels on the shore: 'Albi went,' he says. 'But if you ever needed him, he said to call...'

Fancy is harnessed up – a-dangle on the scaffolding. High up. As high as you can go.

'When they came back,' Fancy says, 'they were all so fucking angry... Soldiers! Some knew they'd lost. Some went to jail – for stealing things, for being rough, for disobedience, obedience. For zeal, for losing faith, for indifference and for cowardice. Some left the front at once, and others took their time. Time – that was what they got, almost all of them!'

She laughs, and Gary too – it's nicely put.

There's quite a crowd below: they don't know why or how she's hanging there. They improvise, some empathise, and some would like to see an end – conventional and swift – that's their temptation. To wish the fall. To see it happen, after all the advertising...

Professionals – they're rescuers, Fancy is unhooked and saved. Gary hovers, doesn't help – it's better so.

'You realise, Fancy,' Gary says, 'I walked away. It doesn't make me emblematic of anything particular – but I see it maybe leaves a question.'

'Staying where I am, that's quite like walking off,' says Fancy. 'If those guys hadn't rescued me – I could have fallen down on Daphne like a bomb...'

'The music, Fancy,' Gary says. 'Technology is not a threat, it's not all about taking power. There's endings, metamorphoses – culture is a sponge. Maybe the jihadis or the other guys are shuffled into science fic...' He shows her – 'Now, Fancy, you put these little claws inside your ears and keep the music to yourself.'

'Oh no,' says Fancy, 'I don't want that stuff to bounce round inside my skull and nowhere to get out.'

'Well,' Gary says, 'I might work nights, and that would solve the noise. What do people here do to earn the cash?'

'Oh,' Fancy says, 'there's things innumerable – but there's the common factors too... There's time and space, and risk, and wearing out quite fast, or lingering in unlikely ways, and telling tales when shifts are done, you go and shoot some pool...'

'That's in the books,' says Gary. 'Old reading doesn't help.'

'Real life is dull,' says Fancy. 'But it's up the slope. It's how the path goes, Gary.'

'I guess they wouldn't want me in the baths,' says Gary. 'Not after the trouble with the stones.'

'Don't give up yet,' says Fancy. 'And anyway – sex isn't on the menu, not for now. Not with me. The soldiers... Being dangled, hung out – it hurts your self-esteem.'

'I wouldn't think of it,' says Gary, and he takes the tram. There's a guy beside him eating ... concealing the treasure in his scarf.

Raw meat. 'I love raw meat,' says Gary, and he looks closely at the guy. They eat it raw in Piemonte... In Ethiopia... so, maybe he's a rasta...

'I love raw meat,' the guy says, 'even though it is a sin. Once we were all friends, the beasts – them and us...'

They pass a sign – The Great Rift. Abyssinian Butchery. 'That'll be the Italians,' Gary says. 'What they're remembered by.'

The guy passes him the bone. They've no common language, except English. Gary gnaws, then shouts – 'Oh no, my friend – it isn't camel!?'

'No, no, it's donkey,' says the guy. 'I read about the slaughtering – the jawbone of an ass. I don't believe it could be done. It's far too small.'

'An error of translation,' Gary says. 'Or someone's ears were plugged.'

'Look,' says the guy. 'I'll tell you how to get a job. Where they shoot pool, you watch them play. Then in a while, they'll give an errand – a message or a package. But, you don't want to stay like that – you'd need to start a bizness...'

'I know,' says Gary, 'I already started one, the caravans... They don't all finish well,' and he remembers Claude – the comic, Deadpool... Claude in the ether now, knowing everything...

Gary hangs around the pool hall.

The day passes, watching guys behind the spots and stripes ... the coloured balls rolling on a pastel universe...

'I read an article,' says Fancy, when he's back, 'about the great life we have here, and how we all muck in and love each other...'

'That'll be Nadine,' says Gary. 'Her writing. Claude sent me here, Nadine writes the fantasy – I bet Chloe's Daphne's boss – so they're all over us, shouting the alarms, like you were, Fancy, suspended on the scaffolding above the drop.'

'They'll know the law, Gary. Not the cops' and soldiers' law, not the faith – a bigger law,' says Fancy. 'More reliable.'

'It's metaphysics, Fancy,' Gary says. 'I made contracts, naturally – it didn't mean a lot. That was the law. Anyway – no law will stop a guy from hanging you outside. I'd help, of course...'

'If you were hereabouts sometimes...' says Fancy: 'You just hang out. I know you, Gary, even if I don't know law.'

Gary observes: the pool balls in their circuits, the players – raging sometimes at the cheats, their own bad strategy, impatient, extinguishing the game, breaking the cues – the balls exploding, cloth gouged, the slate beds incised with new regulations ... fresh ivory carved and shaped, new balls to scrutinise, just off the round, and so the whole game loses a particle, drops into dark, flaring, and expires...

'Fancy!' Gary shouts, returning. 'You've been firing from up high! My pistol – I forget what it was to be used against – the bullets are all spent...'

'Of course!' says Fancy. 'That's the point. You have a pistol for unknown events. I wanted justice...'

'And you fired down in the street – haphazard?' Gary asks.

'Of course I aimed,' says Fancy. 'There's no justice without an aim. The angle's strange – you could hit them if they're lying down – but from up here – they run, they're trapezoids, with match-heads...'

'And who responded to your fire?' asks Gary.

'You bourgeois,' Fancy shouts. 'You think our world is only drugs and whores. That's what you'd like. No one replied. They knew I wanted justice – that way there's respect...'

'Well,' Gary says, 'maybe this way I'll get some work – they'll see we are a feisty pair...'

'Gary,' says Fancy, 'I wouldn't cut you in. You're lazy, clueless. Samir, now – he waits by the sea. There's every kind of thing – the sailors in their wrecks, the mermaids in their shells... And me? I'm sick, Gary: I sell my pills. I'm sicker still – I sell more pills.'

'I won't insist,' says Gary. 'There'll be something more to come...'

'Oh well,' says Fancy, angry now, 'there's asset management, of course: – matchmaking, ops on your genitals, exorcism, divination, first communions...'

'I'll find something,' Gary says. 'I thought I had something before, up there, above. A subject for Nadine, for Chloe. I thought I gave it up, but it was nothing; it turned out it was nothing.'

'Trash,' says Fancy. 'It's good. It's all around, it fills in every space. The word is good. It's the whole habitat, without it, we'd be nothing. There'd be nothing. All you see is dumped, degraded, winding down. The universe! – all stuff discarded, rusted, poured into automobiles, breathed in and out – grit, semen, buried, re-dug, fermented, spat into cuspidors, arms and legs incinerated... Trash. Hah! It's good, the sound...'

'They say it's lived history, life lived, what we were and are,' says Gary.

'Don't be an idiot, Gary,' Fancy says. 'You know that's said to cheer us up. We've made nothing but rubbish, and it's us, all that we think we are and want to be.'

She reaches up a box. 'See,' she says. 'It's not stereotypes. I don't go for those. It's all cops' stuff.' There's buckles, a button, a shirtsleeve, a badge, a broken lock. 'It's just pieces. Not for, and not against – order, quite neutral, that's done its job and is no more.'

'It's like philosophy,' says Gary. 'I thought we all were thinking it. I thought that was me, us, that everything we said was classic, what we thought was like a fingernail of ormolu, or a veneer – fallen off something, waiting to be stuck back on, or a frieze, waiting to be lifted on a tympanum. But – it was just pieces. Junk. Things that weren't worth much ever, and now were nothing you could use them for. Like lengths of twine they

say that is 'the narrative, the news'. How your soldiers must
have laughed – if they had seen TV, instead of their whole story:
a cat's cradle. Against nature, everyone's. A sample: pee in a
bottle, a crust of blood.'

'Rubbish, Gary,' Fancy says. 'Thrown away, and ever near.
Belongs to us, it follows and precedes. Unless, of course – your
Nadine – she wants to buy a house round here – then she can
have mine, and keep the trash... They read the book, your boss
friends, Gary – *The Philosophy of Cash*, always in print.'

'I'm not sure you make the right distinction, Fancy. To me,'
says Gary. 'There's trash, and then there's broken things. Quite
different, even if they look the same, and they're stacked up,
mulching in the same tall pile.'

'It's true, Gary,' Fancy says, 'things in the trash you can take
and mend them – but it's all the same, it's trash. Don't be
judgmental, Gary. There's no hierarchy in things you throw
away, you've finished with. It's time past, time forgotten. It
leads to more time, more trash – no more, and certainly no less.
There's differences in trash, but they're of no account.'

'Tell me how you make your cash, Fancy, and maybe you can
cut me in,' says Gary.

'There!' says Fancy. 'I'm not about you. No one is. I'm
telling you about the whole, not how you can leech on me. And
– forget the goddam soldiers – they don't know a thing. And
they hung me out, over the drop.'

'I'm desperate, Fancy,' Gary says. 'My friends have gone –
Albi, Samir. Franco.'

'I don't think they were your friends,' says Fancy. 'They
didn't let you in, not in on their game. They got tired of you.
You want to play, but you aren't up to it. It's like pool – you
watch, and no one asks you over for a frame.'

'I'd like to play,' says Gary. 'That's what I've always wanted.
The guys here – they take it serious. And they don't pay well.

But right now – I want to know what it is you do, Fancy, how I
can...'

'The guys that wait upon the shore – they're not just there to
count the waves. Containers, Gary! One will come, that
someone's waiting for,' she says.

'What?' asks Gary. 'Arms? Some gold? A preacher with a
book – a new one, maybe one he's discovered in a cave...?'

'That's fantasy,' says Fancy. 'Soldiers don't read books. They
want the money – they will fight for that. They need to eat, like
you and me. It's just – I'm different. They hung me out, the
soldiers did – but I was high, high up on top of them.'

'You look as desperate as me,' says Gary. 'Unquiet. People
who have peace – have power, and lustre: they ... speak to
invisible crowds, like Claude. Write for the unseen, like Nadine.
Chivvy. Like Chloe.'

'Look at me,' says Fancy. 'How can you do what I do? How
can you think of it?'

She turns up the sound, and waves him out, out of her room.

'Look, Gary!' Daphne says. 'How beautiful! This flag! They
all should look like that!'

There's a big hot sun in its middle: 'I'd love to hang it out,'
says Daphne. 'But anyone who's not a Kurd might take a shot at
it.' The room is full of flags, fluttering like butterflies trapped in
a bottle.

'You keep the peace, Daphne,' Gary says. 'Remember,
"acknowledge our dependence": that's what you said – it should
keep us safe.'

'I recognise the end, Gary,' Daphne says. 'Apocalypse. The
book is inconclusive, though. That is their way, the books. And
it's long – longer than a war. And the desires... People will do
anything to stretch them out. Who knows what countries – the
people landed in them – really want? Where they begin, and
where they end... No, Gary, it's best not to provoke. Though it's

a sin against the beautiful,' and she furls the sun-flag, stands it with the rest.

'Listen, Daphne,' Gary says. 'I know the guys that's over everything that goes on here – the writers and the bosses – Nadine, Chloe – and the guy the people follow, Claude. I can be of use. I don't eat much, and never change my clothes...'

'Work, Gary?' Daphne says. 'I know your friends, that count the waves, and wave to matelots. Then, there's the pool – you're a poor fish, Gary, looking for a rock where you can hide ... or an odd job, cleaning up the sharks ... you're compromised, my dear – down here, up there...'

There's a sadness in this dusty room, where few things are decided – because they can't be done, not any of them.

'You missed your boat, dear Gary,' Daphne says. 'You were once an agent, you filled the world with music. It was a global scene – and all that, you gave up – the music wasn't to your taste, the guys that strummed – they disappeared... You didn't understand a thing. Diffusion was the aim. The sound, the noise – it shows us humans walking carelessly, not hiding, and not hunting – just staring round, waving, smoking our spliffs, naming the species that are left... The disappearance – was natural and good. People get tired of guys who sing – the culture, though, is wrapped around like underwear. You had it all, Gary, and you let it fall.'

'It wasn't like that, not a bit,' says Gary. 'Not like that at all. Of course, you could make it up to sound like that. I might have had the fall. That would mean I'm worse off here...'

'Of course you are,' shouts Daphne. 'No casuistry! Nadine, Chloe – what more is there you could have had? You could have played on them and sung so loud! You don't laugh here, Gary, there's no fiddling that lifts you up... This here's a town that gets bombarded first ... before the rest.'

'If only, Gary,' Fancy says. 'I could go down – if there's a stair, a chute – go down into the street.'

'I could take you, Fancy, on my back,' says Gary. 'If you're quite sure. Bad things...'

'Yes!' she says. 'Bad things! And I'll wear my spurs. I'll spit on the sacred fires, and make your pork chops bleed, Gary, I'll spur you in the devil's race – my spit is gasoline, I'm full of it, I'll drive us both, the fires will burn the city down – but not my house, up there, it's up too high, way high... you can see the faithless matelot select the box of tricks and tip it in the surf. You want to know what's in the box? The box that rises from the waves?'

'More than anything, Fancy,' Gary says. 'It's the one last thing I need to make my happiness complete.'

'Oh chuffy-chuff,' says Fancy. 'It'll never be complete. Just add more fuel, you'll laugh your eyebrows off.'

Her spurs are like cocks wear – she digs them in. 'Wait!' she shouts – 'Bring me my spyglass, Gary...' And he does.

'The box is here,' she says. 'Samir is fluttering round, his crowbar ready – I can see inside... Oh – see the people run and hop, throw down their crutches, join the race – the gods have sent their bounty ... gold, arms, or stuff to smoke...'

'Fancy,' says Gary. 'I think you've an idea what it may be...'

'We shan't go in the street,' says Fancy. 'I can spy it all from here.'

It's fruit.

Fruit cold, now sweating in the sun – ripe apples tumbling round your head, pears wedged in to make a cube – pineapples with their shock of hair ... then fruits of no account – the Chinese gooseberries, the pawpaws – that intrusive name, the mangoes crushed ... unlovely cacoes, undecided what to be when they grow up – the advocates, carambolas, infernal leeks pulled up from hell, and mandrake roots ... the marrows flattened, grapes in ferment...

Oh no – they're salty – and they start to rot.

The crowd shrieks, retrieves the sticks it threw away, and waves them in despair.

'Temptation!' Fancy says. 'It doesn't work today ... there is no hope when that is gone...' and then the creatures slither out – the maggots and the worms, the snakes, the pythons and the boas, lying bewildered on the shore.

Samir's at the window. 'I climbed up the scaffolding,' he says: he holds out to Fancy. 'The last, the imperishable...' he says. 'Saved from the sea.'

'It's a crab apple,' Fancy says, making a face.

'The box, the square. It was not the one,' says Samir. 'There is nothing whole and true. Not a peach, not a melba, not a macedonia – nothing human, no place – hope deferred, Fancy. The desire remains...'

'Yes, Samir – the want, the desire. But the whole, the pursuit? The fulfilment, Samir,' Fancy asks. 'When will that be? Now, the theft, the complicity, breaking the law that's set to trap us, put us inside – but, the temptation, Samir, of doing time for what is sweet and passionate – that awaits... In the end, we know there'll be the fall. We'll be entrapped, our striving ... to no avail. And yet – that is our purpose, Samir – to try, to fail, that's to know everything, to see it all...'

'It's all true, Fancy,' Samir says. 'But the true shipment, its landfall – remains intact, integral, pure and ripe. It will all happen, as we hope, expect. The chance will come, lie there, sealed, upon the shore – we'll break it open, the secret store...'

'And we'll be punished, Samir,' Fancy says. 'That is for sure.'

'It will come to everyone,' Samir says. 'We'll all be there. We'll make a city, Fancy, the charcoal buildings, with their

perilous stairs, the flags, the dark... In it together – that is what
they say...'

'That all makes sense,' says Gary. 'I shan't be there. I'd
rather be up high above – bathing with Claude – his followers,
impotent but well-informed. Nadine with her scripts, Chloe with
her rules – it's comforting...'

*

'Those slithering beasts,' says Daphne. 'Out from the crate. You
should have put them into quarantine. The underground is full of
them, they've quite displaced the rats – a moment, they'll be up
the scaffolding...'

'An epidemic!' Fancy says. 'I'm safe. I sleep alone, a pig's
foot underneath the bed...'

'This place,' says Gary. 'Has the equipment for rehab – I'm
sure we can defeat them all – invisible worms, the flattering
snakes...'

*

'It isn't them,' says Daphne. 'It is the plague they bring. The
worms – they'll get us all. And temptation needs no wisdom and
no curiosity... Snakes' days are done. The worms are certain of
abundance – so, no: it's not the certainty of death – it's the
lottery of plague, the sickness that's upon us all. Chloe was here
– she slapped me! "Only the poor get sick," she said, "And here
I see the richness – gambling and good sex, community and
digging drains ... and now you say there's exodus! Put on a
show, a carnival! Daphne! – attract a crowd, display the talents,
colours and the dance..."'

'The guys are leaving,' Gary says. 'Maybe that's what
happened to my city, S: the fear. The other people, who infect...'

'I've no resource,' says Daphne. 'Just the flags... A parade, with twirlers, maybe, in bathing suits...'

'The sickness starts with mottling,' says Fancy. 'The flesh – it is a giveaway.'

'We must be critical,' says Samir. 'What is the cause? What makes us sick? The fruit? Or the competition that feeds upon it – the snakes?'

'No, Samir,' Fancy says. 'It could be the hunger makes us sick.'

'I'm off,' says Daphne. 'A parade of flags. Attract people from all over – each watching for their emblem. Everyone must have a banner. It's an allegory...'

'Allegory?' Samir says. 'It's old hat. We should prepare to run – eat stuff from cans, bind our pant legs so the creatures can't slide up.'

'I have another thought,' says Gary. 'You know how the poor are seen? Poor guys get lent some cash they can't pay back, or given some they shouldn't spend on bets and booze. It's frittered off. That means they're always poor, and now despised, distrusted. Rich people borrow – they pay back, because they're rich. Maybe they lend – it's all the same to them. If they owe cash – they're still the guys that own the banks...'

'Where is the plot?' asks Fancy.

'A gas, a weapon – a plague without a cure, eliminates the poor,' says Gary...

'No!' says Samir. 'Rich guys need the poor to do the work and – just to be poor...'

They stare round – too many theories, none useful for the sweats and buboes...

'I'm safe,' says Fancy, once again. 'The stairs – are broken, so you need to climb outside...'

'Wait, Fancy!' Gary says. 'I go down to the pool hall every day – I have to mix, ingratiate myself. If it's a gas, some germ – it rises... Fancy, you are more exposed...'

'The germs,' says Samir, 'they look like those aeroplanes, invisible, the silent bombers. You can't see anything, the dynamite, the death – it catches you as if your number's tattooed upon your head... It doesn't miss – you think it's random, but it's targeted on the deserving... I wish I hadn't gone to school – all that stuff they fill you with – an hour of vomiting, the buboes swell – those useless lessons: nothing is left...'

'It's like a war for sure,' says Fancy. 'But it's much worse – no one wins, and powerful friends don't help.'

'We could drink,' says Gary. 'It doesn't cause the sickness, and no one's said it's not a cure.'

'You'd have to go down in the street to get the booze,' says Samir. 'You might get the unction on your boots.'

'You might be sniped,' says Fancy. 'I hear Chloe's closed the city. We're in isolation. She says it limits deaths – but it just concentrates them. We're doomed, all doomed. It's been so since the start, of course.' She lies face down on the bed, quite silent.

'Chloe's a pre-war type,' Samir says. 'The old regime. "Live clean, and you can live for ever..." Gary! – your friend Nadine – she takes that line... she writes, "the sickness comes from our behaving bad". Bad sex, bad jobs, bad wages. Coughing in each other's eyes, the spitting while we copulate. Fancy – you're right. We're doomed – we get the sickness; if we don't, we're still as bad as one another. Ignorant, promiscuous...'

'Imprisoned,' Fancy shouts, 'disinfected, under martial law – renegades, defeatists, traitors, cowards all – bomb us, shell us – bring out the smallpox and the clap – fire the bacilli from howitzers, burn us in eternal fires, bury us in rubble, execute us, leave our bones out in the street...'

'Poor Khady,' Samir says. 'The Senegalese – they're particularly prone ... they catch the lot, they're from the dirty continent... Gary – you should go and rescue her, bring her up here...'

'Stay where you are,' shouts Fancy. 'Beware the strangers, their fevers and their chills. They're born with feeble destinies. Genetics has the final word. It always does. Besides,' and she whispers to Gary – 'I have the antidote...'

'Before or after, Fancy?' Gary asks. 'Do you wait until it's caught you, or before...'

'Just as you please,' says Fancy. 'It shows you didn't run. Here it is, you wear it so...'

And she pins it... 'It's a medal, Fancy,' Gary says. 'It doesn't seem to mean you've fought, nor that you've won... Indeed, it's blank...'

'What would you write on it?' she asks. '"For valour"? Wear it, Gary, and remember – hold your breath when you're in company.'

'If I am not infected, that would show it works?' asks Gary, unconvinced.

'Exactly so,' says Fancy. 'Now – go fetch the beer, Samir!'

He's down and up again, a six-pack ... bleach and carbolic on his boots. 'Let's see your tongue, now, Samir,' Fancy shouts. It's small and fleeting – a canary type...

'It's always been like that,' says Samir, covering up.

'The air, Samir,' shouts Fancy, much alarmed, 'you let it in... Now we shall have to flee – leave this unholy city, trudge the weedy fields, the bony oxen gasping in the sand – and maybe found another country, a happy one, a beaming flag...'

'The money, Fancy,' Gary says. 'It always helps – we'll need to pay the masons and the priests...'

'"We"?' says Fancy. 'Gary! You stay here. Parley with Chloe. Your love, Nadine – she owes you something. Have

Claude down to take a bath with you ... steam off those viruses, resist, resist!'

'I'm flattered, Fancy,' Gary says. 'But – those were my friends from higher up the chain... They're shutting us in here ... the fear – it travels faster than the poisoned kiss, the mortal sneeze...'

'They told you, Gary,' Fancy says, 'it's the concrete that you lack. The city – it's gone solid, petrified. And someone here must watch the shore. Now, Samir – ready to give a lift? Don't let me gyre as I'm let down.' But–

Samir is stricken, and his guts rush forth.

Fancy stretches on the bed: 'This bed is made of gold,' she says. 'Something no one can share with me. Samir – this is not a favour. It's your duty – and your interest – to carry me, laid out and legless on the springs, to some flat space, with water sweet and boneless fish, fat animals that graze, blue dawns and purple sunsets... A city, Samir. It might even bear your name...'

'S...' Samir gasps out...

'He's too sick to bear the burden, Fancy,' Gary says. 'And – Fancy! This bed looks like it's made of brass...'

'In the desolation, my new home,' says Fancy. 'Bright City! Making an assay would be out of reach.'

'I'm no expert,' Gary says, 'but – Samir's nearly dead.'

'Oh no!' shouts Fancy, 'here's too high to die... Lash me, Gary, lash me to the bed. Samir will carry me, down and down, down to the street...'

'I'm not quite dead,' says Samir, 'but by the time we're down...'

'That's time enough!', says Fancy. 'Gary! Give him your medal – now you can write "For valour" on it – take me down, you faithful watcher by the shore! Remember – do not tip or jolt...'

'I've cooked myself,' says Samir. 'I'm salty.'

'We'll eat you, Samir,' Fancy says. 'But sparingly, because we love and trust you. You have done fine service. But I fear you're toxic still.'

Gary shouts down, 'I see you lying there, Fancy, spread out. I can't come down. I must watch the sea – and I'm afraid, afraid of death...'

Fancy can't untie herself. She shouts up, 'I need you Gary. Without you, I am nothing.'

Nadine would never say such a thing, an admission – Chloe wouldn't need to say it. It couldn't cross Claude's mind... They're around, always, interfering, nudging – but Gary doesn't give them weight. At last – he's needed.

'All right, Fancy,' Gary shouts. 'I'll think about it. Maybe Samir could manage one last gesture...'

'Not gestures, idiot,' shouts Fancy. 'Untying. Me. Then we can tie Samir to the bed, and you can carry him, as though he is a relative, a father even. And found the city... A Troy, perhaps, bright and impregnable.'

'No, Fancy,' Gary says. 'It's crazy. Two people and a victim – that's not how cities come about. We have survived. Your capital is safe – you're bound to it. Here we belong, along with those who're left. It all starts up again...'

'People die,' says Fancy. 'They leave their jobs to those who don't. Gary – now, you're the marker in the pool hall, right at the heart of everything. Food, drink, games ... it's trivial, but brings you fun.'

'It's not enough,' says Gary. 'Sure, it's concrete – but there's something that's not there – not just the people ... the essence.'

'The essence is there, Gary. You must know. Knowing. That's the essence of the essence,' Fancy says.

'Yes, Fancy,' Gary says, 'I know.'

'I should never have got married,' Fancy says. 'I'm not the type.'

'You? Married? I didn't know,' says Gary.

'That's the point, the point exactly,' Fancy says.

'I'll look for a room elsewhere,' says Gary. 'Nearer to work, silent at night.'

'Go away, Gary,' Fancy says. 'You're dull, with no imagination. Repetitive, unspiritual.'

'That seems the case,' says Gary. 'I'm ready now – for true love. And Daphne says an epidemic's better than a war. It solves the unemployment, there's no ruins to clear up. Maybe it was just a passing sickness, not an epidemic. Not that anyone that's close to it would understand the difference...'

'Oh,' Fancy says. 'I understand all differences. My business rests on them.'

'We got panicky, when there was the epidemic.' Gary says. 'It maybe was a policy. They don't take care of us... A cull...'

Being a marker's a responsibility. There's pool and snooker, billiards with pockets, with *birilli* – the marker's job requires a total honesty, the truth. Complete non-interference, better than the gods or God, there's nothing random, loving, hating – all that is out. You don't much care who wins. No heroes – and no valour. There's essence, maybe, and it's monotonous. It suits Gary for the while, the while he's waiting for his true love.

'So', Daphne says. 'You're with the reactionary gangs? The crooked bosses, Gary?'

'I'm untouchable, Daphne,' Gary says. 'They provoke me – to cheat, to cross the line, give favours, jiggle the sliders, change the rules. It's never in my interest. If I'm not me – I lose their faith. Crooks and toilers – it's all the same to me – the game's self-evident. Everybody understands that if they cheat...'

'What, Gary?' Daphne asks. 'What, when they cheat?'

'They'll sort it out among themselves,' he says. 'The legends get it right. Vendetta – it's condoned. I'm there to keep the

score, and nothing more. It's a record of what they've done –
they have to be content with that.'

'Slim pickings, Gary,' Daphne says. 'Life with Nadine – there
you had more ins and outs, more ups and downs. More rivals.
You were little then – the guys would praise you, maybe – then
off to someone else, another agent, skimming off their work,
their sweat ... their music packed into those black rigid bags.'

'Daphne, it wasn't that at all,' says Gary. 'It's true – I had my
rivals; but the music – that came from necessity, it was
industrial. A habit. Everywhere it came and wriggled in your
ears, new models every day, simple and loud, declaimed, the
beat four-square. I was a step, dear Daphne – just one step in the
stair, the stairway that went right to the top. Heaven, Daphne.
Promising true love – whether in shared mouths, complicit
naughtiness, love of whatever crooked pot, ogival wheel, came
from the oven or the anvil. Love of whatever shape I chose that
day to be – in anger, or in somnolence, indifference or play ...
the groups obedient, patient – packed off to wherever I sent out
the caravans, the guys all singing as they plodded off ... my
camels, or my yaks...'

'No one seems worthy of you, Gary,' Daphne says, and
laughs. 'Yet you're a poor idiot: you doss upon the tables here
and eat the buns they leave...'

'It's not the seeker, Daphne, the dispatcher, the foot soldiers,'
Gary says. 'They're interchangeable. Those are inevitable, part
of the set, the outlets where you plug your instrument. No – it is
the essence. That's what everybody seeks... The mark, the true
mark... That's what matters.'

'It isn't so,' says Daphne. 'Gary – you're just food. You
survive here through your impartiality. You punish no one, you
don't criticise or fight. You tally, that is all. And when some
boss gets taken out – it all goes back to zero. A new match starts.
It's a pool hall, Gary. The lights are bright over the tables:

behind, the tempting fruit in the machines. This is your
beginning and the end, my dear. This is the whole, and what you
see's what you must pot. The game, the game! And after every
game, the score is back to zero.'

'The flags, Daphne?' Gary asks. 'The parade to hex the
plague?'

'Oh, the paraders all ran off,' she says. 'Or dropped dead in
the ditch. I still have every flag. Maybe one is missing, Gary. I'll
be magnanimous – maybe your city already has its banner, its
standard floating on the battlements...'

'It's useless making crenellations,' Gary says. 'There's
always someone paid to open up side gates... You try to buy
them off, the guys outside, waiting to cut some throats...'

'Fancy's gold bed?' laughs Daphne. 'It's true she has a traffic
– but the bed is painted lead...'

'I thought it brass,' says Gary. 'Lead is a good idea. False
gold – it travels round ... it's better than those paper notes on
mulberry cloth.'

'Don't try to court me, Gary,' Daphne says. 'You're a pure
soul in a job. Me – I'm a threadbare soul, in job that's pure.
Power. Making people happy.'

'You're not on my screen, Daphne,' Gary says, his brain goes
back to Claude, who used to say this.

Daphne's face and clothes seem bolted on. There's always
people round who'd want to strip them off.

'My power's made up of all you guys', she says. 'Your hope,
your trust. I'll pour it down upon you all as happiness.'

'It's a big thing, Daphne,' Gary says, quite disbelieving.

'And I'm big with it,' Daphne says, twisting on her big legs,
slowly waving big buttocks to a silent tune.

There's a match on – big bosses – there's lightning, off go the
lights – a tidal wave lifts up the hall, the tables – everything –
goes TILT. The balls – they skidder round, they jump like

pomegranates, bounce off a baulk and stun a bodyguard... The scores slide up and down – the guys shout, some with glee, others are panicking – there's thunder on the timpani – 'game over', Gary shouts, although it's not...

*

'The flood,' says Daphne, 'cuts us off. Worse than a surge of cops. We are an island now. For sure, that brings security. Investment, maybe. Travel's impossible, of course. Your friend Claude,' she says to Gary, who's survived, 'promotes us as a haven. A paradise. The rich will come, sort out our misery. Perhaps we are the only ones who're left – no ship, no raft this time – a land, shipwrecked... This water, full of crawling things – it slows the planet down, we're waterlogged...'

It's true. There's daylight now for days – there's dancing by the mangroves, bars stay open for a week when steady night arrives, indigo and sweet... and then there's sleep, everybody hugger-muggered on the shore, like iguanas blue and green with algae and the dark...

Fancy's building has survived – the scaffolding is swept away, she's isolated, screaming down, 'Climb up my walls and rescue me, and you shall share my golden bed, I'll wrap my golden hair around, and you may share my Fancy name...'

'The first thing,' Daphne says, 'is – build another hall. Pool tables take the violence out the scene, the games will occupy the minds...'

'The bosses,' Gary says, 'have gotten tired of games. Now, they seek an immortality. It's sport...'

There's waterskis and skates, and spearing fish and netting sharks...

'At least there's fewer dead around,' says Daphne. 'The water came and floated them away, it was a resurrection ... ink watered on the registers has blurred the names, the memories are washed quite blank...'

'Samir – he was already dead and now, perhaps, he's gone...' says Gary, finding time to shed his tear.

'The causeway,' Daphne says. 'It sounds a term from your philosophy – but no, there was no overwhelming cause, no push, no pull, no reason, no campaign... After the flood, we saw the deportees, they cleaned them out, they made them walk along the strip, so gay, with white red blue – the plastic bags to carry what they had... Samir – he'd have been one of those, alive or dead, infectious, on the mend. And then – the strip of walkway sank, and left us happy here... The sea, the sea – oh Gary, now, it's all around ... we play upon it like a nursery rug, we stuff it in our mouths and chew – the jellies and the walking fruits, up from the black – oh Gary! it's our box of toys ... the monster swallowed that can swallow us...'

'I never had a childhood, Daphne,' Gary says. 'With jelly babies, soldiers, all that stuff. But – I also fear the endless sea, it reaches for us, its soft mouth, its grasping throat, worms that take us whole, transform us into ropes of kelp, blue lights that suck us down... It has no limit, no satiety, no shame. It has a tick, a tock, a great confusion, animals that's doodled, coloured, gilded – eyes a myriad, a shingle, a cape of pearly buttons, they spot the movements, not the shades...'

'Pity, Gary, pity,' Daphne says. 'Cast it around! Even the cannibals dance, replete, upon the shore. You know – I bring the happiness, but no – it doesn't last. Nothing is lasting, Gary – only the wish, the aspiration. The happiness. All the rest – it changes, constantly – the sea, the land – you know, beneath, is all a raging fire that if it stops – we're done! Not roasted, Gary: – cold and dead. Nothing! Nothing: that does not flow and run away, and change from brown to green to red to brown. That is the essence, Gary, that is why the bosses fight and dare, and tuck the colours out of sight, always the same – the same sequences, the numbers and the shapes – the colours, Gary ... nothing changes them, their order, but the game ... it always starts and every time it's different and ends the same with nothing, and from nothing – a new game is born...'

She weeps.

Gary says, 'I pity you, Daphne, I pity me, and everyone. But – it's not concrete, that is for sure. I'll maybe take a boat. Look for Samir – in a city, or a camp. Or all the rest, the sad friends grey and waiting on the shore. This is not my place, Daphne. You are the counsellor, I know: the happiness you want to bring – it fleets away. Best try exclusively for power, enjoy its slender life...'

'Gary,' says Daphne, 'I can give advice. It's true, it all gets butchered in procedure – but I could tell you, Gary: how you don't belong here, not with me, to me, with Fancy... Her punk life – so true, so punishing... All your friends are dead, sequestered or dispersed, like Samir – the promises, they dangle, "meet me soon..." or never... Then – keeping the score. It might be strategy – for you, Gary, it's not. There's no end game, you have no master play, no winning shot, no rest, no cannon, no curlicue behind your back... You haven't understood, my dear. Power – is happiness, and happiness – is power. There is no "either–or".'

'You underestimate me,' Gary says. 'You see no depth – but that's your eyesight, Daphne. Everybody knows, inside themselves – there's nothing strange, unknown. We're always training for the longer march, the trial from which we won't come back. We're athletes with internal tracks. We are our own competitors. Heroes and champions! I'm off! I'll look for Samir...'

But Daphne – she's gone.

*

Some guys now – they must have a boat...

They land him on the other shore. 'Samir? A person, or a place?' they ask. 'If it's a person – probably he's dead.'

The guys – know all about Nadine, and Chloe: they tune in to Claude. Those three – they're never going to disappear, or tone down by themselves.

'The people on the island,' says a guy, 'they're like a sheep – it trusts you, whether it's sacrifice or feast you have in mind – it trusts you, when you talk of paradise, and cut its throat.'

'I need to take a bus, my friend,' says Gary. 'It's quicker than if I walk.'

The guy says – 'It isn't "quick" you want, my friend: it's "where"?'

*

'Ever hear of someone called Samir?' Gary, waiting at the stop, asks Mae, who stands beside him.

'I know your type,' she says. 'You want to slot guys in, each to a pocket or a drawer. What differentiates for you? A colour? Religion? Class? Some minority? Or you like drama? – money comes in, maybe someone doesn't pay their tax, or someone shoots them while they watch tv... You don't want to do all that, not any of it. It's all been done, and everybody here – where you're going, anyway – we're all mixed up. A melted pot, a salad bowl of dandelions and radishes. I hope it's not you want to find yourself?' she asks. 'Find a pocket, one where you belong? Along the baulk and – poof! you've disappeared?'

'Oh no,' says Gary: 'I'm at peace with all of that. I know exactly where I'm headed for.'

There's military looking trucks, some parked in their direction, others going back towards the sea...

'The deportees?' asks Gary. 'Maybe he's among them... Samir: he was my old friend, I think?'

'Just sit down here,' says Mae, sliding Gary's head on her soft breast. 'I'll take you to Samir. There in the forest, there's a camp. It's all a Disneyland. The animals are small – too small to end up in the pan. They don't grow large – and so they never die – and there are sheep, with little humps...' But – Gary sleeps. He trusts Mae, her haven where they're all mixed up, he dreams of hard nights, hunched down on those slate beds, of Daphne waving flags and Fancy – aloft and screaming in her noisy tower...

He wakes. No bus has come, but Mae has gone. So has his stash. 'Oh no!' he says aloud. 'My document, that tells me who I am. All gone! – and gone to someone else, who'll start it all again, figuring where is S, where we were born and dumped or saved...'

'You're quite upset,' the guy, Viktor, standing over him, remarks. 'There goes the bus! You're lost, you've lost yourself. Let's see what we might build up from what you've left.'

'It's terrible,' says Gary, 'but not as bad as that!'

'In olden days,' says Viktor, 'when you had died, if things had gone quite well before – you found the river, drank, forgot it all – you saw a cleft, a rift – and back you came! But now – it's all done here on earth. You never die, you metamorphose! Out go your beliefs, in come some more, you live for centuries – or so it seems – then there's your return to earthy things, your resurrection, and ... it's full of thieves! Everywhere! But, Gary, you're an honest type – you'll always lose, but keep an aura on your head... Someone must have given it, in another life...'

'Hey!' Gary says. 'It's not reducible to in and out, passing from death to death, the spindle and the light, the river and the drink... Let's think – my identity... I lost my cash – and so, I can afford no charity, that's clear. Circumcised, for sure, and twice at least. And as for prayer – there's nothing in a day I do five times. No sabbath in the pool hall – they just played and played... Whatever I have been – I'd always lapsed. I must have disbelieved. No family, no flag... No origin.'

'Oh, Gary,' Viktor says. 'That still leaves lots of things you might have been. Many many lives you've plodded through. The same for me, until I disembodied! Philosophy on little telephones – you don't need putrefy, you're odourless.'

'Yes, Viktor,' Gary says. 'You won't die – but still – you'll disappear. You could be my old powerful friend – Claude. One or both – recycled, re-fleshed out. Come back to my concerns. There is my past, and that's one mystery. But then – there's now: another puzzle. What am I now, where do I fit? I thought Mae was the beautiful ... accommodating ... peace and provocation too ... might I still love her...? After all, she took my stash, my past, identity. More intimate than that – someone may take my memory, even my soul – identity is deeper, though...'

'Hold back,' says Viktor. 'Identity is past. It's yesterday, even the day before. It's process now, not agency. Your soul's long gone. So's paradise, and paper documents.'

'You're trivial,' says Gary. 'Commonplace.'

They square up, spar together – Viktor lands a blow, and Gary bleeds.

'Now, Gary,' Viktor says. 'Don't be shy. Do you drink? Lots?'

'As an agent, you're obliged. As a marker, no, you can't,' says Gary.

'You see,' Viktor says. 'Drinking from the river. We don't remember that, of course, it's been blacked out, but it's in our bones. Maybe you were a soldier? A fighter? Maybe you sympathised – and that's why you can't remember what you did. Bad guy. It's an alibi, internalised...'

'Everything has its argument,' says Gary. 'You're taught to sympathise, but not too much. The bad things spread around – you start excusing people – they dump on you...'

'I think we've found the nub,' says Viktor. 'Maybe that's as far as we should go.'

'You're wrong, my friend,' says Gary. 'It's not cosmology, or terrorism – it's my stash. That's gone. I used to send guys out – what they did, I've no idea. It's spreading culture, Viktor.'

'You don't need admit a thing,' says Viktor. 'You did it all for profit, I am sure.'

'It was art – like pool, mostly the shots don't quite come off,' says Gary.

'Talking of shots, Gary,' Viktor says. 'Before we see the cops – it's best to ask, are you clean, my friend? The bosses, now, you knew them all...'

'Everybody knows them,' Gary says. 'That's why they're boss.'

You knew? Took part? Nearly took part? You haven't told me everything...' says Viktor.

'There's never anyone to tell everything to,' says Gary. 'What would that do? The time that it would take! It's like Claude's followers – they're naked. There is nothing true on them. And I don't want to hurt poor Mae, the thief – I want my stuff, is all.'

'Of course, she gets to keep the cash,' says Viktor. 'You just want the document.'

'No, Viktor!' Gary says, 'I want it all.'

'We all do, Gary,' Viktor says. 'But your position's weak.'

'Even if you could,' says Gary. 'You couldn't tell everything, not even all the bad, nor write it down, no one does that, ever has ... nor say what you don't know – the consequences and the accidents, – or just you hadn't heard about, or bother with, or just say things are terrible, the wars, vendettas – that supposes every side is right, and wrong.'

'If you go to the police, Gary – be very careful,' Viktor says. 'About your stash, its provenance. Your love of Mae. I take in what you say – it's not about the guilt, or history, responsibility or being really bad, over and over, just for fun – it's that the cops ... they may know things you don't imagine. Or perhaps you have. The other stuff cops deal in – the sentence, and the ethics, reparations, damages – it all comes later, and you do best to avoid part one – the questions, that bring in part two – the answers.'

'I know,' says Gary, 'I'll get nothing back. I'll be a suspect if I go.'

'It's weeds you're full of, Gary,' Viktor says. 'These doubts, the do and don't, and maybes like a hatch of buzzing things that last an hour... That's why you think there is a simpler way... Down with it all! It's had its day! Armed men, sand on their buskins, spraying the defoliant! Here they come! You're dangerous, poor Gary... You don't see the process – it's like boiling eggs. Hard men with kevlar shells, march into the fiery stream – they're soft beneath, then hard again – then cracked. Wait – there's another flurry on the horns – a new contingent – here they come! squared up: they're toasted soldiers, thrusted in – and – my! they're gone again! All, every one, consumed, digested, defecated! Whatever side you're on – you have to fight. Your life depends on it. But watch the process! Don't spin the improbable – the true love. Eggs, Gary! Remember! It's breakfast, Gary – there's no fighting cocks hatched on your tablecloth!'

'I'm sure you're right,' says Gary. 'Although you don't convince.'

'Then follow orders, like the rest,' says Viktor.

'Don't provoke me, Viktor,' Gary says. 'Remember I have had a loss.'

'You want to fight again?' asks Viktor, raising dust.

'Now I remember,' Gary says. 'I owe. Of course! Khady ... she'll be waiting for her settlement...'

'Those Senegalese,' says Viktor. 'On the island – they were down too low. Swept away! Islands are off, at all events, off our horizon, drifting into storms and icebergs.'

'Debts are never cancelled,' Gary says. 'Don't try to trap me Viktor. Khady won't forget me.'

'Nor will she forgive. Everyone's a cop now,' Viktor says. 'It's wanting to be paid back what is owed. I want to see where you are going, head you off.'

'I'm not there yet,' Gary says. 'It may never be.'

'Then it would be too late, meanwhile,' says Viktor. 'Our civilisation's gone to crows...'

'There are many certainties,' Gary says. 'Probably all of everything. The only way round them – is doubt.'

'That's whimsy, Gary,' Viktor says. 'Like wanting to hook on to Mae...'

'She wanted me, needed me,' Gary says, and Viktor laughs. Gary goes on, 'Her life – dependent totally, and yet aggressive – serially. Always destitute – always robbing. It's a poem, Viktor. What's spent instantly – it leaves her with a need, a thirst, a fear of hunger, of torture and expropriation. She's a boss, Viktor, one of those who rule the world. Fear and hunger – lead to grand theft. Does she pray, I wonder, moralise? Feel guilt, do charity, have night sweats, fund scholars? She suffers, Viktor. I don't, not at all...'

'Then why pal up with her?' asks Viktor. 'She's a jigger, boring in and sucking out...'

'Oh well,' says Gary. 'You can't have it all! All that she builds is ephemeral, made not to last. I'm the organism behind her void, the righteous monkey waiting in the grotto's dark. Another path, not taken, not evolved... I could turn into something else that she's not seen before...' .

'Not a human?' Viktor asks.

'I think not,' Gary says.

*

Illegal entry and permanence: anonymity – those are the charges, till the cops think up some more.

'Being and not being,' Gary says, 'That's the charge.'

'Being takes precedence,' Viktor says. 'Not being – that's a consequence of being.'

'Not being creates being,' Gary says.

It seems Viktor – when he's parsed – is a counsellor: – a Chloe–Daphne–Claude, amalgamated, stewed, poured into shabby clothes, mostly brown and checkered ... a philosophical cop.

'Once, it was done upstairs, in castles,' Viktor says, 'Now – it's basements. The accusations, confessions. Incriminations and extortions. A turn of the screws.'

'Which side are you on, Viktor?' Gary asks.

'It's justice,' Viktor says, 'That has no sides.'

'There's something missing, so it seems,' says Gary. 'A structure must have sides, a left and right. I'm sure I'd find something on both sides. That's the right deal for me: here, not here. Not wholly innocent, not wholly guilty... And will I know, when it is done? Justice?'

'You need to be patient, Gary,' Viktor says. 'I hope you're not locked up. They count in years – you'd have quite a different way to calculate. There's rough stuff too, I've heard.'

*

'Mae!' shouts Gary, when Viktor goes upstairs somewhere, 'Nabbed! I hoped I'd see you. I've no rancour...'

'Nor have I,' says Mae. 'I'm lucky. They can't hold me here – you don't exist...'

'You can steal from dead people,' Gary says. 'So of course, if I'm not here, you can rob me, and – I can forgive you just the same. When you've been punished, naturally – and not by me.'

'Your clothes are right,' says Mae. 'You could be a cop, in for the rough stuff. Let's try walking out... As if we're someone else.'

'We can never come back here,' says Gary. 'That's good, but where...'

'I'm sure there's no records on the island,' Mae says, pulling Gary along behind. 'So they'll never catch you. But we can't go there, and can't stay here.'

'Look, Mae,' Gary says, 'I've parleyed with important guys, my powerful friends, and sent the culture everywhere. I'm sure – no one would follow you. Just give me back the document...'

'Oh Gary, I had an urgency. I ate it,' Mae says, giggling. 'Besides – I'm just a nuisance. And you're the guilty one.'

'That's incredible, Mae,' Gary says, much perturbed.

'But Gary – we're free! We just walked out,' says Mae.

'Yes!' Gary says. 'It's incredible, miraculous. A dream! Of course, there's places much worse than that: – you're not in there for years – it's months, and that's the end. One's heard it all – they won't let you go, even if you're one of them, the really bad. You're done for. Done for everywhere, on every side, whatever the beliefs, the goal.'

'You got mixed up,' says Mae. 'You did things reprehensible. There's Senegal. There's bosses. The corrupt, the bandits. You went along.'

'You're not a person that I'd make confessions to,' says Gary. 'You need to hang me on a hook, before I'd tell. You're not a bully, not a thug – you're just a thief, Mae; light relief.'

'You must have friends here, Gary. Otherwise I'd take you to my gang, some are musicians... You could manage them...' says Mae.

'Musicians: the last resort,' says Gary. 'I'll bet they go to anywhere. World music, universal sentiments... It's a sombre way to carry on...'

Mae says, 'Sombre? *Sombras*, spectres... Musicians up from hell – they play their harps and don't exist once they have made their sound. But you could be a spectre too, if you've no powerful friends to intercede.'

'Best not go to them,' says Gary. 'Those up above – they wanted power, not me. Nadine, Chloe... That is the essence, Mae. That's what makes it stand, the species, walk on, like a baby giant. That is the concrete too. Power, big and trivial – that's the string that holds the parts and makes it look like something – whether it's got by adulation or by dungeon... Society, the universe – without the power, it all falls in a heap.'

'That's it, then, Gary?' Mae says, and laughs quite stridently. 'Your conclusion, your great work? Maybe it's your alibi for ending here...'

*

There's a sudden dump of frogs – quite inexplicable. Into the paddyfield they go – to eat the insects, you suppose. The plane drops some by Gary, by mistake: on Mae – 'Hey, don't stamp on them,' shouts Gary.

'The goddam things are in my hair,' shouts Mae. 'If you don't like me treading on them – pick them up. Into the water with them...'

'No, Mae,' says Gary, 'I'm not into that. Not handling. Call it squeamish. Frogs are impulse, not reflection or looking beautiful... Some are quite small – if they are hurt, just deal with them, but not where I can see.'

'Hark!' says Mae. '"Ekekekekcoaxcoax" – they settle down at once... You can trust a frog!'

'Listen, Mae,' Gary says. 'I'm grateful, naturally –you've shuffled off my past, eaten it, digested – and now it's passed too, on to some stranger, looking for his founding motive and a city to go with. But – you've prejudiced my future. I can't substantiate my name, my provenance. I'm a celadon for sure – but probably a counterfeit. That's why I loved the island – we all shouted there, accepted everything, fighting, tricking – causing pain, receiving it...'

'Just come and listen to my musical mates,' says Mae, persisting.

'No,' Gary shouts. 'It's harmonics fiddled on a single string. It goes in my ears, those sounds – I have a job to sweat them out.'

'You're pure enough,' says Mae. 'You've nothing left to steal. You've been stripped, you bleed and shiver – but Gary, you are still a sheep.'

'Rice!' Gary says. 'I'll get work here – here in the rice fields...'

'No, Gary, here you can't hide. The people – they see you, you're not loyal and clean. They're afraid of you, they scent a threat, a war,' says Mae. 'If you haven't read the book, you'll have seen the scroll, the picture: "the stranger in the rice meadows: a general, a bandit, or a common soldier". They won't chance you, Gary. You're stuck, a suspect, stuck in "next": "where next?"'

'I thought I might be taken for a sage, Mae,' Gary says. 'But – no. I suppose I must go where you're pushing me. Maybe you're right – I might be a threat. The people here – they're right to be afraid. But I won't confide in you, not what happens next, or where it comes from, nor the reasoning.'

Mae's used to what can't be explained.

'I understand,' she says. 'You've the idea of what the music wants, where it might end up – and that's enough.'

'More than enough,' says Gary.

'That's why you won't help my friends,' she says. 'What I don't understand: – they drop the frogs to eat the flies. The flies eat the farmers, and the farmers eat the rice. But – who's to eat the frogs? What's the theology behind all that? Where's the law, and where's the vengeance, Gary? Where's the clean, and where's the true?'

Gary says, 'Perhaps I should tell you, Mae, what I have learned. I don't know about the frogs. For the clean and true – you must frequent the baths. For all the rest – I'll tell you my discovery. It's simple. The more you make it simple, the clearer it becomes.'

4

MODERN AND EVERYTHING

THE TWO HISTORY PROFS – of Modern, and of Everything – prepare to eat before the little ceremony. Modern suggests –

'They say society is ending. All spectres, talking to spectres on our screens... the bombers overhead, and crouching in the cellars...'

'It's stressful. But society is made for that. The more there's stress and power that we can't situate, the more we need society, even though it seems quite monstrous. On and on it goes, sweeping us along.'

'It looks invisible.'

'If we're all ghosts – there must be heat, energy, that boiled off all our flesh. If we don't go outside now – it's because we feel the heat. The danger.'

'Wait!' says Modern. 'Of course it all goes on; there's hope and despair when we aren't out there, strolling on the grass. We'd best study those societies that have really died – not just been troubled, but a fracture: not the modifications – the crackup, one that doesn't mend. Look at what has disappeared and left no trace.'

'This Polish restaurant is rather good,' says Everything: 'The spuds are unremarkable – all the rest comes from the marsh.'

*

They're in the garden now – pansies and hollyhocks.

Professor of All History, Everything, stands on a stool... On the earth are Ancient, Medieval, sprawled. Modern has an arm around him, quite timid, upright; Comparative puts a holly wreath on Everything's bald head. He goes to bed with Ancient. He got them these jobs – nothing to fear from them.

They're all clamped to an iron grid, a proliferating plant stand... for the photograph. A replay of the first essays, those pioneers of snapping. They all agree – it was the good old nineteenth century, where it began to go all wrong. Five minutes of rigidity to freeze the image.

There's shouting – the technique's been almost lost. Some glass plates break.

'You're not the sort to specialise,' Everything tells the anxious student, Angus, hanging round... 'In fact, I doubt you'll stay the course. You float, old son, and waver: a butterfly. I specialise, naturally, in everything. I put my foot in centuries, stir the dross, or lift the lid and sniff. There's blood in most of them, and drowning things. I find the massacres, forgotten. I out the gays, and name the bastards. These guys, the lesser profs –' and he stiffens while the snapper finally explodes her powder, the magnesium, brains too are made of it – and the group of scholars flops back into naturalness. 'They're busy in the undergrowth, weeding out. Reptile control. I do it all, the rest, design, earth-moving, heft, chop and stack. I am ubiquitous.'

*

'Gary and Mae,' the student, Angus, tells him: 'Live as a kind of couple. Two hot rooms, up on a hill. They keep goats, they don't eat them. Gary says, "We do moral philosophy. Then, there's the shit to shovel. My advice – keep a thief about the house..." and

Mae, her head and scraggy body bronzed, lightly greening, dangly arms: she frowns and pouts at this. Food? Mae went to the neighbours' plot and stole some cabbages. We didn't eat together... after, we watched the bullet trains, down in the dip. There's a slim bed in each room. Mae's music lasts all night. How do they rest? I slept outside.'

'No flag, then? Nothing valuable?' asks the Prof.

'Mae went through my wallet,' says the lad. 'But I keep my money in my shoes. Gary had a pistol, an old Tokarev. Wrapped in a flag I didn't recognise. I would have stolen it. I hid it in the earth, but then had second thoughts.'

'So your time was wasted?' says the Prof. 'You know, you'll fail your tests.' Angus ploughs ahead.

'Gary had powerful friends, he said. 'I don't want them powering over me'... My impressions? If you don't know happiness, you don't know how unhappy you might be. They'd nothing to be unhappy over. They lived in their sad universe, just the two: it was sad, that's all, all made that way by someone unhappy, who'd then left the scene.'

'That's you, your projection, you presumptuous boy,' says the prof. He makes noises, like a turkey, wobbling his throat. There's no response. 'I said you ought to learn the local language. You had a week. Nothing! I can fail you now. Or you can take the tests. I'll fail you then.'

'I'll take the tests,' the student says.

'And your passport?' asks the prof. 'Did they purloin that?'

'I told him they'd gone, passports,' Angus says. 'They have our eye on file instead.'

It occurs to him – maybe the prof of everything is father, to one, to both? A lover, husband? Son, maybe?

'No other personal detail?' asks the prof. 'You'd never manage as a spy.'

'That's the job I've always wanted,' Angus says.

'The pistol was a good touch: the flag an obvious invention,' says the prof. 'It's your privilege, of course, to add some lies, and keep some delicacy for yourself...'

'Why put me on to Gary?' asks the student.

The Professor of Everything laughs. 'Gary was a famous organiser of the culture ... of the biz. They wrote him up. He came from nowhere, and made good. Powerful friends. Then – silence. A passion for the quiet. Afterwards – a disappearance. A trek – through plagues, upheavals – to total non-existence. And – here he is again! An emblematic figure – Mae as well. The thief forgiven. You found him! And she's leeched on too... It's re-invention for them both, although they stay the same. That is my thesis...'

'You told me where to look for him,' the student says.

'It's necessary in my work, knowing how to trace,' the prof says. 'That's why I'm what I am.'

'You knew him?' asks the student.

'Better than you do,' says the professor. 'Even if not personally. But – that story's not for you. Gary is central – one of my cultural markers. But now, his trajectory is done, like yours, my friend. His powerful friends? He dropped them off. And they dropped him – he sank, from top to near the bottom. Of course, we, upstairs, have the power. The others – they have only loyalty. Even to us. One hopes they'll not recognise what they possess. Subordinacy.'

The minor profs – they've drifted off.

'Did Gary talk?' the prof of Everything enquires. 'He used to, lots.'

'No, hardly anything,' says Angus.

'Well, of course, music was his food and lymph. Then came the fast, rejection of the body – the quest for quiddity. The silence: at the start and finish, it gets covered up – with clapping and the instruments: the racket. That's not the silence that he sought, what I am after too. The essence, which brings understanding. Silence is the purpose of it, of music, maybe of talk itself. Even – of Everything. Eternal rest, dear boy, a steady state.'

Angus picks a flower. There is no fruit. The prof goes on,

'When I started out, I thought the history of everything was Life. Not the blur and blot, the everyday, the happenstance, concatenation – that's just sprigs, reverberations of existence. And then of course I saw – the history wasn't, wasn't life. Just like the epics and the bibles – those were quite uninterested in lives or life, indeed, they didn't start from there, they rejected what there was, and finished far away, in fantasy. History – the wriggly demon – if you bury it, it roots out underground, puts up a leaf with teeth, flower full of stomach acid, then bites you in the groin.' The prof's pace quickens, and he shouts,

'History! When you die, you see it holds your soul aloft. It isn't you, of course, not floating on, having a good, quite disembodied time. No, history has spliced your soul into that great circling kebab, a meaty core of other souls, that turns and spits its fat, and crackles like a powder train. Watch your eyes, young man!'

The grass is mown down to the root. They play a lot of croquet here.

'Listen,' the prof says. 'The bangs! Everything – is firing: of guns or pots or cylinders, or what they call the "letting go" – not orgasm but dismissal. The bottomless sack... Failure, in your case... There's more to know, of course. History's just candle wax. I set myself the task, right at the start – "Be everything: and at the same time, know it all. Know – and be." Look at the flowers, my son,' and the prof holds Angus's arm: 'You're Scottish – I expect you miss your kilt. Pansies there – they are for you... Cross-dressing – that would fit, unlike the kilt... The hollyhocks – I got the holly wreath – for sure, dear boy, you are in hock!' And the prof laughs, a little wild. 'What should you study to come close to me? Mathematics? Too chilly. Physics - you're further off by miles and lengths of twine. Anatomy? The soggy brain? No: history comes in for sure – but it's a simulacrum, a revenant. Gary was right – the detail, the complication – the techniques, hypotheses, and doubts – that can't be it. Everything – it must be simple, simplicity itself.

'That's why I digested History, the gristly lump, and specialised in Life. Even – sometimes, in sex refined, with Ancient Life.'

Ancient history – she's putting seeding onions in her trug. The two males stare, hypothesise. Her folded frame still bears some pounds of plump.

'Gary – he's survived three plagues. He must be on a winning streak,' says Angus.

'He's brave,' the prof says. 'But they're fighting where he is. Or maybe they will soon. He's in a barren place – that's where wars start. The undesirable – is also vulnerable... There's new pictures circulating, sketches for new orders. Shelley was right – the pride, the peacocks – end up in the pot. The new morphs into ruins – they remind you of the thieves, explorers, archaeologists – snapping themselves against the pyramids. The scoundrels posturing before the dead... They say it's all of us...'

'He had a photo on the wall,' says Angus. 'It looks like Portugal.'

'Yes,' says the prof. 'But that's not S, his city – it's L. They say the 'quake is over now. We don't know where S went – maybe the ground plan'll be uncovered when they drop the heavy stuff.'

'Oh, he wasn't worried about the war to come,' says Angus. 'That's just more details. He says, "what you sit there in the sun and think – is always moral philosophy..."'

'Yes,' says the prof, 'Though you can do that in the attic or the cellar, or sat upon the shore. The study of the real – it's much exaggerated. Just sand in hourglasses ... time in the desert... Lots of places simply disappear. So do you, dear boy! Take the present, the new war, the powers that rise and fall. Now, here's the paradox. They want territory – but they've already flattened it! They can't get off their planes to see the landscape from close up. Where is the pleasure there? I like to walk – to see the greenery, the tiny wary eyes, the burrows ... the garden here ... Warplanes! No room for legs!'

'Human systems,' Angus says, 'are always in imbalance, whether it's a couple, or a country, a continent, a globe. It's all a preparation for a war, that prepares a new imbalance, and explodes the old. The bigger the system, and the better it's equipped – the bigger's the implosion.'

'Take your skills, my lad,' the prof says, irritated, impressed. 'And weave your rug. Remember though – you'll need the parchments too, that only we give out. Sheep skins for the sheep, my friend.'

'You're sure I'll fail the course?' asks Angus.

'I have that power, and you have set yourself against me. Your empty head...'

'Yes,' Angus says. 'It can hold everything. As much as yours!'

'Holà!' the professor shouts – and two black dogs come bounding up. Ranter and Snap. 'See – this forked cretin's not a gardener,' he tells them. 'He's set himself against me – chase, boys! Rend him!'

And Angus hops the fence.

*

'Those dogs!' he tells his girlfriend, Julia. 'My! they were obedient! Must be on dope.'

'He means he'll make you fail the course,' says Julia. 'Though you could do his work for him, and just as well.'

'That's quite the problem,' Angus says. 'Everybody can do everything. Maybe I'll take off, stay on with Gary, through the war – though he said he didn't want to see me, evermore...'

'But Angus,' Julia says. 'There's only poor guys over there. The work they do – the fields, the factories – it's out of fashion, doesn't pay.'

'You wouldn't want to work there, that is true,' says Angus. 'Bombs and bambis,' Mae said they make. 'Bonbons and rum babas.' To get through the shift – you have to take those pills: they cost. The bosses ought to give them free. Or, there's the earth to dig – but it's all dumb beanstalks, stood in rows, snakes up the stems, and crawlies everywhere.'

'If it's by the sea,' says Julia. 'You could wait for what drifts in.'

'No, Julia,' Angus says. 'There's capitalism in that place. Who wants to clock in, do the macho stuff, be underpaid...? There must be fortunes waiting to be made...'

'Let the prof stick to his Everything,' says Julia. 'Pack his head with it. Get medals. You – should study chance. That's what looms ... here they come! – the new disease, the gunman, the fresh invented crime ... the city dropping in the sinkhole, the plastic replica full of folk – just there to gawp, a speculation justified...'

'It's not the essence, though, if that is what you seek,' Angus says. 'Chance is machinery made of air and distant flutes ... silent, from behind, it embraces you, sucks your hopes out through your ear... It would be novel, studying it... It would beat them all – Gary, the prof – and even Mae. There's no refinement, no excess, no pilfering in chance.'

'Exactly so,' says Julia. 'You're a sneaky type, dear Angus. Chance – that's what fascinates. Ask the medieval prof – she'd know: those centuries were full of it... They made a doorstop, called it God... and all the same, the draughts came in, and swept them all away. Then, there's its ostentatious partner, luck...'

'No point in asking anyone, even a prof,' says Angus: 'If it's chance – anyone might have a clue. Or else they get it, always all the same, as a guess from off their screen.'

'The prof was right – you've made a stand against him, and his work,' says Julia. 'Expulsion was correct.'

'Being right is no excuse,' says Angus.

Julia tells her friend, Melissa, 'Angus's father comes from Haskovo. It explains a lot.'

'The devil comes from there,' Melissa says.

'Oh no,' says Julia. 'That's somewhere else, that's the Ukraine. Angus has been thrown off the course, Melissa. From jealousy. For insubordination.'

'And you, Julia?' Melissa asks. 'Will you go too, and follow him?'

'Those dogs!' says Julia. 'What luck they didn't get to him. I'm not tempted – I wouldn't take the risk... But – expelled! As for our futures... less bed, I think. More calculation.'

'Is there trouble there?' Melissa asks. 'A forked member? Swishy tail? Those can be unsettling.'

'No, Melissa,' Julia says. 'He's my type of younger man. It's chance. He brings it in where there's no room – in sex.'

'Well,' Melissa says, 'he's not a Scot – those Bulgars! and there's Turks down there. I bet they wear the kilt.'

'Maybe, Melissa,' Julia says, 'but the Scottish thing – is moral philosophy. Maybe that wears a kilt – I see it so.'

'Well,' Melissa says, 'so long as he's human, all too human – it can be resolved. I hope he doesn't talk.'

'The prof is difficult,' Julia says. 'Everything: when it stirs, he writes a book. "Sadness" to "sniggers" – through all our species' time. Centuries, centurions. But there's a logic – the font gets larger every time. But Angus, now – he talks by chance: nabobs and oatcakes, outhouses and napalm...'

'Oh,' Melissa says, 'my course is wonderful. I see the connections here. And Death Studies – that covers almost everyone … and everything...'

*

Chance. It means Angus takes some years to light upon the train that takes him back to Gary, and to Mae. Years of profit, of counter-order, a counter-helix to the prof's – a stretch that ought to end its term in dinosaurs spurred on by apes, and chubby gods who take you in their arms and kiss your tears.

'Hah!' shouts Gary, much displeased. 'Here he is, the random voyager! Oh, the confusion that he's left behind, asking directions, and then doubling back ... smoking cigars before his meal ... chaos, my boy, has no home here.'

'No, Gary,' Angus says, cast down. 'It's chance. That's my aria. Not chaos, not evil, not growing younger every day, nothing perverse or tasteless: chance, that's all. I've found you Gary, Mae – by chance. I might, perchance, lodge here, stay with you for ever.'

'What could you do here, Angus?' Gary, despairing, asks. 'Already we don't do much.'

Mae has a stick for marshalling the goats – she thrusts it at Angus, forcing him outside.

'There is a flaw,' says Mae. 'Here – there's no everything. Indeed, there isn't much at all. Your "chance" here, you silly boy – it has no prof to set itself against. There could be fighting – that's not by chance. They'll drop the bombs according to some plan – though yes – it's chance, who's underneath when they come down. There's bad guys here – robbers, mostly, pushers too... Their friends – those are the cops. It's evident, not chance at all, they're comrades; they brush against each other all the time. So – they are our defence. Maybe, they'll resist. That's order too – not an everything, and still the chance will fall upon your head, explode, whether your cranium full or empty be. The stuff is dropped – but not by chance. It falls on you – by chance – and if it doesn't – that's your luck! There you are! Back in the commonplace – you run and duck quite impotent – just like the rest.'

'Mae,' Gary says. 'The lad is poor and persecuted – he's just the kind we don't want here – an appetite, no skills... Just like the rest. It's true – perhaps – in Everything there must be the good. But, alas, I say! – it's not true the field that Angus works in – chance – contains the evil, the reverse, the contrary. Would that he embody it – disorder, revolt against the good. We'd know then where we stand. Let him go down the hill – maybe the militia has some pants to fit. Maybe they'll welcome him. They'll let him do some bad things there...'

'They didn't have a uniform,' says Mae. 'They made him marker in the butts. He sets the targets up – sometimes they take a shot at him. He's happy. It's a place of chance. If he survives – he'll know he's right, the prof is wrong – and with him, Everything.'

'The militia too,' says Gary, 'is chancy. They'll fight to keep refugees away – and when the battle comes – they'll lose, be refugees themselves. There's justice all around, it's meted out before there is a crime...'

'Angus says his girl, Julia, will come: she's failed her course ... so, she can't stay in that country, so...' says Mae.

'I hope there'll be no whining,' Gary says. 'No justifying. She should say she wanted it that way. I wanted camels – they're too big, the guys here hunt and eat them... I'd try farming some alpacas, but it's too low here, too hot at nights. I fancy woven hats – the symbols – male, female, the sun – the pink, yellow, green, and brown. Just like those snooker games... I don't know how to weave. But see – I don't complain.'

'Hah!' says Mae. 'I hear you shout at night – "some people eat their memories – I pot mine – twelve dark red balls, like on the tsar's table..." "here the coca doesn't grow – I can't do the rites, I can't sell the leaves down in the village, it has to be the alcohol, distilling – white liquor, that's the essence".'

'Here,' says Gary ignoring her, 'there's always firing – they test the munitions from the arsenal, down on the range, where Angus flags and pastes the targets. Those long arms – always at it – the flags ... the black, the red... Angus – if he survives – then chance will win. The everyday's collapsed in anarchy. For sure, it isn't what I sought, but there's satisfaction too. A conclusion reached at last.'

'There's alpaca farms all round,' says Mae. 'But you won't try. You say that stage is past. Gary, the breakthrough – you're always at that point ... it never comes.'

'Of breaking,' Gary says. 'I know much. The island – remember? – it all broke. The people, friends and bosses – they all went under. But here – there's nothing breaks. The people here – you drive them out, beat them with rods, they sleep in sties: just give the sign, they'd all be back, same dwellings, same intrigues, same cauldron bubbling on the peat... The detail, Mae: nothing would change, it would replicate. This society's elastic. They're masters of the insignificant – it's a spit in any rank of order, Mae...'

Julia comes in, looks round. The bed, the shovel, a copper helix, the grainy reek...

'Who are you, Julie?' Gary asks. 'Let me feel you, feel your face. That's how I see, Julie. The blind see better, but to put you in my store, to pot your face – it takes my fingers... I'm a marker, like your ugly friend, Angus, the vulgar Bulgar. So – do you believe? Something? Believe in liberation? Even if you're black – no one says it any more, liberation, and my fingers can't tell you, or even me, what your colour is. That's good; it's good you failed. Not everyone does that – you've a special line – bottom of the sheet, the list of winners – along with someone no one's ever seen. Failed. You and the ghost. Rejoice, Julie. Now – what're you going to do here, before you leave? I'm a marker, Julie, remember that! – I notice you, a presence or an absence... Even both at once would do.'

'That brown clay you're preparing for the wheel,' says Mae, put out. 'Kneading – is Julia. Julia the name, not Julie.'

'No!' Gary shouts. 'Here, besides me, there's women and goats. Julia – I don't know what is, but Julie, yes: she's a goat, and beautiful. She can stay until the curfew.'

'You stay inside when there's a curfew,' Julie says.

'Oh no,' says Gary. 'You don't want to be caught inside – not when there's dark purposes, droning in the sky, targeting; or guys, looking for a place to sleep. You need a disguise, Julie – or Julia, both of you. Maybe you are doubled, an infant travesty, born with the mask: Julie the failure, proud of it. Julia – a stuck-up, before she takes the final test.

'Me – I'm a drunk. Again. Mae's unique, you can't hide her. You're safe with her – you feel her hands slip in your trouser pockets. You're out of cash, so it must be sex she's after...'

Julie and Mae stare, quite unamused.

Gary pushes on, 'My city... There were people there of every size and every colour. Temples for everyone. Now that's disappeared, for good or ill – what's left, for me, except conclusions?'

'Yes,' says Mae. 'A conclusion would be good. I was a singer, Julie ... we had a group, and Gary here ... he let us down... Now, it's my turn to make inventions...'

'Your group, Mae,' Gary says, 'was tired. "Mirth, admit me of thy crew" – that stuff. Your transgressions, Mae – not worth a row of beans: one pod of peas, perhaps.'

'Angus is a marker too, like you were, Gary,' Julie says. 'I saw him running with his flag. The guys down there would shoot at anything. His ears – they've had to grow – they're like a hare's. He cheats the hunt – but the noise is deafening. He frolics. Death wish – I can't rely on him. Who do I put my trust in, Mae? Angus has a life set to be brief, its shortness justified by his aims. He's in the lap of chance, where he would want to be, but – he could end up on the floor. I'm afraid the righteous one – the prof that makes us fail – he has the winning hand.'

'Oh no,' says Mae. 'Where I am from, dear Julie, there's a saying, 'the bad guys always win'. They're always caught, chastised – but in the end, there's always more of them...'

'Julie here,' says Gary, lightening up, 'could sleep outside and feed the goats.'

It's her chance! 'I hope I'm worth being in your city, Gary,' she says, 'when it opens.'

'I'm not sure there's water for the baths,' says Gary. 'Don't make plans.'

'There's my friend, Melissa,' Julie says. 'She's failed too.'

'We'll have to get more goats,' says Gary. 'You've no principle, Julie – does Melissa have one? I don't want a house full of aimless people, mostly dossing down outside.'

'What we need,' says Mae, 'is a pistol. Ours was stolen. Getting one could be my principle.'

'Melissa agrees with what I want,' Julie says. 'She's quite gabby on her own account, though.'

'There's firing everywhere,' Gary repeats. 'It keeps this society together – we're prepared for victory or defeat. You can't do better than that.'

*

'Why, it's Julia!' Angus says, pushing through the door.

'Things have changed,' says Julie. 'I'm Julie now. You, Angus – are the past.'

'That's good,' he says. 'Exactly as I hoped. But – Gary, there is surprising news.'

Gary sits down on the bed, then stretches out. His feet are bare, not clean.

'I saw – they pinned Mae to the gate,' says Angus. 'She was breaking in: the armoury. You must remember Mae, Gary – she was your *grand amour.*'

'We have to take her down!' says Julie. 'She'll be in such pain!'

'No, Julie,' Angus says. 'When I say "pinned" – it means she's gone beyond the wall that holds us breathing people in, like skin... She's tacked out, splayed upon the village gate.'

'You can't be soft on thieving, Angus,' Julie says. 'Societies unravel if you do... The pistol – maybe they thought she was an enemy. It's such an insignificance, until the trigger's pulled.'

'That's terrible,' says Gary. 'That doesn't mean, dear Julie, that you can take her room and play her songs, and have Melissa sleep outside. I know we're fatalists, more or less, the three or four of us – but we should set aside some time to grieve, and wonder if they'll come for us... Too bad Mae never reached the principle – a life quite disappointed – disappointing too...'

'That may be so,' says Julie, 'though we could say that thieving was her principle – that way, stealing the pistol was the apex of her life. It's classic – two justices come into conflict.

Property is theft comes into tension with the converse, theft is property.'

'Yes, Julie,' Angus says, 'but if those weapons can be seen as stolen property – suppose you steal them... Is that property? Or theft?'

'Oh Angus – your education lets you down,' says Gary, quite angrily. 'It must be both. Poor Mae – she should have stuck to singing – when she went thieving, she was always caught.'

'She's spread out like a stoat,' says Angus. 'The dogs...'

'We should go down...' says Julie.

'They'll think we're organised, that we have a plan,' says Gary. 'We don't know who's responsible – a faction, possibly. You educated guys – you maybe have a guess...'

'We didn't do it in our course,' says Julie. 'Besides, we failed.'

'I know how cops and bosses think,' says Gary. 'Us making a fuss when someone's caught stealing a weapon...that won't go down so well...'

'I wouldn't cross them, Gary,' Angus says. 'They're dead-eyed shots.'

'My powerful friends – I gave them up,' says Gary. 'And the eccentrics ... well... Let's not think of Mae as body, let's forget about the gun. Think of a memorial. I have in mind – Matisse – *La musique. La danse.* Emblematic, and quite still, and silent. She might have danced. There is no room. Her music never stopped at night.'

'That's you, not her,' says Julie. 'Pathos. Besides, they're in the Hermitage.'

'Exactly right,' says Gary. 'We should need to steal them, then. She had a soft feeling for Russia.'

'They're too big for her room,' says Julie. 'We need something that's useful, but no theft. Peace, honesty...'

'Of course,' says Gary. 'A llama. It can even bear her name. We'll put it with the goats. I hope its identity's secure, with other species all around...'

'What are we doing?' Julie asks. 'Finding a new normality? Ridding ourselves of the past without a suffering?' She weeps. 'I'm too young for all this – I only just dumped Angus.'

'Don't take responsibility,' Gary says. 'Give it instead. Hand it around. Seek justice, if required. A judgement for the dead. It doesn't change a thing. My search for something at the core ... how does poor Mae, disappearing, affect all that? Someone has responsibility – they won't own up. It wasn't me. The verdict's open...'

'The guys will need me,' Angus says, swiftly exiting. 'More firing. And Julie – you're right – my life hangs on a hair in someone's sights.'

'Now he's gone, Gary,' Julie says, 'I wanted to say – this looking for the essence, the quiddity. I don't know if you found it – but it seems there's everyone been looking for the same – and finding it.'

'What if they have?' asks Gary, 'And good for them.'

'Oh,' says Julie, 'the silence – think of Malevich. Klein. Stillness: the colour. Where it is, and isn't. Here, not here – always both together in your head. And all the rest of them, in garrets, hoping to tramp up that same track. The image, real, graffito, scribble or daub – poised, receding into past time, existing when the life it had belonged to, all around, has died. But still there, in its frame. Coloured earths, Gary, lumps of them, stuck there and for sale. What's Mae's essence, Gary?'

'She didn't have one,' Gary says. 'It was just her. What's the essence of death? Evidently, what's there, left pinned on to the gate. Over is the song. No mirth, no crew.'

'That's my point, Gary,' Julie says. 'It's there. Or perhaps not there. Nothing to be found. Essence: it's in the thing itself.'

'I've heard all this before,' says Gary. 'It's everything and everywhere, like daisies in the grass. It's good, Julie, that's for sure: good, like everything and everywhere.'

'Just a dead end, probably,' says Julie.

'Mae's another one,' says Gary, 'I suppose.'

Julie sleeps, silently, in Mae's room, Mae's bed, that night.

Since she arrived, Gary has had some problems he doesn't know how to resolve.

'Come on, Gary,' Gary thinks. 'It can't be so difficult; after all, Julie failed the course. She's not so bright. The thing itself? There, that's the flaw. The thing, pinned on the gate – it isn't Mae. Maybe the llama – you could say – that's a thing itself, in and for itself. But it's not here. Where'd I find a llama? In the village store? In memory of Mae, bring in a creature of the camel race, to safely graze... Mae's memory – a ghostly thing. Quiet! Silence, Gary, Mae...! There is no thing, nothing, no "every thing" at all. The everything should contain all things – and none at all, if there's no things... Is everything good, then? Indifferent? Bad, perhaps...'

At dawn, he sleeps. The village is a threatening place. Best to abandon it.

'There was drumming all night long,' says Julie.

'Not me,' says Gary, 'I couldn't sleep.'

'And shouting,' Julie says. 'You can't do philosophy like that any more. You have to get it right, or else you'll fail.'

'Failing and not, it's just the same,' says Gary. 'You've nowhere else to go, Julie, except where we end up. We'll pack the stuff into this handcart, go down the track, and then...'

'And Angus?' Julie asks. 'I've abandoned him.'

'What a lot of cash!' says Gary, ripping up Mae's bed. 'We'll donate the goats – that way the neighbours won't pursue. The debt is paid.'

'It never is...' Julie starts, but they are off, away – Mae isn't on the gate. You never know where they've been put.

'They'll eat the goats, Gary ... you realise,' Julie says.

'That's politics,' Gary says. 'Not much to be done. They won't fit on the bus. I'd fear too, for Angus. We're in a miserable part of the world. The guys aim well, but they're full of rancour.'

They push the handcart, full of banknotes, past the walls, the castle... 'You could stay here, Julie,' Gary says, tiring of prodding her along.

'No, Gary,' Julie says. 'But have you thought – the cities now ... they're museums. Everybody's poor, then rich, then poor again ... the bosses were warned against the workers – where are they now, Gary, the workers? Serving food, going to shows. It's all museums, Gary, day-trips. The villages – full of memories, but everyone's illiterate ... that's the front line, Gary – sacks of spuds...'

'Lots want to live in villages, Julie, especially if they live in towns,' says Gary, breathless. 'Stay, Julie, and enjoy.'

'No Gary,' Julie says: 'I'm a social. You were in the arts...'

'Oh Julie, absolutely not!' says Gary. 'I was in the biz! The critics are silent, but there's millions of them. It's police, Julie. Their voice is cash. Mae was helpful – theft's my cushion. I don't hang around, not anywhere. I'm the sort who gets away. You, Julie – if you want to risk yourself, the people round you – you could stay!'

'It's good everyone here's illiterate, don't you think?' Julie asks. 'They've not yet started writing it all down.'

'Nothing's renewed, Julie – it erupts like whiteheads. These guys kill before someone has even thought to screw them. And those animals – bulls. What sort are they, Julie?' Gary asks.

'They're all the same, Gary. Male animals. We can go round. But – if we're to travel, I must ask: where are you on mercy killing? I need to know,' says Julie.

'Nature's all around, Julie – it sorts out death. We can't take the bus – there's villagers. The train is full of tax inspectors. Nature, Julie – I don't give a fuck to it. Let's hurry on through, quick as quick,' says Gary.

'We should be fasting, Gary,' Julie says. 'But I need some soup. I'm sure I'm pregnant – but the inn is closed.'

'The owners have to eat,' says Gary. 'Force a way in, and ask.'

The soup is mostly flour – 'It's paste,' says Julie. 'It's good for you, it's like you're sticking manifestoes to your gut. And – Gary – if you want to reach some intimacy – we'll sit and you can plumb my psychological depths. That's what we're put on earth to do. Too often, we don't have the time to hook on people ... they flitter by, you never know the impression you have made...'

'Most people think the rest are shits or arrogant, or that it brings a disadvantage knowing them,' says Gary. 'And, Julie, you're a lovely person, I am sure. But I don't want a family. I'm not ready – and, remember: – I am recently bereaved.'

'Forget all that,' says Julie. 'It looks like rain, I'm tired. Mae's been taken down and stowed. Let's sit here – don't let them poke about inside the cart... And Gary, you're archaic. I've known the others – archaic all, from profs to Angus. They've wriggled their way in to me – unstoppable. You're the worst, Gary, you're a bigot fighting bigots who gather round you...'

'Yes,' Gary says. 'That's true. What's to become of me? And you. The new – it comes to us as rendered meat... On, on it comes – the people here – new revelations, repetitive as ocean waves...'

'Your values, Gary. Politics, perhaps. You should have had more of that, shipped as crew and climbed some masts. Maybe those boats all sank ... but there were radicals, the groups you managed ... they could have warmed you up...'

'Those are singers, Julie,' Gary says. 'Or they strum and drum. The songs are doggerel. Their fathers used the pistols: the sons cried and threw them down. Most people run from new upheavals, Julie – I am one of them. I'm not a cop and not a martyr – which might you be? Maybe both...'

'There's no hope in you, Gary,' Julie says.

'I'm a city boy, Julie,' Gary says. 'And people here – they've had the soil conjured from below their feet...'

'We've all had that,' says Julie. 'At least they have the memory.'

'Drink my booze,' says Gary. 'It's chickpeas – I planned tequila: the aloes were the wrong variety... The drink's supposed to make you think of sex – we could experiment.'

'Oh, Julie says. 'Some always think of sex. But thinking doesn't prove a thing. It's an impediment for forming fours, of course – the military kind, I mean. The child I may be going to have – that's sex as far as I would want to go... Maybe it'll inherit Everything from the professor – for sure there was an element of chance as well – that's Angus pushing in...'

The inn – there must be an upstairs – their profit doesn't come from soup. The couple, Julie, Gary, find the stairs – they're made of gingerbread, and tumble down, there's ginger cats in suits, bean tendrils – the ceiling's chocolate, the walls – they billow in and out with every breath ... at last, they reach the room above... They lie upon the bed and think of other people, other countries. Julie says, 'It's all a copout, me and everyone I know – you, Angus, and the prof. The thing is, to use our philosophical axe to cut prescriptive thought. Away with those presumptions – maybe there's no truth to reach, nor compromise: chance may be error. Angus said that chance was sin. It might be just mistakes – I've cleared the ground with my philosophy, dear Gary. I'm ready for the start. No metaphysics, no imperative of any kind ... I would begin my reasoning here – but maybe I shall need to enter into labour first, bathe a child, buy rides on Shetland ponies...'

'If Melissa comes,' says Gary, 'she'd lend a hand.'

'That's so,' says Julie, 'but there's Angus – his wish for sacrifice... He could start with me. But a father who believes in chance – maybe's not suitable for rearing kids...'

'It happens to all kinds,' says Gary, not committing: 'Procreation. Chance could be an explanation.'

'Gary!' Julie shouts, suddenly alert. 'It's not a whim that's struck me – it's a craving. The chocolate ceiling – my! just what's needed for a happy child... I could eat a kilo... Those pale walls, flapping – could be sauerkraut... And lying here – I just had some good sex. Someone you wouldn't know, Gary, I'm sure he'd love a game of snooker, though, at any time...'

'Come away, Julie,' Gary says. 'Out the window – let's take a leap: the panes are frosted sugar, and the grass is candied artichokes... There'll be someone at the crossroads, waiting – maybe it's Melissa, maybe it's our bus. Perhaps there's news of Angus – everybody's wish is coming partly true – maybe his death wish...'

'Not that,' says Julie. 'Spirit of sacrifice, that's it.'

'I understand,' says Gary. 'The spirit. It's like me, distilling the essence of the chick pea.'

'You shouldn't sell it in the village,' Julie says. 'It leads to vengeance, feuds – it's impure to boot. Melissa's converted – she will not approve. I told her, "You'll not get far with Islam, dear – what gains respect here's gasoline that powers their automobiles and tractors." I said, "Now you've seen the video, you should read the book."'

'We're flakey Europeans, Julie,' Gary says. 'We want rest. Only the Chinese work, and in a while they'll stop. The energy – it's running out our legs, theirs too, and then – all will be over. Our governments, and theirs as well, will bomb us, maybe put us in jail because we haven't paid our bill... We're all the same, we're anarchoid, traditions quite repressive, innovation's cash – immeasurable fortunes, migraines to the rest.'

'Oh fiddle, Gary,' Julie shouts. 'Is that Melissa at the crossroads? That shrouded figure, waiting for us two, like Oedipus who's got his story wrong... Away we'll go, you, pushing the handcart, finding other spots... Me – that chocolate's fired me up. If I don't have a child, I'll think of something else to drop down in the world. An algorithm, space walk, maybe a song.'

'Go easy,' Gary says. 'Remember Mae. Remember Angus, pasting over bullet holes, fiddling the scores, reaching for his targets – until some guy aims treacherously... I've seen it all before. Then, in Dark City, it was nature snapping at our pants. Next time...'

'There, you see?' shouts Julie. 'You aren't depressive – it's just melancholia. Next time! There's hope... We had good fun in the inn...'

'It was a spree,' Gary agrees. 'But we broke the bed.'

'Pay the innkeeper with hooch,' says Julie. 'Distilling. That's your destiny. Your genius is in the bootleg industry. We'll find some kids to help us trade the stuff...'

'If you have twins,' says Gary, 'that way we could make a start at once...'

'Call it "Chickliq",' Julie says, 'to remind everyone of me.'

'It's more desired if it's not called anything,' says Gary.

'Like *belle de jour* and Coca Cola,' Julie agrees, 'but we should travel on. This place is collapsing, though they're all still here ... it's bleached ... they'll be taken over ... they need so much stuff to keep them going on – there's lines of trucks ... how can they pay? What can they sell? Once it was horses...'

'Mercenaries,' Gary says. 'That's what you sell. Some with arms to shoot, and some with arms to sweep and hammer. Everybody does it – some make cash... Others – they have work like Angus. You get to want short lives.'

The figure they've seen – slowly nears the crossroads.

'I was above the game, Julie,' Gary says. 'A marker. Before – I sent them out, not to return. But now – it seems I'm in the game: the game's a whirligig.'

'That person's not Melissa,' Julie says.

'Of course, it couldn't be,' says Gary. 'It's a villager. She knows where Mae's been put. I'm sure wherever she's been taken, it wouldn't suit. Come on, Julie – help me push the cart.'

*

'I prefer the old kind of poverty,' Julie says. 'There was hope. Now, the new...'

'They were rich then, Julie,' Gary says. 'The villagers. Even richer than us now.'

'Angus is tireless,' Julie says. 'He has every virtue – it's absurd. He's a priest, a holy man – just watch his fascination with every vice! The scurrying, as the bullets whizz above his head... never a moment still, his head bobs high, up in the sun... I shan't see him again, I'm sure.'

'This sociology,' gasps Gary. 'Enough with it! The slope is steep. We'll take Mae's cash – it'll be our memory of her. Some booze, the copper coil – and ditch the rest.'

'That's all there was,' says Julie.

'Then take your share,' says Gary. 'Why should I carry everything? There's a town here – you can see the architecture. We'll rest here till we go our ways, and, if you want to leave your child – here, at the crossroads, it will give a choice. That was my fate...'

'A child?' Julie cogitates. 'Maybe something – more lasting. Brighter. An edict. In a frame. A figurine in bronze...'

'If you get caught with those,' says Gary. 'Even if it's just a gift – you end up on the griddle... And I've some news. Angus...'

'You won't see him again,' the shrouded lady cries. 'He raised his head...'

Julie and Gary can't hear right – does she says 'into the sun'? 'Into the sin?' Not his, surely, the sin – except he gambled with himself, and so with Everything – maybe some guy, impatient, saw his lofted ears, squeezed the lever, simplified – and sinned: so we suppose.

'Carry me, Gary,' Julie weeps. 'I'm so heavy.'

'Yes, Julie, you're a weighty case,' says Gary.

'You're light, Gary, a feather. I carry other spirits, plus everything I know. You may fail – but you can know as much as if you pass. Besides – I'm tired.' And Julie climbs aboard, on Gary's back they reach the town. 'Now,' Julie says, 'there is some space. I'll grieve. There's birds that sing and birds that peck and tear – the life was sweet, in tune, the death gives nourishment...'

'The gates are closed,' says Gary. 'There's always a side door, but – we'll have to pay the guys to let us in.'

What luck! There's a guy, Gabriele his name. Gary, Julie – crawl in through a tiny door, no wider than a rabbit hole.

'Being pregnant, Julie, costs you more,' says Gabriele. 'And be clear – women and children are not wanted here. A risk to themselves, and even more to us.'

'I've always thought that way,' says Gary. 'Maybe Julie will change her mind – transform her bundle into something more desirable and well designed.'

'Oh yes!' says Julie. 'Most anything you wish! Just think of me as fruit – inside a pit, a kernel – discarded or preserved indefinitely. Think of it as aspirations, my sadness, a frolic on the sands – a tree, a creature carved in chestnut for the totem here...'

'Yours is the choice, of course,' says Gabriele. 'But if the soldiers come, it's best to have a something you can hide...'

'I've had experience,' says Gary. 'Powerful friends. Those saunas. Then there was Dark City – I know how to fix the scene.'

'Forget all that,' says Gabriele. 'Your corrupt friends – disgraced, replaced by others quite the same. Now, to have some hope of safety, you should dissimulate; and don't drop names. There's shrouded figures at the gate, come knocking at all hours... There's crossroads everywhere, with messengers and relatives...'

'Oh yes!' says Julie. 'We've had our message, not a welcome one, alas. Maybe my friend Melissa's already here. She keeps abreast of news – it sticks to her like lint on taffy. If being shrouded gets you in for free, I'm sure she's here. Of course, if my pregnancy should come to term, we three'll all keep mum.'

They wander round the town. 'Who commands here?' Gary asks a guy. Is that a kaftan that he wears? or baggy pants, a greatcoat, or a sheet...?

'Who brought you in?' asks the guy. 'I'd have done it cheaper, bestowed a blanket from a charity.'

'Who rules this roost?' asks Gary. There's pigs and chickens here, so the people can't be Vegans. The pigs are troubled – seeing black distant pudding like a thundercloud ... their destinies assured ... they know. People are forgotten, only the greatest crimes remembered, then it is too late – when the soft wind blows, you smell the slaughterhouse... Pigs don't need telling, they pick it up at birth.

'I'm Yuri,' says the guy: no one's quite sure of that. 'Once, the Russians ruled in San Francisco. They were friends to Indians – and then all got sold off. Remember, I can get you two a Lada, cheap,' he says. 'There is no gasoline. You can push it in this quarter, anywhere: the rest is tricky – each has its boss, its faith, its flag.'

'Oh well,' says Gary. 'We're both quite used to that. You have the choice – a city, or a village. I've tried them all. The countryside's a freefire zone...'

'I think,' says Julie, going slim. 'I'll not be pregnant after all. Another time, perhaps... We're used to continents divided into fiefs – a city's just the same, but small, like me.'

This city's full of groups – your leisure time is occupied: – there's martial arts, and prayer, and reading heavy novels, writing poems, drawing flowers ... swordplay and doing plays... There's things to buy, and demos, sit-ins, evictions, squats – nothing is alien, nothing unexplored.

'You'd best decide,' says Yuri. 'Where's you're territory, who gives the best protection, develops your creative sides.'

'Oh,' Gary says. 'We're not creative – no, we got away from that. No longer do we tend the goats, nor do we steal...'

'To live here,' Yuri says, 'you need beliefs. Or a descent. Gabriele – he's agnostic, he just takes your cash, and dumps you. Those notes – they're pretty, but you can't bring them in. Where do you come from, Gary? Don't say S – it doesn't mean a thing. It's just a hiss – it changed its name, it was destroyed, the guy they called it after – he turned out to be a crook.'

'Right,' Gary says, 'I've no descent. My colour's vague. Julie's is flushed – maybe the royal flush? Beliefs – well, they've got overlaid. There was my uncle, then a conversion for my girl, and then free dinners – it's got quite confused. The best thing is to take the charity when you are poor, and give it back when you are rich. The outward sign – convinces. Stay off theology. Wave your quarter's flag, and keep your own, your private one, stitched to your heart. Be very careful though – those stitches, if they penetrate, can stop the pump.'

'Oh,' Julie says, 'we pray a lot, but flags are perilous. My lover, Angus – he waved them in the butts, so's when you missed the target you would know ... and someone got pissed off,' she goes on, weeping, 'and shot him right between the ears.'

'Or maybe faulty sights,' says Gary, repairing Julie's improvidence. 'They were the cops, or free-shooters – our protectors. We aren't subversives – not when we're with others who are not...'

'You put things awkward,' Yuri says.

Gary asks, 'Suppose we stay with you, Yuri, seeing's you've taken all my cash. Must we believe about the Russians, ruling California?'

'It's a belief. We celebrate. So, is it true? You'd need to ask a prof,' says Yuri, and Julie weeps some more, thinking of the Everything that's fled far off, her failure, that of Angus too...

'Enough, Julie,' Gary says, 'Make some new friends, replace the old. We're Russians now. Not much is asked of them. You pray two times a year, but out of step with all the rest. And you're protected too...'

'Bombs from the air,' Julie snivels. 'Bombs on the ground have more effect, and better aimed.'

'It won't come to that,' says Gary. 'We have nothing here, this city ... modest people, scrabbling. There's just us.'

'We're in the way of somewhere else,' says Julie. 'They hate us for our strength and weakness. And you've no job...'

'That's fine, dear Julie,' Gary says. 'Russian women – they do all the work.'

'Everyone has powerful friends here,' Julie says. 'They won't cross each other. We're in a system, bigger than the world, maybe it's too big to crash.'

'We shan't see Gabriele, not round here,' Gary says. 'He's Italian. So is God. They took over the Americas, when the Russians were bought out. The Italians don't trust them, not Gabriele, and not God. When it's dark, Yuri will take us round the wonders of the other parts: the Indians – their baskets with the pythons. The Chinese – the dragons, those white Mercedes you get to drive in hell. French novelists in brocade and tricorns... Then, there's the ruins – we'll be spared, all of us, so's they're preserved. Just terra cotta blocks, with numbers on. And every faith has built a spire, or many of them – the faience, glass, the gold mosaics, the turquoise, lapis lazuli, the shrines – the gods with trunks, and doves and fires, and eagles – gods with lovers, gods without sons, or mothers, gods by parthenogenesis, gods you see and gods you don't... Protection, Julie – we have everything. A hundred pantheons – and sacred texts – on bark, on clay, on goat, sheep, and human skins. We're covered, Julie. That is what I lacked, when I was higher up, up the fine staircase, bathing with Claude, those interviews with Nadine... Protection. Daphne – twirling flags... They didn't fold me to their traitors' hearts. They gave me rights and documents – it didn't mean a thing. On tanks, on camels, in the air and from the underground, from spies and cousins ... the bad thing will come... The Prof stood silent in his garden, he sniffed the air. He knew.'

'You didn't even take the test,' says Julie. 'You didn't pass, you couldn't fail. Here in our two rooms again – I'm sweating, grafting every day ... and in the end, from scraps of brass and bronze and iron – we'll cast a kolokol. A bell so large we'll need to strike it with our sticks – no tower will hold it, it would shake the city down. And when we see the dust far off, the danger on its horses – then the alarm will sound! The bell will fill you with its breath, a brazen wind that snaps your brain off its supports, over and over, like a nut it spins...'

'I understand all that,' says Gary. 'What good will it do?'

'The bell's a rich thing,' Julie says. 'But it's made of scraps – brass earrings, copper tubes, iron hinges. It's to be given to the city – but the city's poor – each quarter's rich, but we're all poor who work. Before they came here, everyone was poor, and when they leave... Don't tell me, Gary, how it might improve – that way, we'd lose our warriors... The bell – it can't be lifted ... if it doesn't crack, it'll stand there on its plinth, struck *en sourdine* – when it sounds, it's the knell for death...'

'It pays our rent, Julie,' Gary says. 'The rest is moral philosophy.'

'If we're to command again in San Francisco,' Julie says, 'we'll need more pregnancies.'

'It's not my thing,' says Gary. 'This is not my home. I've lost, I haven't found. Julie, your way's not mine.'

'I do things,' Julie says, 'that's the difference.'

'Maybe the bad thing's us,' says Gary.

'Gary, you're sick,' says Julie, not much caring.

'Yuri took my money – was it to get me work, or so I didn't have to?' Gary asks.

'It wouldn't matter either way,' says Julie. 'Your face, Gary – people tire of it. They want to drive your nose – right in!'

'You don't get anywhere, Julie,' Gary says, provoking her, 'unless you first work out where you stand on all the bigger things.'

'It's clear where everybody is,' says Julie. 'There's a million galaxies – people like us don't live in most of them. Think of this particular city like a galaxy...' She falters.

'You're right, Julie,' Gary says. 'Most people, they may drift a bit, but they've decided more or less what side they're on.'

'No one has ever doubted that,' says Julie. 'So, where have we got? What's your past done for you? Where is Melissa – all your friends dropped you, Gary, but I've still hopes for Melissa.'

All night and every night, he hears Julie crying out – 'the bell! the bell, the kolokol' ... black, greater than the one's that's chipped and passive, back in Moscow – she chuckles with delight, anticipation, then she does the voices, all the twelve, the tones of bells, she sees them hanging in a row above the people, five seeding onion domes around – tin-tin-tin they go, calling to life and burials ... then tangled in a carillon, a mish and mash of conversations...

Gary, sleepless, walks the walls, all night and in the dawn when first birds rise and bulbuls crawl back to some stranger's nest ... above the sinking walls the balconies arise, the roofs with twisted furnishings above the levels of defence, the new glass spikes are higher still ... there's plum and almond, fig, rooting in the masonry – even blue aloes – 'the right kind', thinks Gary. 'I could take the portion of Mae's cash that Julie's stashed, pay my way out, into the hinterland, the sandy gardens, the empty hoses coiled like pythons waiting for the flute...' and tramp and rest, and make new friends... and down below the hammers sound, a tin-tin-tin recycling bicycles, the clapped-out putputs – in gardens there's the circles of the earnest, cramped and crosslegged some, others – arms wheeling like a windmill, into their gymnastics, some in martial arts, some still and timid, ingratiating with the literature – 'the hive!' he thinks: '"Perhaps we may suspect the bees persist without an aim – which makes the ardour of their quest the clearer, purer, more independent, nobler..." I could make tequila here,' he says aloud – already guys are winding down, the bottles and the flasks come out, the hammers drop ... forget the bees, their quest ... the bad thing happening to them, their procreation under threat, the flowers unfumbled, death in the hexagons...

*

'I can't keep you, Gary,' Julie says. 'We don't have sex, even.'

'I could be a warrior,' says Gary.

'No, you have to take a test,' says Julie. 'And if you plan to leave – you have to take a test. Now you've no cash. You won't get out.' She's satisfied, not pleased: 'And you have to go to sermons too. Another test. The enemies within, the questions it's not discrete to ask. You're protected here – that's what you need to know.'

'I could look for Melissa,' Gary says. 'Since you're into bells.'

'You aren't good with people, Gary,' Julie says. 'Try for something concrete. You could interrogate some prisoners.'

'For sure I could,' says Gary. 'Maybe I already know what they'd have to tell. As for those bells – remember the Prof's foxgloves? The life of bees – crossing the threshold into the fleshy part, fertility. "Ring my bell" – recall it? Apiary attracts. The dance before the hive, the rite of spring...watching those Russians dance their pants off...'

'There's a lightness all around you, Gary,' Julie says. 'It's irritating – lightness of weight, not revelation.'

*

Gary asks Yuri. 'Yes,' Yuri says, 'There is a way. A treachery. A tunnel, but it costs.'

'I must leave,' Gary says: it gets more urgent. 'What's the price?'

'It's Gabriele shows the way,' says Yuri. 'He's reasonable when you arrive – but if the place is not for you – it's hard to leave... He's incorruptible. All the money that you have, he takes when you go out. It's logical – you must have made it here, so there's a tax...'

'I could have made tequila here,' says Gary. 'But I'd rather leave.'

'Then take a bath, and purify,' says Yuri.

The baths are full of young guys, greasing up, and maybe having sex – it's hard to see, and indiscrete besides; the corner's dark... 'The gel will keep the bullets off,' they chant...

Philosophy here has had its day...

Here's Gabriele. 'Now let me out,' says Gary. Part of his stash is in his shoes.

'Barefoot, please,' says Gabriele. 'A mark of humility's required. I'll carry them, your heavy boots.'

'Maybe I should stay,' says Gary. 'Now I see it's you gatekeepers who command. I looked at the old permanent guys, the elders who command the quarters – the thunderers, the holy rollers, the elected ones, who try to act as if they are immortal, and the young gabby ones ... but in the end, it's you who hold the gate, the tunnel's mouth – you decide if it's enemies who enter, or it's saviours.'

'Oh,' says Gabriele, 'there's not often saviours. And if there were – what have they left that's saved now? It's guys with cash who come and go – not welcomed and not missed. Then – there's those coming from the desert and the tundra, who want to start a new *arrondissement*. That's it. There's tribes and clans, customs, inventions ... we let them in, we let them out. They come like you, Gary – they have in mind the essence ... they leave impoverished, or else they don't...'

'Maybe...' says Gary. 'Might I stay?'

'Don't think of it,' says Gabriele. 'The ones that stay, they have their Julies tight in hand. The pregnancies – they come to term, there's kids and ancestors. Not you.'

'It was the goddam voices,' Gary says. 'Continuous. The sound of bells they couldn't hang.'

'Well, anyway,' says Gabriele. 'You weren't in any fights. You don't believe, and so they didn't burn your shrine. You have no property, so socialism was no threat – nor yet a goal. This is the essence, Gary, that I'm describing now. Do you want the details, friend?'

'No,' Gary says, 'but – a curiosity. Gabriele – what do you spend your money on?'

'You cheeky boy,' laughs Gabriele. 'You must understand – that poverty and wealth are both a spur. There's always schemes that drink my cash... The city's rather cramped – lots to knock down, some things you can't, and then the glass spikes, grown taller than the walls ... they cost, and so the walls need building up ... new people come in through the gate, the tunnel, they like at first to shop and gawp ... maybe we should have another city... But it isn't possible. We're finite, Gary, this here's more finite than the rest. Not many, destitute like you, want to spin off, out of your quarter... Not this city, you say – but, Gary, are there others? Different? Maybe somewhere they live all hugger-mugger, undifferentiated – but the aim, the context, is the same. The fears – identical. But – I guess you've no nation, and no passport, no customs – no glue to stick you here. There's guys who fight to get more room, have you believe in them and follow their commands... You're not like that, Gary, you're the passive kind. You like the heat – but in the sauna and the baths...'

'You mean,' says Gary, 'you finance it all. The buildings and the wrecking balls, the dynamite, the concrete, protocols, commandments, the cement...'

'There's not just me,' says Gabriele. 'There's gates and tunnels that you haven't seen. Guardians.'

Gary says, 'When I think of the arithmetic – I can't believe you generate enough...'

'Believe just what you want – when you're out beyond the walls,' says Gabriele. 'If you need company, just take your pile from these – a parting gift, a stirrupcup...'

There's heaps of vinyl discs, mostly without their sleeves. 'It could be stuff my lads had made...' says Gary, as Gabriele pushes him along.

There's manuals. *An Easy Way to Vamp, Walking the Dog, First Steps...*

'Here,' says Gabriele. 'There's inspiration,' and he holds out a disc, *'Kolokola', Rachmaninov's The Bells*: 'It's out of fashion now... There used to be a 'Kolokol' designed for you, the Herzen mag. He'd be more the friend you would appreciate – but that's all gone. There's a City of Nets – this will be the City of the Bells. They tock the time to come and go. All this, remember, all your past – you leave behind. But – it's you, Gary. Old music, old mags, old actors in The Bells. You *are* what most has turned you off. That's irony, my friend. We see it – but you don't. There's nowhere else you can belong. '

'I understand, Gabriele: the usual sendoff – a tribute that's a kick up the backside too,' says Gary. 'I've left it all behind so many times – and here it is again.'

'Where you're going, Gary,' Gabriele says. 'No one survives. Because there is no point. There's nothing there that you can call a life.'

'I'm leaving,' Gary says, 'before there's fighting – not just from drink and wanting urban lots, but a redistributing of the whole...'

'There's always fighting:' Gabriele says. 'You're in the abstract, Gary. That won't suit this time...'

'You make me sound quite harmless,' Gary says. 'And uninvolved...'

'Oh Gary!' Gabriele says. 'It's not my job to make the judgments. Think of me only as taking obols – one when you enter, another – if you have it – when you leave.'

'That's fatalism, Gabriele,' Gary says, holding tight the gatepost as Gabriele hammers at his thumb. 'See how we all live longer, eat our grains, we humans – betterment there is ... I deeply disagree with you...'

How sweet, if he could stay, to walk the walls, to hear the birds and see the trees ... they're trying out the kolokol, the greatest bell, that brings both peace and war, and calls to prayer, salvation for some, damnation for the rest...

'That's casuistry, Gary,' Gabriele says. 'You live longer, some of you, but there's always more – and more – of everyone. It evens out. Learn from the camels, Gary: the torrid sun, elusive water – tough problems for us guys. See how the camels manage those...' and Gabriele breaks the hold and closes up the tunnel mouth.

5

LA FACE DES ETOILES

THE GRASS IS SPARSE. The tinny leaves are bluey-green. Far off, he sees a line of humps... A cactus thicket – could hold a sleeping tiger, a nymph, a choir of flutes. The sun's right overhead ... but on the horizon there are many suns and moons, spots, stripes, the colours go from yellow, brown, and pink to black. Gary's barefoot, of course, the city's far behind, the bell is striking twelve, or maybe more. He's ready to give up, hallucinates – there's no one to surrender to...

But here's an inn. 'La Face...' it says.

Inside – what merriment! There's no bells here – 'We had a water clock,' the aproned guy behind the bar declares, 'but now it's sand. We don't sell water here...' he jokes round, to all the company. They roister, laugh, guffaw. It's like Café Voltaire, without the art.

'You're welcome here,' the boss tells Gary. 'Don't stare as if you've left the world. We're people here who don't enjoy the country things – trampling the snakes and snuffing pigs and planting roots ... and don't aspire to towns – shuffling the forms and changing plugs and paying tax... Here – is New Life!'

'I appreciate all that,' says Gary, 'but I've no cash.'

'No problem,' says the guy, uncorking a dense bottle, pouring. 'You run a tab, for just as long as you are here... Now –

forget tequila – here's some pepper vodka: better than a sauna or
a bath... It purifies you from within – you can drink all day, and
pray – not by the clock, the bell, the call – but when the dove
descends ... you'll shout out loud, in tongues, perhaps, you'll
sweat, you're shriven, forgiven...'

'I guess without the boiling water...' Gary says, 'It's a better
option,' ... and he drinks. It's like fresh charcoal, Romania's
pride, obstinate at first, quite twiggy to get it down inside...
Better by far than those hot stones, or greasy baths... It fires each
organ, strips each tube – better than caustic... 'Yes!' says Gary.
'This is love, divine, profane. This is New Life, this reams out
every sin and misbelief...'

The others laugh to see his joy. The long log tables wobble
with their mirth ... it's true their faces fade and flicker – red and
sweaty with the drink, the women's teeth are rocky, and the men
have axmen's arms now gone to curds – but there is jollity, tall
stories, defences flattened...

'I didn't expect this,' Gary says to Spiro, the boss. 'Someone
to make me happy...'

'Not happy, Gary,' Spiro says. 'Drunk.'

'Where you came from, what your family did, and did to you
– it's gone, over – irreparable,' says Annie, a sweaty-looking
lady with big arms too, tossing down the pepper, hiccupping. 'If
you're straight – you need to find a pal. And if you're gay – the
same. If you're a loner – you know it all by now. Just sit, enjoy.'

'I'm not sure.' says Gary. 'I had a city, I'm quite sure, at
birth. I'd friends – I didn't do much for them. But – Spiro seems
a good guy ... free with his resource...'

'Spiro pours,' says Annie. 'He doesn't need to wash a glass.
He lets us run a tab – there's business always going on beneath,
there's wealth that wanders to and fro.'

'Where might we go from here?' asks Gary. 'If we decide to
move, or look for other people, other places ... all those things.'

'Oh no, dear,' Annie says. 'We don't come here to move. We come to die.'

Gary's amazed. 'Die? Not at once?'

'Of course not,' Annie says. 'You look quite fine to me. You need some shoes, that's all...'

'While waiting, there's stuff to do.There's nature. And good works? Building a herd...' says Gary, then, provoking, 'Whipping up some crowds...'

'Not here, love,' Annie says.

'Why's the inn called that?' asks Gary.

'From here, all you see's the stars. When the stars look back at us – all they see's the inn,' says Annie. 'Maybe they hear the bell. We can't.'

'Why's that?' asks Gary, who has suffered from its boom.

'We are stars too,' says Annie. 'Have been, could have been – or didn't want to be. Now, we're black matter – we're the larger part of everything, but we're invisible. We whirl, accelerate – but no one sees.'

'It's logical,' says Gary. 'But – "La Face" ... it's a quotation. The great poet, on the still greater *douanier.*'

'This is a customs post,' says Annie. 'An *octroi.* If you have baggage when you come – you must declare it: or if you have a plan, a vision... No one ever has. We stay here, this is where we sleep. Fear not – there is no sound but sleep! The others who pass through – they may be terrified, or warlike, but that's it. They're passing through. No sound. Nothing to pay if you're in transit, naturally.'

'It sounds transparent,' Gary says, 'but still it leaves some questions. You stars – I understand your lives and deaths – but all these others ... passing through...'

'It's not a mystery,' says Annie. 'You've said it all. They're people passing through, they leave no trace – the desert round –

it's quite exhausting. Even if you've transport – you rest awhile,
out in the yard, then you move on.'

'They used to let off rockets, drop those bombs, here in the
desert,' Spiro says, listening in. 'Those spacemen – they were all
soldiers. It was a punishment. The training – a Leavenworth:
they never took a prisoner, won a skirmish.'

Annie laughs. 'Spiro!' she says, 'we're just your honest trade.
The facade. Gary's keen to know – where the money really
comes in...'

'Gary doesn't look so naive he doesn't know,' Spiro says,
shaking a bottle with a sediment.

'You've a sharp glance, Gary,' Annie says. 'If you want to
rope those camels, you'll need my big arms too.'

'I'd hoped the principle could be made voluntary,' Gary says.
'Most principles are that.'

'A camel corps?' enthuses Annie. 'It's impressive – quicker
than elephants. But they're robust beasts to harness and to drill.
Gary! You don't eat, don't sleep, your frame's like a Thai
puppet's. Your vision...'

'I've not quite given up on that,' says Gary, 'though I see
effects on the horizon here ... we see for distances immense...'

'It's just refraction,' Annie says. 'And because there's
nothing here. This is a take-off place. You're launched from here
– when it's your time, you're primed, and then – you are no
more. No more upon this wild expanse, that is. Remember –
Spiro has us make our wills, and everything is left to him.'

'I've nothing left,' says Gary. 'I am clean. I don't see many of
us here with treasures hidden...'

'I told you,' Annie says, 'Spiro does well with you know
what, and you know who. Our legacies – it's faith we leave
behind, the last thing we have left. No one has family to stick
upon a tree. It's not the cash, for Spiro. His costs are minimal –

the hooch he distils himself, the peppers grow in trays beside his bed ... we don't do dirty on the sheets...'

'Annie,' says Gary, anxiously. 'Don't get me wrong – I didn't leave those other places, upstairs and in the basements, because I couldn't sleep. It's all a question of my thinking time. The flat expanse ... time. My time.'

'I don't believe it, Gary,' Annie says. 'You are a finick. A connoisseur of the immaterial. That's right for here – we're on the way to being it, the lot of us. Those who come by night and leave by dawn – the warriors, the slaves – the traffic we don't hear because we sleep – they too are near to immateriality. Your singsong groups, the rockets, and the sound of bells – they too disappear... They travel round and spiral, then – they go, they don't come back...'

'I know, Annie – and it's banal,' says Gary. 'A while ago, I thought there was the essence – of what there is, has been. But now – I'm not so sure... Maybe it's there just to console...'

'Ah, true love,' Annie says, squeezing and dropping him, 'That's what you need. You'll end before it does!'

'I'm at the start, you know,' says Gary. 'Just trying out.'

'You don't seem young, Gary,' Annie says. 'You talk like it, but really... And you're on the right... I see your patronising self, you've suffered, but you're smug...'

'Oh no, Annie,' Gary says. 'I'm young. I've always felt quite left...'

'You know, what saves you, Gary dear,' says Annie, 'is loving camels. It's true, they can survive – we can't... But they have many of your vices too...'

'Maybe it's all changed,' says Gary, 'while I was studying my destiny – and living it. I have in mind to join the travellers in the yard, to try again...'

'Are you a warrior, or a slave?' asks Annie. 'You don't quite seem a warrior, but no one elects to be a slave.'

'Let's try to form a herd,' says Gary. 'A clan. A troop.'

'I'll help, of course,' says Annie – 'but maybe they don't want...'

'There'll be ropes here,' says Gary. 'Tomorrow we shall wrastle up our herd!'

*

They sleep.

'What do you want ropes for, Gary?' Annie asks: 'We're tied already...'

'They're to corral our camels, Annie,' Gary says. 'Remember...'

'I don't remember anything,' says Annie. 'I'm hungover – but you're mad. I have a blackout – you've a mirage. Maybe those distant humps ... maybe they're animals – we hear them sing and roar, when we are gone, they'll run the land... But – not for now, dear Gary – maybe it's Spiro catches them and puts them in our pies...'

'Nonsense, Annie,' Gary says. 'It's been my mission all my life, to bring them in our history, give them our chrism, designate them as our heirs if we slip up...'

'Oh Gary,' Annie says, 'for sure we've slipped. But after us, there's wilderness.'

'The truths you told me, Annie ... my failings, and my character?' says Gary, trembling.

'The truths – yes, Gary, those run past like racing camels,' Annie says. 'They're beautiful and white, whiter than the lies that go along with them. You catch them, Gary, put a halter on... One kick – they're off again: your ropes – they trail behind. The beasts are most uncomfortable to ride – two humps is best, you don't fall off so much, one hump – you must decide – in front, in back, or on the top... It is your crucial choice... You need a destination too – those camels tamed – they won't just wander round. Think, Gary, the sun – up in the sky? Or skating round and round? How long it took to work it out... It took all science, for millennia – and that's the truth, my love. That's how it is, the world, and truth.'

'Annie,' says Gary, desperate – he needs her slabby arms to hobble them, the creatures that survive – and throw them down, brand them, put woolly nosebands on their woolly nose... 'That's crap, Annie – you've ridden them, you know them... Without them we shall not survive – Spiro will do for us, this is our end...'

'Are you surprised?' asks Annie. 'And did you think it went for ever on? You reach your death, and on it goes, this world, and spinning round, and all the other suns go wafting up and down, like in a shooting booth, and off the rockets go, and Spiro tips your ashes in the sand, and all your friends go on, until they reach La Face ... and in the sand they'll go, and still the music plays, the ditties, they get written down and played on Fenders in the village hall... Is that all what you think, dear Gary? That it's a narrative? Like *War and Peace* and *Don Quixote* – you read them under Judas trees and eat the fruit and think it's passion, and the end is inconclusive, on and on it goes, the story, and you're in it and your part is good or bad and gives you satisfaction – maybe not – but that is what there is, that's Everything?'

'Yes, Annie – that's what I believe,' says Gary, crying now. 'That's Everything. It's like a bottle – drink, it frees your mind, and like a bottle, it has dregs – that could be you, or me – but there's a mouth ... it's true, the mouth is mostly silent, but it opens to an inconclusive universe, vaster than the bottle, where there's no intoxication, no liver and no brain – just the mailships flying round with loving messages for you and all your chums – planet to planet, dodging those rocks and flying bombs... Yes,

Annie, that is how it is. Everything, dear Annie. An empty bottle...'

'If you haven't left yourself to Spiro,' Annie says. 'You could walk ... go back, find the city, S, touch the pillar of the gate – if that still stands, move on...'

'You could come too,' says Gary, quite reluctantly. 'You're the best thing in my life...'

'Of course,' says Annie, 'but that is how it goes. "Maybe on another night, another traveller..."'

'You mean there can be company? I might join a band, that's leaving here? But – those who pass through: if they're either warriors or slaves – those options don't attract,' says Gary.

'It's true,' says Annie. 'You would be a flop at both. Remember La Face, Gary – it's the only place anywhere you can live without a myth. None. Upstairs, downstairs – everybody knows exactly if they're going somewhere, and where they may end up... Even if you're pissed all day – you know. Remember, Gary: be just. Purify yourself. Take baths and wash. Justice is more important, though. Remember that, Gary.'

'Oh, I will, Annie. Yes, oh yes,' says Gary.

*

After all, it isn't far, walking to the next place.

'Come inside,' says the guy on the gate. 'I bet they burned your house. Your family...'

'No, no, nothing like that,' says Gary. 'I saw it coming, that's all – but it's not the reason why I'm here.'

'Well, come in,' says the guy. 'Of course, you can't stay long. It doesn't matter about the house, if it was burnt, if you had one even – same for the family... You're quite anonymous. You're not a snail, you don't carry a house around, so I'd not expect to see one on your back. If you'd lost it – you'd just be a slug!

Some animals carry their little ones on top, or in a pouch...
You've nothing – and that's smart. But of course, you are not
trustworthy. You could trot off, stealing my gold and jewellery,
looting the places where we worship. Any goddam thing. Your
face – it's like a thief's, your breath stinks, probably your feet...'

'Tell me, please,' says Gary. 'Just who commands. Who'll
take me in. I'll pay, of course.'

'No family?' asks the guy. 'That's good. Betrayals?'

'Essential,' Gary says, 'if you want freedom. Promises –
open, tacit, to the species ... if you don't make them, you don't
know what kind you are. But to make your way – they all betray,
your friends, and you in turn... Just one, and she was dead...'

'Yes,' says the guy, 'a little guilt – it's a good spur. But not
essential. As for the dead – they're quite indifferent, and you are
out of reach. They're pieces off the board.'

6

THE GATEKEEPER

'PLAY IT RIGHT, Gary,' says the gatekeeper. 'This could be your paradise. You can do everything you'd never done.'

'No, no,' says Gary. 'You mustn't let me! Besides, I like the puzzling... Action: letting it pass...'

'That's fine,' says the guy. 'No one can tell your difference. You're irresolute. Get signed in.'

'Is there law here?' Gary asks. 'Or is it struggles, all about resources, and how you may not get enough?'

'There's no one else waiting,' says the guy. 'It's all for you.'

Even so – it's never easy. Waiting for the gate to open, your turn. Turn and turn away. Gary thinks:

'... the people all live in a hole in the ground' – that's what the song says, but only the rich people do. The rest are blocked off, vulnerable, up high, in their tenements. You have to descend, reach the street, buy stuff, expose yourself. It's only fear, of course, that there'll be a buzz, a silence, a rocket on your head. Some far off suspicion about your life-world: not quite straight, hmmm. That's enough to...

'Francine here,' says the gatekeeping guy, 'gives you your number.'

Maybe – carry a fake bundle ... fool the far-off targeters, bearing your baby innocence, an unexpected birth, insurance against your sudden painless death, *tombeau* and requiem. At peace – or just not.

... random attack is worse, more dispersed, it drops ... no buzz – instead, a shepherd's whistling, then you get your bang, but you'd have better spent your buck ... or...

'You must tell your project. What do you think will happen to you here?' Francine asks. 'No number without an aim.'

'To own everything,' Gary says. 'Not buy and sell, just ... silence – and so, everything I see is mine, all of it!'

'That's much too vague,' says Francine. 'That means you'll wander round, walk into gardens. I'd tell you my project, except you'd cheat, and make it yours... You might not think it – but we all have values here, though everything we do is different, it has to be. If you don't share them – I can't assign a number.'

'You're joking, Francine,' Gary says.

'Yes, of course!' says Francine, laughing along with the gatekeeper. 'Come on, Gary – I am the gate. Should I open for you?'

Francine! What an invitation! Not bad looking too...

Gary thinks: Are you the one, Francine? Am I the one? Two numbers us – the very first. Whole numbers. One by one – is one. That's a relief! Two separates – multiplied, end up identical, without a history, a future. You have your fling – there's no result, no effect and no affect.

'I have my number, Francine,' Gary shouts. 'It's number one!'

'You cheeky boy!' the gatekeeper and Francine shout back, the gatekeeper adds, 'Don't tell it to the cops. Come, Gary, come, have a bath. Bathe, purify with me. The hot stones here – turn us into iguanas. The flames, Gary, burn our feet like desert sand ... they roast our bones away, until we're like two leather sacks...'

'No!' says Gary. 'Justice comes first.'

'This is your place, then,' Francine says. 'We've models! Lawyers, judges – prisons and rehab. The very best.'

'The system's good. The laws – they're rubbish,' says the gatekeeper.

'It isn't what I mean,' says Gary. 'The Law – is something that you know, and follow. You don't invent. The rest is destiny.'

'Oh Gary,' says Francine, pulling him along. 'You're such a Loki. A sense of humour! How you make me laugh!'

'Don't pull so,' Gary says. 'No rush. Your gate ... unlocked now...'

'In here, Gary,' Francine says. 'I'm semi-rich – this is a semi-basement. We'll be safe – the rent is paid.'

'What is this, Francine? Sex?' Gary asks.

'I told you, Gary, I'm the gate. Open me and find out,' Francine says.

'What's the exchange, Francine? You let me in for free...' says Gary.

'Me and the gatekeeper – relax, rest, Gary... We are your parents, me – your mother. The man who keeps the gate, Giulio, your father,' Francine says: 'You're home at last. Reclaimed. We love you, always have. All – now yours.'

'It's all a cod,' says Gary. 'Recruiting me. What's the game? Importing slaves? Forging warriors? A civil war?'

'Don't be banal,' says Francine. 'You'll make me cross. That's all around, import and export, making, breaking. Saint-Bartholémy – one massacre at least as large, it happens every day. To stabilise. We all abjure. We change from night to day, without a glance up to the sky. The greater good – it's always on the move. We don't need you for that.'

'That's evident,' says Gary. 'What then...?'

'Of course I let some good people in for cash, and bad ones free. Like you. It's right and normal – and it happens everywhere. We buy some stuff, we sell some rockets; they send us their bad things – the Terror, like in France, the guillotines, the severed heads like jugs upon a shelf – we send them back those flying things that make you jump... It's normal, Gary, everybody does it. That's how people go around and round, and change their minds – instead of thinking this or that. A revelation strikes from out the blue: it's smart to have a dog, a samoyed – I think dogs are unclean, myself – Gary, don't you?' Francine asks.

'It's never come my way,' says Gary. 'You can't have opinions about everything.'

'Oh yes you can, you must,' says Giulio, the gatekeeper. 'If you have one opinion, you can have them all. The mechanism is identical in every case – it's like the guillotine.'

'This place, this cellar,' Gary says, 'it's all boxes – don't you unpack, Francine?'

'No, never, Gary,' Fancine says. 'I repeat banalities until you say, "Let's have this sex you've talked so much about ... and not just you, Francine! It's happened, times before." Giulio! – maybe you should leave, or turn your back...'

'You're a joker, Francine,' Gary says. 'But you're good-looking too. There's nowhere here to sit, even to lie down...'

'Oh,' Francine says, 'see – there's a foam mattress, in the shade – you could imagine you're on the waves, the movement, Gary, maybe the foam brings mermaids to your mind? The wine-dark sea – you did all that at school – probably a mixed one, if you remember it?'

'Yes,' Gary says. 'I think my education was quite mixed.'

'You see,' says Francine, 'I don't unpack. I have all my things about me. I never break relationships – I'd never be divorced from Giulio. Gary – men like you, they have some easy sex, and then they find the other is – well, complicated and with a past quite intricate: opinions, the full set. Everything is covered, don't try changing them. Concentrate upon your own, and keep off mine.'

'I've no response, Francine,' says Gary. 'The gallop is all yours.'

'Good,' she says: 'It should be that way.'

'You must always have been here, Francine – you don't unpack because you never packed,' says Gary.

'It's my materials,' Francine says. 'You ought to know – the future is both certain and unknown – it's a box. We don't know what time is, but we can measure it quite accurately.'

'I guess it's like the sex we didn't have...' says Gary.

'Exactly so,' says Francine. 'That's what keeps the city walls upright, the numbers in their place.'

'You and Giulio,' Gary says. 'Must know lots...'

'We know everything,' Francine says, 'about everyone. Consider: we're your parents. We forgive you, but we'll hand you in.'

'I haven't started yet,' says Gary. 'Not being good or bad. Too young.'

'You've been in foreign parts – the hospices, the rehab dumps – places too like this, with people of high class, free spenders, flexible ideas...' says Giulio, turning round, staring the couple up and down, Gary and the wife, mother, lover – his Francine.

'Don't make it out a caricature,' Francine says. 'This here's a city, real as real. No plots, nothing unreasonable...'

'It's not my city, S, the city once I had imagined, wrecked, incorporated...' Gary says.

'You can't have everything,' says Giulio. 'A story, city life – that's ended, gone utterly. Parents, old as rocks or trees – they've forgotten you, the drama, their cowardice or foresight – they've long separated, maybe taking different trains, on rails with different gauges, different rhythms – different sleeps... They've forgotten you, Gary – if they cry, it's just dementia...

Forget your story you've made up. We – Francine and me – we are your parents. This is where you must belong. Societies don't end – they may go underground, and then we dig them up and put them in a box. It's our curse, poor Gary – the species being – it's our speciality, our long heavy scaly tail. It stops us running fast enough.'

'You've missed something, Giulio,' Gary says. 'The city I imagined – wasn't there.'

'You said,' says Giulio. 'You imagined it.'

'I had no memory of it, but how it must have been – it wasn't,' Gary says.

'That's true of everything,' says Francine. 'There's guys that study Everything. It's gone. You don't remember how your parents were – still less how they are. We're them, Gary. Welcome! Be good, be just. Take your bath with Giulio.'

'No!' shouts Gary. 'To have justice, you must know the truth.'

'Stay dirty, then,' says Giulio, much offended. 'And fuck you.'

'You've seen my semi-basement, Gary,' Francine says. 'I don't live there – that's for my trysts. Maybe you'd like to see the rest?'

'Everywhere?' asks Gary. 'We can go in all the streets, the gardens, sit under the lime trees, drink our bock? And you, Francine – my mother, lover – goddess of the city ... my father, keeping the only gate? We'll see everything? Everyone? Even the least presentable?'

'Of course,' says Francine. 'The most, the worst, is – one day, they may decide I am not worshipful. You may be too young to get your bock... But, yes, Gary, it's home, it's safe...'

'I don't know I can take all that,' says Gary. 'It sounds a patsy kind of world...'

'Of course,' says Francine. 'That's so, if it only was a world. We know everything that happens here, and can... But the threat, of destruction and abandonment – it starts elsewhere. On the outside... Then, it comes inside – not through the gate, but through the walls. Up from the drains. You must have lived outside, seen something of it... "Red rain", the song says...'

'Yes,' says Gary. 'Remember Jericho. Remember Babylon. You mean I'm not safe, not at all, not for a moment, no matter what you say...?'

'Oh Gary,' Giulio says. 'You must have realised...'

'My aim?' asks Gary. 'You required one. What weight now does that have?'

'I don't remember that you had an aim,' says Francine. 'You should have wrote it down.'

'It's why I'm here,' says Gary. 'But to set it out – it's not so simple. The method – I thought it should be silence – but like you say, there's influences from outside. Music and dance, and drink...'

'Well,' says Giulio, 'we've had militias and occupation, civil war. Each takes a toll, it isn't easy, finding some way to outlast. It wasn't what we had expected, even though it always happens.'

'Gary knows all that,' says Francine. 'He wanted to go back a bit, that's all.'

'Like you,' says Gary. 'Being my mum and dad. Francine – Giulio could be your father. Maybe he is. A great uncle, easily.'

'It's glue,' says Francine. 'Keeps the place together, fruits tied to the family tree. He got me the job as well.'

'You're permanent you two,' says Gary. 'No elections – you can do anything...'

'Oh no,' says Giulio. 'We have the urge, it's true – volition. But no action follows. Our intentions, what we do – it makes no difference. There's no tragedy – anything can happen any time to anyone: no one's brought low, no one is rising up. No irony:

there's no security, and so there's no illusion, no one to know what's round the corner. No hero mounted, proud – about to take a fall. There's lots of turmoil, though,' and Francine begins to cry.

'We suffer so,' she says. 'You Gary – you come in off the sand, maybe the sea – an urchin, a crude beast – a camel, or a lizard – full of intent ... all due to fail. Chance, Gary. Strikes us all. How does that fit to your intentions? Fortune has deserted us. And yet it can't! That way there'd be no fortune. A fortune's what we need to set us up, a small investment where we are not known...'

'Oh,' says Gary, muted and appalled, 'I'll find a place out of the eye. A place where there's no happenstance. Maybe I'll rule there. Write an epic. Not be pitiful.'

'Impossible,' says Giulio. 'So far you've survived the lot. You've been respectable, nature has had a snap at you, you were on death row, the poisoned chalice in your hand. Now, it will happen, like it has to us: chance, Gary – something you'd not accounted for... Not vendetta – indifference. The movement of the handless clock, the chimes quite random, the bassest bell that dumbs your ears...'

'My mistake,' says Francine, 'is fear. Here it comes, rolling down the cellar steps! – fragging, the Americans call it – to do with fragments, everything becoming them: a kind of bottle, tumbling down, a paralysing drink, a drunk into the party. The only solid thing, entire, is death, death in the eyes ... the light that leads us to the tomb...'

'It's not at all like that,' says Giulio. 'You're morbid, Francine. Things changed before, from side to side, to left and right, from faith to faith: belief in nothing, belief in what you're told, belief in everything. What's best, Gary? You have to change your clothes as regulations change, but that's a little thing – you still bathe in the nude... Quite personally – whatever

John Fraser

I believe, it ends in nothing. That's the best. I like that – it's clean and flexible.'

'Some people,' Gary says, 'are rubbish. You can't make me live with them.'

'Forget all that for now,' says Francine. 'Put it like this – chance is an unpredictable recurrence. But recurrence, means it's permanent – forever it returns. It has a maths, it goes on happening. Chance things turn up, they always do. So – pure one-off chance – goes out the window! We're victims, victims of chance – always, and always the same eternal chance.'

'It isn't chance,' says Giulio. 'It's interest. Other people envy us, or we're on the way to where they want to go. They're out for pillage.'

'They're all good people here,' says Francine. 'Just some are neglected. Turns them rough.'

'They don't want you to be interested in them,' Giulio says. 'They want cash and getting their own way.'

'Maybe – let everybody win?' says Francine, laughing.

'I know,' says Giulio. 'You're going to say "we've gone the wrong road – there must be other ways". It isn't true. There is no other way. We can't escape. Others can.'

'That's not what I mean,' says Francine. 'You can have convictions, and you keep them to yourself. They are your secret you.'

'The conviction people have is, "if it's good for me, it must be good for you". First it was religion, then politics, now it's science,' Giulio says. 'No one keeps quiet when they have found the truth. Look at this place – all the experts in immortality we have! The noise!'

'Immortality doesn't change a thing,' says Francine. 'You're just here in the mess for longer, that is all.'

'It's got too complicated, living for eternity,' says Giulio. 'First you could do it – everybody could – for free. Your body could be blown to shreds, your brain like jam – but up you went – an interview, then you were housed. Wars were fought, about procedures, the good books, vestments, prayers – all that: but in the end – eternity. Now – it's clinics and expense, and quotas too. Your body's just a wrapping – the pizza crust left on your dish. The brainy guys are only interested in your brain.'

'Gary,' says Francine, turning her back on Giulio, 'I know the book you get your ideas from – truth, essence – all that stuff. It's all exploded, out of date – it's so attractive in you, Gary!'

'Life is revision, Francine,' Gary says, quite flattered. 'Maybe we should try to bond. But Giulio – he's such a weight – his science too. The first immortals from the lab'll be mice and sheep. They'll wait for us, so we'll have food and something for our cats... Those French Immortals – we can read their stuff. Everlasting flowers – that's them! All will be provided, as was written down.'

'Where shall we go, meanwhile?' asks Francine. 'We should find a map, and see where there's a spot that's plentiful and quite unknown...'

'I don't feel fit,' says Gary, 'to push that stone again, up to the crest ... and Giulio, he has muscles too, maybe some help...'

'Oh no,' says Francine, 'Giulio is spent.' She's taller, stands over Gary, fingers his arm, and whispers, 'Giulio – I'm through with him. I know a well – we'll cast him down – his torments, his finicking in bed – enough, dear Gary... Stun him first, of course – he should not suffer like he's tortured me... My culture is pacific. Be merciful, move on, that's what it says.'

'This Giulio affair,' says Gary. 'I see myself rather as complicit in some awkward stuff, accomplice, maybe. The deed itself I always ducked... Of course, if there's violence that he's done – even the verbal – that would serve, an excuse that justifies a dire reprisal. So, why did you choose me, Francine? It's true – you attract me, you have the looks...'

'Of course there's violence. Especially the verbal. Arguing, refuting, differing. And my family told me I was beautiful,' Francine says. 'Some time I'll tell you what happened to them all. But Gary – you don't listen! Chance! That's what brought us close as close, together till the end.'

'I'm not sure, Francine,' says Gary. 'I'm clean. It feels good – like a snail who's shucked its shell. We could stay here, or go.'

'You haven't understood,' says Francine: 'It's not about Giulio's job, or running off, to a place with plants and animals... You've a mind that wanders, you're a butterfly. Listen, Gary – it's not about you being clean. That's always temporary. You're only clean because there's dirt. The dirt – it washes off. It's easy – if it goes inside – you sweat it out. This – this affair – it has to do with justice. That comes first, Gary – you'll have heard.'

'Justice. Of course,' says Gary. 'But what you plan – for me, it's parricide.'

'Think theatre, Gary,' Francine says. 'Think complex: – the figure at the crossroads. Surely you've seen them, hovering. There's always been a shrouded stranger there, a mystery. Now you can put a face on him. You don't need to know him well, just enough to get it right. The deed. Justice, Gary – it's always better if it's not too personal, too family, too medieval – justice knows no favours, and does none. You're the scholar, Gary – you have grasped the essence: – first the crime, then the punishment, yours the righteous arm, that holds the righteous rock... First the blow, and then the justice...'

'It's not my kind of tale...' says Gary

'Ding dong bell, Gary, Giulio's in the well... You know all about casting bells, Gary. The tune – a classic. One of your groups could have picked it out – it's not so difficult. Remember the music: the great bell in Moscow ... our gate, the great gate of Kiev. See, Gary, it all hangs together – the bell, the well. Even your groups could see – that's a good rhyme,' and Francine improvises, ventures into variations.

'No casting into wells,' says Gary. 'I run, Francine, but I don't want a vengeful huntsman chasing after me. Killing no murder, maybe – but you talk murder, and that means there's blame and verdicts.'

'Oh Gary,' Francine says, quite patient still. 'You don't understand. Some drastic things have happened here – searches, abductions, dumpings by the road – torment and mutilation – "Eyeless in Gaza" – you remember that, I'm sure. You can imagine what you dread, and multiply by what is real. That is the sum, the essence, Gary.'

'The city,' Gary says, shifting the ground, 'it used to be an economic site – now there's the great powers – secular, up in the skies, sacred in the cellars. We're just little powers, compared.'

'Come on Gary,' Francine shouts. 'Half-hearted punishment's not punishment at all. If you're in doubt about the crime – let's call it an atrocity. We're used to those. No one's still counting, taking notes and writing names.'

'So, that's your analysis, Francine?' asks Gary. 'The troubles we can see all round – it's due to bad guys? Nothing more. And now you want me, us, to be the bad guys too?'

'Let's focus on the little things,' says Francine. 'Though for me – they're large.'

'Maybe there's bigger things than being just,' Gary starts. 'You talk about the bad guys – as though they're wild things on a ramp, like rakehells...'

Francine says: 'Think of all the guys – bad, good, in between – who take up arms against the guys who live next door. The reasons? Gary, the list is long – the effects, we've seen them here. Giulio's your "guy who lives next door" – secessionist, sectarian, a radical – and off he goes, hoping to plug you in the eye...'

'I know, Francine,' says Gary. 'It's all quite complicated. But Giulio ... his case, to me, especially to you, is different...'

'Case? Case?' shouts Francine. 'You're not his lawyer. If you don't act – there's no crime, no resolution, no liberation and no victory.'

'You confuse these issues,' Gary says.

'No,' says Francine. 'It's so simple you can't see.'

'If the trouble isn't bad guys – you think it's neighbours now, Francine? When you don't pursue the essence,' Gary says, 'you lose yourself. You're a throw of grit, tossed haphazard. It's strange – that pursuit. It's hunting something alien, that runs. It has its life. What do you do with it, once caught? Eat it? Stuff it? Maybe it'll have been torn to pieces, sweating – its heart a clinker. Hunting isn't beautiful – you win because you're more intelligent, and strong – but if you catch your prey ... you come out crass, a dullard, impotent. A slobbering craw. Not so clever. Just quicker, once. Better armed. Desire, pursuit – they are the best sightings you can manage – but they disappoint.'

'Vanity, my dear,' says Francine. 'You try anything, so's not to act. Help me. Come down to the detail, the concrete. It won't take long. It's memorable, the act, but momentaneous. Armies won't clash because of it, no victories soar with wings or sag with wreaths. Silence – for ever, if you can.'

How will it be done? Wrapped in a rug and trampled – no shedding of the innocent's blood. Like the Mongols: Francine has that air ... a Mongol princess, bargained off down South ... bouncing in a buffalo cart with solid wheels, bumping on the grasslands, into concubinage and higher politics. Concubine? – it's not so bad.

Or – with a slab of concrete: the very concrete Gary's been exhorted to admire. Francine – she has something of the heiress – Minneapolis, perhaps, class and fragrance! – rocks you back, and she can whip up an afro if it serves...

Or – the object of the crime made drunk stupid, dropped in the well... Francine has something of the apache dancer, farouche you'd say, the eyes glow with the kohl, the vaseline around, a promise of good times but swift – expensive too.

*

No one mentions Giulio. Nevermore. Nor do they take their water from the well. Gary, his son, born of an unknown father, lost what was left of innocence – he won't confess. What to? Maybe he'll be taken on by some militia? A risky deal – but you can hide, secure. At least, he's offering himself – but no! – not bold enough, nor fervent. Not hungry, not macho...

'Giulio – was a beast,' Francine says. 'But I'd not harm him. I talk baroque because of what I've seen. Keep the gate, Gary, I'll give the numbers out. Don't let the cops come in. Your Russian friends – they must give the bell, to hang over our great gate. To knell, to toll the tales, clang in the wind. Give an interview, Gary – that gets you sympathy. It covers you. Your old lover, that Nadine – now, she reports on wars. Her friend Chloe – she is said to drop the bombs... Get them interested in you. You're well connected, Gary – though your father – he was better at the sex...'

'Should I miss my father?' Gary asks. 'I may have seen him – what should I have done with him?'

'Peace now, Gary,' Francine says. 'No anguish, no regrets. There's orphans here, and fathers too. You could take your pick. Everything here is over quick. No nurseries now, and so the rhymes are all of war, of bells and crackleshells, of roses in a ring and all fell down...'

'The Governor's gone,' says Gary. 'Who knows the state we're in? The market works...'

'But don't go down,' Francine says. 'Have them bring stuff up...'

'This gatehouse – it's like when I was up high,' says Gary. 'In Rehab. With Fancy. Where do we end up, Francine? Back at the start?'

'Oh no, Gary,' Francine says. 'Don't be reactionary. It'll be better, better than you can imagine.'

'Yes, Francine,' says Gary. 'I believe that too.'

*

Here in the gatehouse – life is good.

'You know,' says Francine. 'Better than justice is the truth. That's the foundation. Now – don't say it, Gary! We all know there's definitions, but the point is – we each know, for ourselves exactly what is true. The story of poor you-know-who, his end... Each has their version, and must stick to it. Who made the Eiffel Tower a heap of scrap? Sold off as souvenirs ... diverting tourists to New York? It's dangerous stuff, this, Gary – but if you know the truth, just keep it to yourself. You've troubles without telling everyone what's true for you...'

'What I wonder,' Gary says, dividing roots into red and white, the wurzels in ungainly heaps, 'is if I'm looking for some thing beyond the true and just. That means – not true, nor just. Meaning, Francine. That seem to fit my bill...'

'Taking a life, Gary,' Francine says, 'should take you closer to its meaning, or its nullity.'

'A wandering bullet, what they call a slug,' says Gary. 'Some guy, fired up, runs down the street – he shoots – you're gone... Does he get meaning? Do you, as you lie and watch your aspirations make dark puddles round your groin?'

'Maybe not,' Francine says, 'but nullity's too strong. There's just irrelevance. That must come in. And Gary – what's so special about meaning? Most people don't inquire. In your own life, the driver is not getting caught; not being punished, just or not, according to a truth, or to a lie.'

7

PUMA

ONE DAY, Francine says, 'This is Puma. I don't know what he is – he was a cop, but they weren't paid, so he was nothing. Now, he's here to protect us. Gary, you should always do what he says, and you'll be safe. He knows everything about the threat.'

'Oh come, Francine,' says Puma, putting an arm round her and sliding a familiar hand over a breast. 'It's up to him if he obeys.'

'What exactly...' Gary asks.

Puma has a small head and reddish-silver hair, a slender body that moves bonelessly. 'You have faults, Gary,' he says. 'Anyone can overlook your misogyny, misanthropy as well. But your defect goes deeper. You don't take responsibility for what happens to you.'

'I don't see how you can,' says Gary, overlooking the crimes witnessed, the murders committed in his name, in the cause of self-defence or justice. 'At least, it's not easy.'

'The people, Gary, you must have noticed them, while you were thinking and making your way. You should have helped them. Instead...' says Puma.

'It wouldn't have been easy,' Gary says. 'They were quite autonomous, all protected ... or else broken up, like chicken livers in a sack.'

'You've much to learn,' says Puma. 'And on all sides there are potential enemies. Your efforts at a toleration make you esteemed, it's true, but also vulnerable.'

'People who want to do you harm and force you into things, or giving them all up – they don't give a fuck what you believe,' says Gary, bridling.

'It's best,' says Puma, ignoring him, 'to make the city in here, in the gatehouse, since you can't wander round outside. I'll do the wandering from now on – here, there's mostly what you need. You've had an enviable life – escapes and struggles, forefront and depths, renunciations, conquests... You're guilty and redeemed. Now you can take things easy. Sum it all up.'

'What does Francine say?' asks Gary. 'Where do I stand with her?'

'Oh,' Francine says, 'I keep my options – but I think of everybody else ... they threaten, but they've aspirations of pure gold. Puma will shield us from the hard ones, and the soft – both in their own way damage you. The hard smash into you, the soft – they run away. With Puma here, you don't need make a judgement. He sorts it out, makes the alliances, pays; he calls the guards. Don't worry about anything.'

'Forget all that, Francine,' says Puma. 'The problem is – Gary has no idea where he is going. You trust me, Francine: now it's Gary's turn, to take care of that: fidelity. What goes on is really simple, but not if you try to tart it up, and wonder where it comes from.'

'It's good to have a philosopher about the place,' says Francine. 'Gary may see that as a sentence – but sentences are sometimes what can rock the world. Puma,' she tells Gary, 'will read, and listen to his music. You, of course, are free to leave. Up here, over the gate, we don't know who comes in and out – it might one night be you sneaking...'

Puma installs his pussy cats, cooks chops, as meagre as a comma, on a brazier – ruby coals. Sometimes Gary hears him with Francine – sex: growls and squeaking, chuckles too.

The gatehouse – full of street furniture, lampposts, bags of tarmac, boilers for boiling tar, graders for grading snow – there's every convenience, no space. It's a nutshell, all the detail that you need to make a street, or pave a market, finish off a town.

'I see no threat,' says Gary.

'You're too high up. There's stones, graffiti – those are normal everywhere. But I go round: the mood is grey to black. No buys, no sales. To and fro the people go – what do they talk of, Gary? I don't know... A bad sign, that. It came to me,' says Puma, turning to Francine. 'That time is like a cabinet, containing Everything, displayed. And we walk past, and out the door.'

'Nonsense, Puma,' Gary says, 'time is not like anything at all. It is itself, unique. An essence of the essences, it's Everything inside an empty box.'

'Let's postpone the subject,' Puma says. 'Until Francine can set us straight. We're getting nowhere. That too's where time is and isn't.'

'Oh how good it is to have some active minds around,' says Francine, braising small cadavers for the cats. 'Those Berber songs are excellent, dear Puma, and let's hear some rousing Chabrier – poor Gary never thought to bring his discs...'

'Francine,' says Gary, in despair, 'I told you. Music in your ears – it's just a set of fiddlings. Once you know what it is all about, you don't need explore the graveyard – every bang and scrape, the divas dead and dying, the santurs plinked and plonked. A danse macabre, skeletons with tempered bones.'

'Oh Gary,' Puma says, stretching out his wiry length upon a couch. 'You're too refined for me! I like to hear the hammers on those silver anvils, watch the throb of thunder sheets, see the strobes like darts of sun in jungle thickets ... those monkeys playing and the crows in wait...'

'What are your cats called, Puma?' Gary asks.

'Nothing,' Puma says: 'Cats don't come when they are called.'

'Oh Puma,' Francine says admiring. 'Don't you two boys get involved with names and things. You'll tumble over worse than with the time.'

'If I thought,' says Puma, 'that Gary had a crime lodged somewhere in his past – I'd hand him in. I'm still a cop. Dealing with names, and things, and time – you'd call me an unusual guy, a super-cop.'

'There's street lights here,' says Gary. 'They could be from ... they could be for ... the City; S. I might already have a mother – but why was I abandoned?'

'Listen, Gary,' Puma shouts. 'Forget nostalgia for what there's never been. We're all abandoned, there's no motive except the way things are. The way things are contains the meaning and the motives too.'

'The walls here,' Gary says, 'are in bad states. If there are bombs – the ring will all fall down.'

'We'd open wide the gates,' says Puma. 'Let the people out! Everyone! Abandon everything!''

'That's terrible!' says Francine. 'We should bomb first, then root the bad guys out, and wait for peace. Block up the well, and pave the market.'

'You're right, Francine,' says Puma, hugging a cat so tight she yowls. 'This place has history. It lies here like a turtle pegged out in the sand.'

'From up here,' says Gary. 'Cathedrals look like pimples on a face.'

'It's the productive things you need to see,' says Puma. 'Hear the clang and feel the heat.'

'A foundry,' Francine says, 'for where they cast the bells. It's picturesque. People come: if we had rooms, we'd rent them out.'

'You need a world view, Francine,' Puma says. 'Not promiscuity and passing trade. You need to differentiate – of all the people passing through the gate, some barbarous ones, with burials quite sumptuous and odd, have stayed. They're quite awful, and their powerful friends are worse. The point is – do we live where everyone is useful, but there is a hierarchy? There's things for everyone to do, but no one should get so uppity the ship is compromised. The singers sing the songs of everyone: and that is where it ends. Or do you want eternal flux? A stew, paella, broth of sea and land, of animals that roar, of tiny beasts that eat the timbers, a caucus-race of fur and scale?'

'Oh,' Francine says. 'I'd leave it all to history. I love a race. That is – I love to bet, and study form.'

'We've spread beyond these walls,' says Puma. 'The poles and bulbs stored here – they were for new cities, suburbs with a bench and shrubs...'

'It's all stopped,' Francine says. 'As if we're set in aspic. Or in brawn. Shall we lurch forward on our path again?'

'Remember,' Puma says. 'Here is a sentence: I don't know what crime Gary did, but here's a sentence that should give him hope: "In philosophy, we do not draw conclusions." It's a life sentence in itself, of course, but Gary's safe for now. There's too much else to ponder on. Up here, we could make a sniper's nest. You could cover that descent down to the metro...'

'Puma, you have friends,' says Francine, looking scared. 'Feathering a sniper's nest, up here – we could be crows... You could lead us, Puma ... a militia ... Those fatigues – my, how they suit!'

'Not yet, Francine,' says Puma, laughing. 'There's regulars. It's true – I don't trust essentialists like Gary here – it all rests on conclusions. For me – the march is what signifies – the songs, the tramp, the dirty jokes, the roistering... Of course – I'm ready to join battle, you can predict my action from intention. I'll not abandon guys like me – and you, Francine,' he joshes, hugs her.

'The trouble,' says Gary, knowing he's left out, 'is Francine – when she signed us in, she put our beliefs down wrong, our origins. I'm down as theist. You, Puma, as a fundamentalist. It was her joke, but if they come for us...'

'It's easy,' Puma says. 'We're jackals, hyenas – wearing skins from our last meal, the carrion had for dinner. That's our camouflage...'

'You're plausible, Puma,' Gary says. 'I'm not from here, so I might go...'

'You look as if you *are* from here, Gary,' Francine says. 'Except – if you were, really – you would love me more.'

'Here – is a big place, expanding,' Puma says. 'Europe has got much bigger – they wanted it that way, even if there's lots of slum – it's over to the Pacific, that's for sure, from East and West.'

'Of course, there's always something to preoccupy,' says Gary. 'I've been in many places – China, Brazil – you need to watch yourself. But beliefs is new.'

'Nonsense!' says Francine. 'You two old philosophers – you ought to know, the strife's eternal. Bloody, too. It's people like me who have a job and offices – we have to pour on oil, make the engines run.'

'I don't find myself here,' Gary says. 'The menace, bad theology... Graffiti...'

There's an urge to cry, or even throw Puma down, down into the street far below.

'Your interview?' asks Puma.

'Nadine, people like that – lackeys of wealth and noise. I wasted time when I could have been sweeping them away,' says Gary.

'Then do something great,' says Francine, 'and go! Leave! Never to be seen again.'

*

It's not so easy. Not going, nor staying round. If you're innocent ... you walk your height... But otherwise...

There's Francine on the bed, with Puma, the pussycats between, all nude: Puma's arms and feet twitch as if he's running, pulling triggers, his mouth dribbles, spits as if he's giving orders.

'Nothing bad is happening here,' thinks Gary, and he pulls, so gently, Francine's spirit, its whole shiny length, from her sleeping nose.

'She doesn't use it,' Gary thinks, 'and it's my memento...'

She and Puma look quite clean, but Gary tingles with his grease – he hasn't bathed since walking here. 'Claude,' he thinks, 'another lackey of bad noise. I should have spent my life struggling for the guys oppressed, instead of ending up as one of them...'

If no one pities you, self-pity is the only way. He weeps.

At the gate, there's guys – look you right in the eyes. 'I'm a theist.' 'I'm not a theist' – strong, the urge to confess to them, leave a truth to be scooped out, drop phrases that provoke and irritate. He scuttles past.

In the distance, camels in the sand. Little do they have to browse upon... Grassy knolls close, to left and right, no lambs, no shepherds. There's two roads – Gary takes the one without the trees and ditches – there'll be a city; unannounced, as there's no longer rising smoke, and claxons – when they flood, it's silently.

Puma's ready: as for the rest, it's inconclusive. If you know which side you're on – it's all a risk. Best not to talk so much.

What's it all about? Not cosmology, for sure, 'old wrongs and present woes' – that must be right...

8

RAOUL

'YOU CAN WANDER anywhere,' says Raoul. 'I can give a ride, my friend. But since you don't know where you want to go and what will happen next...'

'Right on!' says Gary. 'That's a sporty car you have, Raoul! It'll take me near to where I want to end – that last city was too complicated...'

'Oh,' Raoul says. 'You're only at the start. And you sound like you still search for where it was that you began. That's a mistake. I bet you live on stolen cash, leave disappointed brides, tout round a whimsical philosophy – a puffed-up self. There's many like you, on this road...'

Wildly, he drives. It's a DeSoto Fireflite – 'See its nostrils flare', says Raoul. There's no abyss to race towards, but there are other things to dodge, more trudgers, cops in helicopters, animals escaping, their eyes dark and wild...

'No,' says Gary. 'I'm a measured soul. Something great. That I shall do. Each pace a metre, precise, Napoleonic...'

'People don't last, Gary,' Raoul says, honking at a swarm of people pushing prams and toting bales. 'Your city's fallen. Out they come, looking for another S... Wave to your sweet old mum... We can't stop, they'll cut our throats, or try to pay us for our charity... "The world is one, it's ours, we'll find some tin to roof our hovel." Hah! We all prefer a hovel to a tent!'

'All this crowd,' says Gary. 'Locking their doors, leaving their souls inside – it's hard, and it's not caravanning ... cold, but not the Altai... Nomads without their beasts. Return! Those stone houses, ripple walls to catch the sun and double it ... marigolds, hollyhocks. That's a fine dream, Raoul!

'You ride along in mine, my dream,' says Raoul. 'It's trivial, but fun. I'm not like you – I have no guilt, no urge to confess, no destination... I'm a lucky devil – neither all good, nor bad. That choice! Quite impossible, the good! the bad! Fiddle! Doing the accounts – the good do bad, the bad do things that end up good, or just hohum... It's good I don't need bother – it's all diplomacy. A can of fudge. Now, I choose the time I live in, make my collection – cars, gewgaws – lovely things. Nothing's irreversible. Mastering time – that's the great enterprise. That way, you turn it into space. You can go anywhere – some gas monkey'll be around to fill you up. Do nothing you can't deny, can't ignore. The sound goes out, Gary, catch it, put it in your hat, under a bell like cheese ... that rock hard stuff, they dry it in the sun – Roquefort... I don't enjoy it, but you see my point. You have to cancel out, Gary, or else you cry with all the rest. It's useless, sharing hardship if it isn't yours.'

'Oh, I'm sure they don't see it quite like that,' says Gary, remembering Mae, splayed, and Giulio ... his distant splash, unnoticed, Gary hopes, like Icarus in the pic...

'They don't see it at all. It all rolls on,' says Raoul. 'You mustn't roll away as well – not you. It's all beyond you, beyond good and evil, like they used to sing. I'm not selfish, Gary, I'm appalled. Willing the good, the bad – it all ends up the same – the fires, death rays, the row of sulky heads...'

'Good? Bad? You remind me of the woman – my mother,' Gary says. 'Those were all the words she knew. If you're bad – what are the consequences? If good – you're missed, until we find another, similar.'

'Always do what your mother says,' says Raoul, giggling. 'That way, you should at least be clean.'

'There's justice, and there's politics,' says Gary. 'There's doing what you're told, or what you'd like if it was true – or you're afraid, ambitious – or at loose ends...'

'Let's stop,' says Raoul. 'If there are baths. Find some company too. A game of cards. I've cash to lose. Fancy that, Gary? They'll never spot you, if that's what scares: that's why I drive this automobile – they look at this, not me, not you.'

'I'm good at cards,' says Gary. 'I can win or lose, just as I please.'

Raoul stops the DeSoto. 'No more discoveries,' he says, taking out a bottle, a yellow stuff, like gasoline, inside. 'A gift!,' he says. 'Drink, Gary – like the Russians say, 'Goodbye brains, see you tomorrow,' and they drink.

'Let's finish the bottle,' Gary says. 'There's no one here to play. The city's complicated. They run. If you run, you die younger than if you stay.'

'If you stay, you're dead,' says Raoul. 'Don't get attached to soil and stones – the road calls, smooth and slick.'

'I don't need tell you anything,' says Gary. 'You've no hold on me, you're indifferent to my story, to anything I have to tell.'

'Oh,' Raoul says, 'if it's new – I'll dress it up, and spin it back to you.'

'*Christos anesti,*' Gary says. 'Wasn't he the lucky one. No one need leave Paris, though, unless they want a job. Let's go to Paris, Raoul – over here, to our right, is where the Yankees dropped the atom on Ukraine... Left, there's France.'

'Don't puke,' says Raoul. 'My gifthorses might take offence, and bolt. I don't exploit, but I must buy and sell. When you've no cash – you have to sell yourself. In your case, Gary, you are worth exactly nought. The people here, who run away – they think to save their lives they need to spend. You and I, Gary, we know it isn't so. You live the longer if you don't spend cash. That's why you haven't offered me to pay the gas.'

'Oh Raoul!' says Gary. 'My money's stolen. I wouldn't lay it on you so...'

'All money's been stolen many times, unless they hand it over at the mint back door,' says Raoul.

'The booze...' says Gary, passing out.

'The cash...' says Raoul, sweeping up the pot. 'You've lost your stash at cards, my friend! It has been noble, what you did, to play when you can't count the spots...'

'I don't remember that,' says Gary: 'It's best to forget what is to come, not what is past and quite untouchable.'

'A Studebaker Avanti!' Raoul shouts. 'That's the next delight! I've won! New life! It could be mine, my spirit and my soul!'

'I saw you as a slaver, Raoul,' says Gary. 'Not as a playboy into rust.'

'You got me wrong,' says Raoul. 'I guess, now you are destitute – you've come to depend on me. Just when I feel... there's no more to be done, be seen. Sound, silence – it's a movement, plod, transition – like sun to moon. Good to bad and back again – we've said all there's to say on that. I take my step back, sit on the leatherette – and here it comes again, scrolling out: everything, new, seen before. I know it all, of course. The peoples gyre around, they settle, they grow strong – and drive the weaker down the roads...'

'I don't remember anything,' says Gary. 'Were they Lithuanians, the guys we played at cards?'

'There,' says Raoul. 'You do remember – they were honest guys, it's me who won. You sang, you danced, you fought and chanted – then you prayed – it was the best of times. Besides, you don't remember lots of things – stalking an oryx, putting poison on your darts... Invent, dear Gary – that is what they say.

Oh – I invent. Every day, and all the time. But what good does invention do? You live for more, and in the fear of death. The fear – it starts off young, it's part of what you eat, and when you run to burn it off, your veins pop out, your heart balloons – and in the end, there is the end, and all the rest of us go on.'

'This doesn't seem the right way out, Raoul,' Gary says. 'If the species doesn't satisfy, then it's transcendence that you seek. One on one – if you do it right, comes out eleven.'

'Help me lift this poor beast up,' says Raoul. 'It's one of those, I think, that uses front legs first, to stand. Help me, you idiot. You're mine – I don't know what to do with you. I might even fire you ... you're no mechanic,' and together they raise up the Fireflite's hood –

'Oh no!' says Gary. 'There's no motor here ... it's full of useless stuff – sheet music, pianola rolls – look, the Charmaines, the Roquettes – I never handled them for sure, and here's the boys, the Sixty-sixers – sunk without trace, I'll bet, and this stuff's hair straightener, and there's rigid underwear...'

'The motor's underneath, or at the other end,' Raoul says. 'I cling to this old stuff – like sailors clinging to a stump, those grey sea waves around my neck like scarves – unwanted gifts – or boas...'

'What's to come, Raoul?' Gary asks. 'Rescue? Another ship?'

'Yes, Gary, that's what I hope, of course,' says Raoul. 'I enjoy my story. Nothing I do will make it end sooner or later than it should. And you, Gary – you have things upside down. People don't run from cities – they run in from the countryside. They make cities so immense, you can have civil wars inside them. Whole countries are the suburbs. You might see people running from the little cities – they run towards those larger still, more dense: you live in clotted blocks, your villages are vertical, your brothers are all round you – under, over, in the schoolroom they sit beside you, and in the cemetery – that's them, snoring in the nearby hole...'

'You're right, Raoul. I've been sidetracked,' says Gary. 'I've lived all that. It wasn't what I wanted: my city isn't on a map, you know...'

'Don't tell me it was roots you wanted, Gary,' Raoul says, and laughs. 'You don't want anything, and what you get you throw away. You seek right answers, so you say, but first – you must find the questions. Me – I'm on the road. No one asks, and no one tells. It's good.'

'Cleanliness. Justice...' Gary says.

'A message from a drunk – her name you don't remember,' says Raoul.

'I'm tired of the cave,' says Gary. 'I want light. Things as they are. The thing as it is.'

'Magritte?' asks Raoul, laughing some more. 'Boil the Things down, you have the Thing. Inedible. It's all coked, dry entrails balled together in a cauldron, a hot pot. All there, unrecognisable, fused and frizzled up.'

'The question's right – the answer's the wrong one, that's all,' says Gary.

'Go away, Gary,' Raoul says. 'I'll give you cash. Get lost, more lost. You're too old for doubts, adventures. You stink, there's a corpse inside you. Corral your camels, charge some kids to ride on them around the park.'

'I'm not satisfied, Raoul,' says Gary. 'I'm guaranteed my money back.'

'Oh no,' says Raoul, pushing Gary out the automobile, and revving up. 'You're bound to wandering. You must go everywhere, see everything, keeping your head well down, risking a stoning for your beliefs, your disbeliefs. The world has taken shifts reactionary. We all cling to our stumps amid the waves ... you've had your life quixotic, lived through war and peace – your crime is inked in on your back – you think it is invisible – it is to you, but not to justice, Gary, nor when you take your bath...'

'Raoul,' shouts Gary, as he disappears. 'My money! At least – give me a percentage back...'

Too late. It always is.

Another city – one too big to cancel, and too poor to loot: too populous to bring conformity, too superstitious for the sceptics – too laborious to edge towards a magic – long afternoons with samoyeds and houris by your side, a flask of wine, a tale of rescue in extremis from the waves...

There's a whisper – 'Houris? You see those when you're dead.'

9

AMBER

'I work the road with Raoul,' the lady, Amber, says: 'He makes more than me. I can sing, but I can't dance. Amber's my colour too, like the name, look!' And she pulls up her skirt. 'You – for instance, are you black?'

'It's close,' says Gary, put out.

'You could pass,' she says. 'I give advice on it. Your fears – if they're global, or just what will happen next. I soothe. You pay.'

'It seems not much,' says Gary.

'I know,' says Amber. 'People are mean when they're at ease. I can tell about you from your music – Rhythm and Black, maybe.'

'Don't go down that rutted road, Amber,' Gary says.

'Something to confess, then?' Amber asks. 'A homicide? A suicide? A bullying?'

'I guess I'm quite naive,' says Gary. 'But – my purse is empty – that time has come. Begging, borrowing, to eat. Confess? That's empty too. I don't see the point.'

'Come and eat, then,' Amber says, tugging at him. 'There's Parsees here, in crisis. They need the vultures, that clean the dead and perch upon the roof. Zoroaster – now, there's a guy, the first green god, who thought of leaving everything clean – except ... someone's been polishing off the birds.'

She's right – that Parsee cuisine is exquisite. There is a heavy smell comes down the stairs: that's nature too.

'Eat up!' Amber says. 'If you're to do great things, you need to start off full. These people – the cooks – they're on the move again. The fields back there –' and she waves, 'are full of them. The vultures look like bin liners. They're full too, but they get shot. It's a clash of cultures.'

All she says is true: the Parsees run out the door, leaving the dishes uncleaned. 'I could sing,' says Amber, 'and you could dance. Work the road. But you're so fussy about music styles.'

'Oh yes, Amber,' Gary says, belching. 'If you don't get the philosophy right, you're loaded with guilt and regret. That way you can't dance either.'

'Finish up your flask of wine,' says Amber. 'There's no samoyeds here for you to pet. Let's not go on the roof – it's not our time...'

'Adventure?' Gary asks. 'The great deeds? Am I prepared? The food is free, but even so – I'm skint – just like the antelope we ate.'

'Oh Gary,' Amber says. 'You've so much to learn! Poor people's adventures – they're so different from the ones that if you're rich.'

'I'm ready, Amber,' Gary says. 'Teach me. Let me forget the rest.'

'No, not at all, and it'll take time,' says Amber. 'Starting with the trivial...'

'Sex?' asks Gary: 'There's a fourth sex, abstinence. The best, and longest.'

'You've been happy, Gary?' Amber asks, watching skeins of supergeese, far overhead. 'It's the most, for us. We're animals, Gary. Trial and error – that's our method. We can make bowers, like those little birds that finick with their scrawls of red and blue. They're limited, my friend: there's not so much that you can find, beneath the bushes and the rocks.'

'These Parsees,' Gary says. 'They're generous. They recycle themselves.'

'Hmm,' says Amber. 'Zoroaster was quite keen on sacrifice. Blood and gore – you sacrifice someone so's not to be cut up yourself. The goats don't see it so. It's true, we've gone beyond that – the sacrifices now are only humans. It's all quite workaday and counted now – the dead; and all you eat and leave there on your plate. I tend to be a Buddhist, Gary, though I don't believe. At least with him, we shan't need another chief – he's been and gone. Alas – we'll always be, and never gone, they say. Up the ladders, then dangling down again like spiders, disgraced and persecuted. Not my ideal. For me, it's the uncertainty principle that attracts.'

'You talk of animals,' says Gary. 'We're monkeys, scorpions and foxes, all in one. Hybrids. We're poisonous infantry, we run and massacre – but our fear, it makes us want to live in trees and hope our brothers can protect. It's true we talk about transcending what we are, of solving problems that we've made. We do things big, we've tools to match. There's that desert – beautiful, where the camels roam – and they've stacked all our atoms underneath – a savage pot, waiting to explode...'

'No, Gary,' Amber says, 'you've lived too long in villages. Few people, lots of contact with them all, and knowing what's within the families, like they were clocks that always lose their special key... You go to cities – lots of guys, and hardly know a soul. But – they know a lot, they think much more than you: they do their science off in little rooms with gas and water laid ... they think they'll tweak the universe – it isn't so. Go there, if you want hopes, my friend. You think it's splendid, like a dream?'

'Take me, dear Amber,' Gary says, 'and show me. No tricks? No sex – you seem past reflecting on it...'

'No, Gary, there's no scam. An apartment, no rent, the tenant's you,' she says. 'I'll show you how the culture and the fellowship have flowered... It's your habitat, Gary – friends and cleanliness abound. In the morning, you can hear the bells...'

'They ring for vengeance, Amber, or for punishment,' says Gary. 'I saw it made, that bell, too big to hoist it in a tower – maybe chipped and out of tune... They go to prayer, the faithful – kneel and wait the axe. For some, the knife. The cleanliness – it wouldn't be a cleansing there, by chance, of people in the wrong?'

'The city's much too big for that. Now, hurry Gary,' Amber says. 'Why, you remind me of Othello, you're so dark and dashing now – it must have been the Parsee lamb with fenugreek!'

Amber has a little dark moustache – Gary looks close – it's even started going grey – lots of Southern women have one – maybe it's passion brings it out, the poppy's heart, the sweet plum, pollen and purple skins ... up North, they've done away with it, the tache, the mole, the strawberry mark, along the upper lip...

They tramp along the metalled road. 'We'll find a taxi,' Amber says. 'They have them here, they're communal, old classics, with checkered duck tape all around.'

They're pressed together, on the back seat, a guy with chickens in a plastic bag before them, a lady with a comb of cairngorms in her silky hair, as black as feathers ... her mouth droops, and drips a little. Gary sweats. 'This apartment – has furniture?' he asks.

'Oh yes,' says Amber. 'It's all class.'

There's suburbs – unfinished tenements and massive food stores closed. Gary's apartment, high up – 'Hey, Amber,' Gary says. 'It's rather stark.'

'Oh, you're so picayune,' says Amber, nipping at his cheek with a claw. 'Books, they say, do furnish rooms – here, there's no books, there's pictures, topping it all off.'

'There's naught but pictures here,' says Gary.

They're stacked – some look like Twombly, others look like everybody else.

'They're insured,' says Amber, 'so – no sweat. If guys come in to rob, just show them where's the best.'

'Amber, I'm going liquid,' Gary says. 'I'm finished.'

'Gary, of course I love you,' Amber says. 'But I observe you. You've a crap attitude. You look at people suffering, women too, and note their weaknesses. It stamps you.'

'I'm sick,' says Gary. 'Yes, it's true. I see how it starts – decline, liquescence. Everybody's, mine too.'

'Well,' Amber says, 'don't draw on the walls, or chip the parquet. Down the slope you go in your soggy basket, your soiled sheets. Don't complain, respect the others going down with you.'

'Oh Amber,' Gary says, retching. 'I do, I will, I do.'

*

The guy who comes to steal the pictures jemmies his way in. 'Gary,' he says, 'you're dying. Dying dirty. Fading among your jewels. They shine, they glister like the humming bird, and you are silent. Yes, this is it. You've found the quiddity at last. The only noise is you.'

'That isn't what I meant at all,' says Gary. 'And – what jewels? They have their backs to us – I'd call them canvasses, but they're on chipboard, laminates, stuff found, discarded, formica, gasblown bark...'

'Oh Gary,' says the guy, 'you're not a bower bird. You don't appreciate what's gathered, or what's hunted down. You think you're a sophisticate, but really – it's convention. You want a portrait! – friend or saint. Outside – the street is full of them, that you don't recognise. Or else – you want a face, a simulacrum – but no! The spirit isn't in the face – why, look at yours, the creases sown with what looks like molasses, it's a vomitorium, the stubble like burnt cornstalks, pustules that cluster green and yellow round those marbling eyes...'

'Help me!' Gary says. 'I blame no one. Make me whole.'

'A landscape? For your hols? Or bleak, to avoid? I have to load the van,' the robber says. 'Hold on to life, and maybe I'll be back to put you vertical again. Above all – don't croak, little toad,' he smiles, kindly. 'We need a genuine tenant to live here, alive. For the insurance...'

'Amber!' Gary gasps.

It's not about insurance – it's about stealing stolen pictures.

'This city – it's full of laws and calculation,' Gary says.

'Yes,' says the bandit-robber. 'It's the best. There's trams and shows, and parks with nursemaids: rockets at night, and Malagueñas till the dawn...'

'I'm amazed,' says Gary, 'though I don't need anything of what you say...'

'It's like a store,' the robber-conman says. 'You can't eat everything, nor carry it. Now: we need these images – they're our finance.'

'You must be into terror, then,' says Gary. 'No doubt you have that too.'

'Help me roll these up,' says the robber-terrorist, scissoring some large ones from their frames.

'I'm sick,' says Gary, angrily. 'My life's been full of breaks, right from the start. Good breaks, and fractures. And so – you look. If you can find a stable place, you'll see how it all holds, how you all grow in lockstep... Find a glue that fills the cracks.'

'You're delirious, Gary,' says the crook. 'Look back at what you've done and what's been done, and done to you. You're sick because you're tired of plodding on. I know – I've been in rehab, had those straws stuck in my head and all that's bad sucked out.'

'They'll say you're pretty bad,' says Gary. 'I'm quite sceptical, of course – although it doesn't change a thing.'

'That's maybe,' says the guy who's been in analysis and even had some engineering in his head. 'I do the things I do much better now.'

'I'm not clean, just now,' says Gary. 'Justice? I've tramped the world – it's my eland, elusive, savage. But I'm hollowed out with sickness – organs shrivelled, nutmegs. My tongue clacks in my bell, my head...'

'It's identity,' says the guy. 'We did all that in jail. I'll get you a new one, you'll be cured. I'll get you parents, siblings, a birthplace. True – you might end up illegitimate... How about Samarkand? There's all sorts there, and you can dress up...'

'I'll take the risk of bastardy,' says Gary. 'I'll be new! Amber wouldn't recognise...'

'That isn't so,' says the felon-benefactor. ''Twere better that it were.'

'I feel better,' Gary says. 'More irrigated. But – these parents ... who were they? The city, mine – it's not this... And social space – where do I stand, what do I have? I'm stood before you now – but false documents or true – show me what's changed in me.'

'Well, Gary,' says the guy, the robber who broke down Gary's door. 'You're one of us. You're an accomplice. Stealing an identity – of course, it gives you one, new, enjoy it, try it out

– your new social space as well. If you are a Parsee, though, maybe the lamb had made you homesick? Bellies are a tender plant, you know. Who knows what grows down there?

*

Gary's in Samarkand.

The heat! The dog – runs slow, experienced, will make the crossing ... no, not quite ... the truck hits. The sun, the tiger, high tiles – sabre teeth into Gary's flesh. He boils. The broken mosque – they've done it up, the dome, long since... That isn't his S, the city, it's all new – even though it's long ago.

'Don't bother getting the door fixed,' says Amber, hasty, suddenly, looking round. 'I didn't expect you would be here... You're finished now. You leave.'

'Where's the other guy?' asks Gary. 'The thief?'

'Oh,' Amber says, pushing Gary down the stairs and out. 'There was a mixup. He got sick and died. Probably got what you should have had. Those Twomblys – someone else will call, that's one sure thing.'

'One picture,' Gary says, trying to resist. 'Has a meaning. Two in a room – or more – it's a museum, or a market. Unless they're all same, the pictures, best turn them so you see the backs, and they look in the same direction as you do...'

'Yes, Gary dear,' says Amber, getting frantic.

'Look, Amber,' Gary says, 'I feel your strong will pressing in my back. It's not that you have in mind to ask me to do some thing uncivil, unpardonable? – it's been done before. I still have the great thing I must do...'

'Not now, dear Gary,' Amber says. 'The dreadful thing! – it will be done to us, if we don't hurry on ... And yes – those pictures, they all look the same, and so they can have a life of staring at the wall. The same fate awaits us, you, me – or worse!'

'No, Amber,' Gary says. 'You can't fool me with talk of crime and penalty. Crime – it's ideological. Punishment – it's personal, subjective. My ideas have wilted – from cosmology to minimal. Work it out Amber. I'm in your thrall – but tiny and inedible. My great thing – where's my space? Who recognises me?'

'Oh Gary,' Amber says. 'If you want space – rent a stadium, that's what you do: and for yourself – you need do pub. I know our fate is trivial – but mine, it resonates, inside my skin. I tremble like a bell, just after it's been tolled...'

'Told what, Amber?' Gary jokes. 'This hurrying along, when it's you who put me in your story and its rush...'

'I gave you food,' says Amber, 'and dwelling-space.'

'No bed, no chair,' says Gary. 'Not a room – a lair.'

'You think it's broken down,' says Amber. 'All the comfort and the heroism you thought would come, be yours. It isn't so. We are the proof, the caviar, that there's richness here. No transcendence, it is true – but that's the price of being born with hairy legs and wheezing hearts.'

They run: guys toting beams, churning cement, they cheer them on.

'Clubs, Gary. Machetes, pistols, scimitars,' says Amber, scared. 'You can't tell ... it could be any one of them...'

'No, Amber,' Gary says. 'That's of no consequence. Uniforms and shaven heads – that's the real. Without them, civil conflict is a no-win game.'

'It has to have an end, all that,' says Amber. 'The knockabout. I've my own idea. No good and bad, no gods and God, no reincarnations and no novelties. No romantics either – no destinies and no destinations. No sovereign who prays for guidance before he drops his armament – no! We want a compact. Lines drawn. No bureaucrats, nothing written down. No contests, voting green or voting blue, the hats, the caps, fomenting combat, Peter versus Paul. The rules – all here, in our heads...'

'There'll be a boss,' says Gary, 'and she will break her word. I remember Chloe, and Nadine...'

'Oh,' Amber says, breathing hard, 'those two – they're always in the square. They follow so that they can lead, when guys are tired of demos, being clubbed and being on the street – they'll start it off again.'

'I had a friend – I used to bathe with him. Into comix, now...' Gary says.

'He's into games, I'm sure,' says Amber. 'For sure he's handed in his body – it'll have been worn right through. They recondition, but you mustn't run, or it will all pop out.'

'This agreement, Amber,' Gary says. 'The compact. It never works. We'll always be in civil wars.'

'Of course, they break their word,' says Amber, starting to run once more. 'There'll be a boss. I have one now, Gary – so do you, though you don't know – his back's turned to you, and he stares against the wall. He's just a scrawl, a pair of specs, a toupé, and some names...'

'It doesn't seem a satisfying end,' says Gary. 'Your state. I guess we have to vote for it, vote the ticket...? Round and round, and up and down.'

'Well,' Amber says, 'better that than fight and lose. It leaves it open for you, your great thing... There is no end – until it comes. Until we all decide we've had enough, and lie down in the gloam, we can't devise another way to carry on...'

Live clean, be just, Gary recalls. It isn't easy to be just, but even harder to be clean. 'The cypress and the palm,' says Gary. 'And water ... flicker far beyond my sight.'

'Dear Gary,' Amber says, 'you're quite exhausting. Think again on what you've done, and where your friends have ended up... It's not been pure...'

'No, no,' says Gary, 'I don't belong in this. I'm more at home on top... I have to pal, I know, but... Besides, who are we running from?'

'Oh, the other boss!' says Amber, pulling Gary into a doorway. 'His friends! Miscreants, liars, bad people all around.'

'Where next?' Gary asks, bewildered.

'Don't worry, Gary,' Amber says. 'Trust me! It's clear your libido's slack, your sperm count must be minus. Otherwise, you'd bond with me. You aren't in the opera house, waiting to present your three-hours show of boom and busts, high song and frolic dances, to Josef Stalin, alone up there in the imperial box. Not a snappy dresser he, but the pall is there. The lead. Quite avant-garde, the hero's not on stage! See, he's covered up his mouth, that big bush – what goes on behind it, on the heath? Cut-throats, seducing? No, Gary, your big moment isn't here and now. When it all starts – in your platoon ... they're all lawyers, computer fixers... Mine – they're all gunmen, forgers. Guess who'll win, survive as well!'

'Be serious, Amber,' Gary says. 'It won't be happening here...'

'If you've the cash,' she says. 'As boss, you'll send guys off to do it somewhere else.'

'I'm sure here's beautiful,' says Gary. 'There's pictures all around. And piles of salty sand waiting to be stood on end and windows, elevators, chiselled in.'

'It may surprise,' says Amber. 'People, lots – aren't happy here. So, when you come to the gates of hell, Gary, and take your courage, knock, or ring that great black bell... They'll know you were indifferent... You weren't creative, Gary, and you didn't make your splash.'

'Those gates are just a sculpture,' Gary says. 'I saw it in a book...'

'What is not a sculpture, Gary?' Amber says, quite stern. 'And don't imagine they don't know what you have done ... and all the sad people you saw and did not comfort ... and the favours you withheld. That death, Gary ... it puts you in an awkward place.'

'I deny it,' Gary says. 'I haven't filed it, not under anything, except maybe a stone.'

'I can get you straight jobs, Gary,' Amber says. 'But you're worth more than that. You've brushed against so many people: and you didn't penetrate. You're a poor man – that, I like. Fancy I realise – was right for you...'

'Fancy!' Gary shouts. 'How did you know? I realise, I should choose my confidants when I'm delirious and rave... Fancy was so taken with her fantasy, it filled her time and everybody else's...'

'And camels, Gary,' Amber says, and laughs. 'What are they to you, you naughty boy?'

'All those people!' Gary says, brushing aside the dromedaries. 'People. Some with the same name, all different in their suffering – and, oh my most grave fault – I never shared theirs ... too satisfied with my own.'

'You've only just begun,' says Amber. 'Let's take respite.'

There's a khaki tent. 'Join here!' it says.

'It's a movie for recruits,' says Amber. 'It's like that diorama that they've made in Waterloo.'

There's sand and sandy uniforms, the colour of fresh sand. 'Camels!' shouts Gary, but he's hushed.

'They're there to fix the scene,' says Amber. 'Back projection. Not for real.'

There's guys, loaded up with heavy gear, who kick in doors, apologise, hand out cubes. 'Turkish delight,' says Amber. 'Rots your teeth.'

There's a sandy track, cubes of sandy houses, people streaming out, some in tears, some pulled along on kitchen chairs. Someone takes names, and someone frisks. 'The cats!' Amber whispers. 'They'll all come back to find the cat.'

'It's war,' she whispers, 'so there's noise, and being hustled into pens. Nothing to read, no paper to note it all, and tests of loyalty; indifference is best..'

'I'd sooner be irregular,' says Gary, sidling out. 'It's very intricate. All kind of tasks. Where do the heroes fit? I hadn't thought about the cats. I dare say they go native if they're not fed from cans.'

'You see,' says Amber, patiently. 'It's better stop the bad guys there than have them here. Yes, Gary, we are bad guys too, but in a minor scale. Old colours, under the fresh paint. When you clean the canvas, or the lens, you see tracks – of purple, red and arsenic green, where there's been pictures done before, or fruit flies, their bodies or their prints entombed. Are they part of the new scene, or to be ignored? You'd have to ask the artist, I suppose. We could search for them, dear Gary, get an answer. We have ways of asking questions... Oh Gary – I love you so. It's unrequited. That's the best. It lasts. Of course, it fades – like Athens, or like Babylon. But you can tour around – that's what life is for, re-visiting. Your memories, and memories of what you've never seen before.'

'I can't object, Amber,' Gary says. 'To anything you've said. I'm quite convinced.'

'Then, my dear,' says Amber, teasing her stringy thigh against him, 'Don't spout out about the cats. Don't mention camels. Their fate – not in your hands. People'll think you're snide. Even disloyal. There's issues here, of history, future, morality – beliefs. Where we all go next.'

'I haven't doubted it,' says Gary. 'I thought – it's a movie, you react whatever way it strikes.'

'It isn't about art at all,' says Amber, sharply. 'You have to feel it, personally. That's what life is – in your case, is not.'

'Of course I feel,' says Gary, puzzled and annoyed. 'If you could take my lid off, you would see. I know how to convince you. You have beliefs, I'm sure. No one has seen so much they can't be made a sacrifice.'

'Oh, Gary,' Amber says. 'I'm much too old to fight. I'd go and volunteer – they wouldn't have me. But – I'm not too old to love. That flash, back on the road ... epiphany! You! Gary! I'd clean you up, though. But – how I prize your innocence! Better than you – they've only made an inconclusive few.'

'I could cleave to you, Amber,' Gary says. 'It's a strange word. Cleaving, like cutting meat, and sticking to someone... I must admit – there's many loves I've had, that went to ending, some did not – but, Amber, here we are... Alone, for now...'

'Gary,' says Amber. 'Cleaving. That's a cavemen's word. They met few people, so love and murder often went in lockstep – now, it ends in compromise, and understanding. That's what the movie that we saw was indicating.'

'You must be right,' says Gary. 'I just didn't see...'

'Oh, naturally, some cases end in total zero...' Amber says. 'The every last one hunted down, tried, jailed, executed. No example comes to mind – but think! – those places that once were, and now are not. Gone, gone entirely, like a fragrance or a boil, gone like a breeze, a dawn, a storm, a beefsteak, a caress...'

'I quite see,' says Gary. 'Gone like yesterday, like us tomorrow; yes, yes, oh yes, I see.'

'OK, Gary,' Amber says, pushing him along once more. 'Don't forget today. That's where all that matters is resolved, or not. Don't ignore the sharp edge of the present...'

'Don't hustle so, dear Amber,' Gary says. 'It's true – we're allies. When I was in the gatehouse – I had an ally too. You do things for them you don't always understand, agree with – but alliances are that. You just suspend your doubts – for everywhere, there lies some doubt, some ignorance, some lack of empathy.'

'Good, Gary,' Amber says. 'If you want anything, some help – you know, I'll give it. Maybe some ally made you overstep your mark. Forget it. Peace. Do what I ask, we won't fall out.'

'No, I don't remember anything like that. Besides, I only remember what I am responsible for – not what others make me do. Now, this job, Amber...?' Gary asks.

'Capitalism – it hasn't worked,' she says. 'Not if it's just money, hiring poor unemployed and hayseeds, sacking them... We need the criminals to grease the wheels. When capitalism starts to stink too much, or when the minions hassle us – maybe we'll take a bath... Come out clean, and insurrectionary. Socialism, Gary. There'll still be lots of deserving poor around. The undeserving poor as well, the saints, the envious... We'll have socialism, and put the rich on lampposts.'

'The job, Amber?' asks Gary.

'What do you care?' asks Amber. 'You're not qualified. Do anything, well, or bad, you'll get fed up, or persecuted. They'll catch you thieving, and get rid of you,' says Amber, looking stern and knowing. 'Meantime – wave your flag, don't go near the crowds. You know what soldiering says – leave yourself a way you can retreat. Think victory and heroism – plan for defeat.'

'I'm reminded of the Cabaret Voltaire,' says Gary. 'Laocoon withdraws, and leaves the snakes in peace.'

'Oh, you take it all too serious,' says Amber. 'No one is following us. We can have fun. The future's ours again. But – tell me – what do camels mean to you? They're a reference point, it seems...'

'They come from so long back,' says Gary. 'Long before us. Then – the haughty service, the trade in fables, epics, the exotic places, high on the icy ridge – and singing proper songs, and fellowship... We've been for ever tamed, Amber, always unthinking and desperate in a clan, under some ancient beast...'

'Well said, Gary,' Amber says. 'We shall work well together. That's your job – to be with me, do what I do, do what I say you ought. I told you that before. You're a good anarchist, Gary. I'm a bad – an evil – one. It'll be easy to turn you. You're not political.'

'I'm an anarchist because I can do exactly what I want,' says Gary, irritated. 'I'm a power, a great power. You're just a follower, *carina*, a sweetheart. No substance. Doing what comes easy, that's all. And you know what they say – "You must lend yourself to others, to yourself commit yourself."'

'I bet you saw that on a wall,' says Amber. 'But it was written there for you. They saw you coming.'

'Now, tell me,' Gary says, 'is Raoul the boss? Does he run guns?'

'Guns is already everywhere,' says Amber, and she laughs. 'Raoul works that stretch of road, and boasts about his wheels, is all. You're quite primitive, Gary – no one makes cash from selling arms, that's why states do it – the profitable thing is money. That makes money, lots of it, like rabbits, fruit flies, maybe – procreating. Give it invisible hay, an intangible caress – it ruts. Don't be so complicated.'

'Love is revolution, revolution – must be love,' says Gary. 'I know – it's hate as well. The movie says – "we live in dreams. Dreams live in us."'

'It won't happen here,' says Amber. 'If it did – we would be ready, I can promise that. I was little, in Iran – in 1979. What did "ready" mean then, I ask? You can trust me, Gary – I'll see you right. But – be very very prudent with your friends, and joining things ... and chatting too.'

'Amber – comes from the Baltic, Amber,' Gary says.

'You're so smart!' says Amber, irritated. 'You talk like one of those guys – short of cash, tired of life, follow anywhere and anything. We know – we all can know – everything. We accept it, all of it, whether we're informed or not.'

Amber's hungry, again. She knows all the best spots. Here they make an excellent hotpot. Amber makes Gary sit... 'One day, the Mongolians will rule the world again,' she says.

'Maybe,' says Gary. 'Not in my lifetime, though. You know – I'm quite off Parsee food – that pasanda, it was goat. I love goats, not on a plate. Perhaps it was for that, I got so sick...'

'Oh, your memories, Gary! I'm all for them, but you do nothing useful with yours,' says Amber. 'At least the pasanda wasn't camel,' and she laughs. 'Of course, it's called Mongolian hotpot – they're not Mongolians here...'

They sit and wait.

'You've never known how things work, Gary,' Amber says. 'I'll start explaining it, right now.'

The hotpot is cold. 'Every city,' Amber says, 'is really two. Imagine two bowls, fit snug inside each other. Each bowl has figures painted round inside – the outside of the whole's irrelevant. The design – could be parking squares or spires – no one who is within could care about it. In the smaller, inner bowl, there's brightly coloured folk, in silken clothes around, taking their ease – who make the laws, and tot accounts, write poetry, count the hoplites' suits, and so and so. And in the bowl beneath, the larger one...'

'I know, I know,' says Gary. 'I was there. Dark City, or the Rehab that doesn't cure... Don't persist, dear Amber...'

'The larger one, there's maybe figures painted too. But you can't see – the two shells fit so snug.'

'And that's where all the toil goes on – beneath – the songs are different, short and sugary. There's grumbling – but the whole circles round. The upper and the lower bowls – they don't touch, but they revolve together. And what makes things go round and round – is us... We are the grease that stops the crunch, the grinding of the bowls together, friction, then combustion... Yes, Gary, I know the image too – it starts to creak. But – the sense is there. You thought you lived in that top bowl – but no! You were already in between – the laws, the customs, and the poetry, your groups sang and pacified the guys beneath, they simplified, those lyrics bitter-sweet, hooked everybody in... Injustice and hate, Gary – it was set in four–four time and easy chords...'

'This is old stuff, Amber,' Gary says. 'Whatever trade you guys are in – you like to think the spheres can circulate because of you. Everybody thinks like that – the butcher, tax-farmers, jailers... It isn't so. You – the fiddlers, *passeurs,* snake-oil salesmen, provocateurs – you leech upon the multitude, you're opportune, and opportunists – you're a fault in the design itself. Get the system right – if that is possible – then you disappear. You stabilise, you don't facilitate...'

'That's why, dear Gary, you got sick and boring – went to rehab. Frustration. The system can't be fixed. And it never works,' says Amber. 'Not better than hohum. It's good – if it was better it would be a paradise. Most people – after the weighing, they would go to hell. With you – your curiosity becomes an unrequited lust... Up and down you float, between the bowls...'

'Forget the image,' Gary says. 'What's it all for, the bowls, the figures in their silks?'

'It's life,' says Amber proudly. 'Probably the universe. On, on, it goes – if there's a catch, and grinding, stripping, fusion of the gears – there's sparkles, bangs that you can't hear, everything is gold and purple for a while – and then there's dust and wandering rocks.'

'Those figures on the upper bowl,' says Gary. 'Who put them there? What do they do?'

'Oh, some say,' says Amber. 'They are in the clay, the frit. We all come from it, so it's said, and go back into it...'

'No, Amber,' Gary says. 'For sure there's painters who have put them on – some portraits – gods, athletes, warriors, that sort of guy. Me – I'm sceptical. Why's you have figures on the inside of a bowl...?'

'Then leave them out,' says Amber. 'They do give a lilt, a rhythm, to the whirl, is all. It's my embellishment. Though – it's true – if it's a dance, it is monotonous.'

'Well,' Gary says. 'Whatever is the universe ... don't put me back where I came from – in the music biz.'

'Oh Gary,' Amber says, 'I'm sure there are some plans for you. Adventures like you've had – can't go to waste. The boss will tell me where your destiny may lead...'

'Aren't you the boss, then, Amber?' Gary asks. 'You know the places for good eats – I haven't seen you pay a bill...'

'Oh come on Gary,' Amber says. 'The hotpot – surely passes on the hots! It's made for that! I'm ready now... Initiation – you're a student of the rites... A hop upstairs, in this fine hostelry – a frieze of buddhas on the walls ... the flesh forever rising in new beastly shapes... New life! Gary... Don't think love, think porno, in 3D...'

'Wait!' says Gary, desperate. 'I hear the roar of Raoul outside ... that Studebaker...'

'Rubbish!' Amber shouts. 'Enough of your procrastinating crap! Raoul got lifted. He's inside, now staring at some walls. The motor – went for scrap...'

'A pause!' says Gary. 'Poor Raoul. Don't you think, dear Amber, this walking on the edge, you and your crew – forever stuck in purgatory, between the smaller and the larger bowl –

you surely long for cannonades, revenge and vindication, a
ceremony, recognition of your labours...'

'Yes, yes, of course,' says Amber. 'Jenny the Pirate is our
favourite song. You might have sent your groups out, chanting
it. It is the song for all musicians everywhere ... art unrequited,
guys with long hair, gals with short skirts, jigging the usual
jigajig – longing for a blast to knock down those hotels along the
front, their palmstrewn ballrooms, pianos out of tune, the
stadiums where wrestlers top the bill and you get booed ... the
covers and the repertoire dragged out, the managers who flit,
your druggie mates who don't show up... Yes, every trade is full
of it, and so the hatred grows, you pour the powder in the
culverins, take the slow match – and BOOM! Yes, Gary, that
outweighs all images of heaven and all hell... The biz! You're
right! The universal song ... it's plagiary, you're hired just to be
fired, you're blacked and ridiculed...'

'Oh no!' says Gary, 'I didn't know, poor Amber – you were
one of them... A singer, dancer – all those hopes, twinkled round
the room from glitter balls ... into oblivion...'

'Well,' Amber says, preening. 'That was long ago. I had a
voice ... once, I could flatten seas and dissipate the clouds, and
turn the world from dawn to dark...'

'It's a gift,' says Gary. 'If you're lucky. If you aren't lucky...'

'Oh Gary, I guess we're colleagues,' Amber says. 'Of a sort.'
She looks at him with deference. 'You were a big guy...'

'Music is the biggest thing,' says Gary. 'It's immeasurable.
Like the air.'

'Invisible,' Amber says. 'And better so.'

'Yes,' Gary says. 'I've been pondering ... my big idea... I
thought – why not a bandit city. Like those villages – everybody
equal. In a gang, a band. All the exploiting done outside the
bounds, a pacific skimming off... No lifelong jobs, no offices
with staring at the walls, no cops and robbers doing their scenes,

like in a town. It's just a tax, on guys just passing through, who want a profit too...'

'They'd bomb us, Gary,' Amber says.

'Yes,' says Gary, 'sure they would. You're right – the idea's bygone. Besides, there's precious animals that carry precious stuff... We've no rights on them.'

'It isn't always so, perhaps' says Amber. 'That there's always stronger ones that close you down. Sometimes – you do it all yourself, and screw it up. But, Gary, you should think again about those bandits. Even if we made it work – it all ends up the same. Or worse – normal...'

'It's transition, that's so slow,' says Gary. 'You speed things up – with a disaster. A flood, and massacre, a war. If you leave things just to work out – it takes millennia. Guys forget – they go through what there was. They think it's new – but no ... it's a version of the antique. And yet – these civilisations. You don't know you're in one, but if you aren't, you're a barbarian, a nameless – it's as if there's something to move towards, over and over, trying without knowing what, and if the limit's what you grope for, touch it, then – fall back. No further. Nothing to be done.'

'I'll show you Claude,' says Amber. 'He has worked with games – they play with us...'

She brings him up, and lights him. There he is, Gary's bathmate – lying on a slab – maybe he's naked, but his body is a cloth, a few bones collapsed inside, a desiccated jaguar – there are sprouts of hair, and empty skin in flounces, brocades of liver spots – he tries to rise, can't make it, rolls on his knees and elbows, his macaco's rump rears up... 'He knows there's a connection,' Amber says, 'but he can't see you. Anyway, his eyes don't work so well...'

'Games, Claude,' Amber shouts. 'Tell us about the games!'

'No one's interested,' Claude says. 'The games now – they're just for playing.'

'No, Claude,' says Amber. 'Liven up! Games are our pyramids, our magic mountains, our heights and hells, the plumed serpent, the flayed one. You remember? You said so – it's all we've been and knew...'

'Blasphemy!' shouts Claude. 'That's blasphemy. We're just fiddling now... Fire! Eruptions! That's how it always ended, while all we show is projections, reflections on the wall – it's all happened, all that's left is epic, actor guys running up and down the streets, shooting and setting fires. Those cities – of priests and warriors – even bankers – all so long ago. The Best, my friends – it was tried, it all exploded. There were real pilgrimages, on foot, on camel back, or inside real animals, prowling, growling, rattling – the snake, the croc, the puma... Mescalin days, my friend! We had a hot line, direct, to power, and the divine. No more!'

'There!' says Amber: 'Now, we can turn him off. He wouldn't recognise you, Gary. He gives these audiences, from his slab. Guys tune in, I guess. Purity and justice – he took so many baths – now look at him – covered in a spotted pelt, and reeking, that's for sure.'

'You need account for everything,' says Gary. 'Of course. For Everything. That done, you keep arriving at the limit. It's a meniscus, you push and push – quite impenetrable. Whenever you have lived, whatever exercise you take... Even the mescalin – it doesn't help. There is no other side. No beyond, no higher up, no resolution. We're animals, dear Amber – there is no way out, no beyond... Claude's games are like the scrawling on the walls – the hunts successful, the feasts that end in satisfaction, not in brawls ... the hero and his dog – immortal. But in the field, it isn't so.'

'Oh Gary,' Amber says, 'you're such a poet! Poor Claude ... and yet, he's lucky, he's too far degraded to have fears of death, he's gone outside himself...'

'But not to anywhere,' says Gary. 'No justice, and no purity.'

'He was your friend, that's all,' says Amber. 'It does good, seeing where people have got to, decades after. You thought they had the clue...'

'Getting together,' Gary says. 'To do what? Ten people – you could put on a play. But thousands, millions – being a civilisation. Does that put a shine on your eye?'

'Everybody asks that,' Amber says. 'Don't be banal. They ask that all the time.'

'That's odd,' Gary says. 'It's the first time I've thought of it.'

He thrusts Amber past a sign: 'Queen-size steamboat', it says.

'I'm full, Amber,' Gary says. 'Although my head's quite empty...'

'Oh Gary,' Amber says. 'You're so conventional – city, village, then and now, this mode or that, this or that sex, or country, colour... It's fluid, now: thoughts flow and scurry, irrigate the dust. We're pools of mercury ... planetary, scored deep, with canals full of liquid methane – we hiss and bubble, Gary. Of course – I could eat you up! Yumyum. Long pig – and you're so fresh and pink. But – of course, the decision doesn't rest with me. Hurry and have your big idea – or you could end up bad.'

'This food,' says Gary. 'It says to me – enough. That is enough.'

'You haven't followed, then,' says Amber. 'The Parsee food – it told you: we are carrion. The hotpot – we make half-forgotten empires, end up small. As the great statesman said – the fuckers fucked. Everyone's a halfbreed, born of male and female. If you'd had the steaboat – it shows, you boil yourself. Your spirit rises ... steam. You end up edible, not pure.'

'The message, then,' says Gary. 'Is quietist. Fixist, in a word. Those epics – they end so good: in finding love, or god, or vengeance, or all three.'

'Convention, Gary,' Amber says. 'That's for publication. In the real – the epic never ends: you sing the thousand verses, reach the entrepot and sell your stuff, buy new camels, then you're off again ... back. Not where you came from – you don't come from anywhere, no home, no rest. You sing to do your trade, not to achieve the silence that you want, Gary ... and your silence – it's Pax Eterna. That, we're given from the start.'

'What then, dear Amber?' Gary asks. 'Claude has boiled dry. He's back down, in the hypocaust, he hears the conches, sees the demons, pops the tabs – he's rattlers in his eyes – he sees the buckets full of blood, probably not his... But, Amber, you say there's none of this, no result. You don't get set up in the priesthood, carry the statue, win the medal, or the prize you have to gift to charity – you don't emerge. Down in the underground you stay. The rite is rite. It leads to nothing. Someone else takes on your trip. You're not even clean – there's snakes and cobwebs. And – where is justice, Amber?'

'Oh Gary – I'm not competent. I can ask around. But in the end – you'll have to ask a higher-up,' Amber says.

'And will they know?' asks Gary.

'That doesn't matter,' Amber says. 'It's not "know", it's "do". What they do, is justice. That is how it is.'

'Why do you cling?' asks Gary. 'Am I another voyager? You pal, do a few steps together, then... "Put another nickel in..." What's changed, dear Amber, is, there's no more nickelodeons – the rest is just the same. Out comes the "music, music, music". It's easy to think it up – each of us can conjure out a thousand tunes, all junked, until – the lucky strike: you are a millionaire! Hummed everywhere. Or – maybe not, so try again, again...What will you get with me, Amber, take from me?'

'Raoul,' says Amber. 'Got done for an absurdity. Cheating at cards! A victimless offence, for sure. So, this stretch of road – is mine alone, to work, to master. Maybe I'll be mayor. Or boss of all the bandits here... Liberation or dictatorship – or maybe both. I can't do all this alone... Nothing,' and she starts to weep. 'Alas, is ever done alone. No one's prepared, or has a store. You dump your kid in bushes – she can't hunt or speak. She'll need some guys to tell her what the story is, how to button up her frock and launch her spear...'

'It's true,' says Gary, thinking of the bell and all the sweat it takes to make a boom, a bong – 'Nature – no one is doing it. It rollers on – and so, it must be science, nothing cuddly, or motherly, at all. Things happen when some sum is totted up, makes stardust trickle in your eyes, equations balance out – and then – here come the rocks!...'

'Yes, Gary,' Amber says. 'I'm old. It's all old. Mathematics – hasn't changed for years, it's always been. How can we live so little, grow so old, and all around it's been here, tocking along, always right...'

'It's not that you are old, Amber,' Gary says. 'You're small.'

'It doesn't bother me,' says Amber. 'But – you mean that maths and physics, all the stuff we didn't follow when we were at school – is God, and all his purpose? Eternal, right, and logical? It seems so... What point in us, then; we slither round, fornicate, send messages of bland farewell...?'

'It doesn't bother me,' says Gary. 'If you're right.'

'It's death, Gary,' Amber says. 'That bothers you. Of course things like arithmetic don't bother you. Remember the Parsees' roof, the smell – not armpits, Gary, the whole shoot!'

'Bathe, Amber,' Gary says. 'That'll take it all away.'

'When you smell your death, Gary,' Amber says, 'it's getting late. You think – Paris, Moscow, Damascus – places where it's best not to be young, though you don't see so much; nor old –

though you don't have so long to look at things. But – we both know the middle size, the provinces.'

'That's where systems don't work – not at all, or bad...' says Gary.

'Or else a system's too high up, in the sky where you can't reach,' says Amber. 'So, people believe in providence, and saying "right!" without a thought too much...'

'Providence – a lottery,' Gary says. 'You never know if it has worked, for who. And where does it all lead – the logic and the brotherhood?'

'Adventurous guys like me,' says Amber. 'That's what it takes. We are the grease.'

Gary says, 'Maybe this has been my paradise, like the guy said, at the gate. Eating, being loved and watched – doing nothing. Speculating.'

'It's time to go up the road now, Gary,' Amber says.

                                    *

'We've been waiting ages for you, Gary,' Paolo says.

There's a hierarchy – guys in t-shirts and Bermuda pants – maybe they make connections, keep the lights a-buzz. Then suits – up from wool to aluminium, pewter, Sheffield, solid silver. Uniforms – the firemen – arsonists from Troy, stokers from hell with all the latest ... admirals from luggers and from packet boats, mine-trawlers and medusa rafts... The soldiers, with their plumes and whisks – 'My,' Gary says. 'You're some big cheese.'

'Oh no,' laughs Paolo, 'I'm at most a brie. We want to hear you big idea – Amber has sketched it in...'

'Oh no,' says Gary, backing off. 'I'm limited. People and places, that is all...'

'It's the meniscus,' Paolo says. 'I've samples here of many kinds. How to get through, to penetrate... Transcend. That's the word I want. Here,' and he pulls out paper cones. 'Here's where I command.'

There is no map. They're lists of middling cities, smaller countries spreading round about them.

'I thought you just lived in one space, manipulated one system, got chased out...' says Gary.

'Oh no,' laughs Paolo. 'A system is a system anywhere. Just like providence – though there's some dispute with that. We work it all a different way. Like draughts. Before, you governed just one middling city – say Vienna, San Francisco, Lima: now, with draughts, your piece takes all those of the same dimensions. When you reach an end, meniscus you would call it – you are crowned. You don't go off the board, don't go beyond – just get some boots with lifts, a bouffant wig, a golden hat. Then you can go to bigger places – like Montengrin princesses did, all that time ago...'

'It's true,' says Gary. 'Meniscus was my image, but...'

Paolo pushes on, 'You've heard of Modernism, the modern *Stil,* how it was adopted everywhere – remember those bars in the Sahel... It trumped art nouveau, and as for gothic ... they're... Nowhere, nowhere, Gary...'

'But ... the looks, beliefs...' says Gary.

'Oh, there's delicacy. Being robust. But it's lots of processions, martyrs, tall buildings...' Paolo says. 'The issues, Gary...'

'It sounds, put like that, quite opportunist,' Gary says.

'I knew you'd understand,' says Paolo. 'The point is this. Meniscus – on water, or on methane... You've heard of surface tension? That's what we deal with every day. The philosophy – well, remember the song about the long-legged fly – not a true fly, of course – moving on the water. Normally – a leg goes through – fly, or human, it's the same. A struggle, and you drown – fall into the hot, the other side, the other shore – the far, far side. What we don't want is fancy – saints and sinners. Saved and damned. That's not at all transcendence – rather, a provocation.'

'It's not meniscus, then,' says Gary, floundering, broken through, into the spate, being sucked under, sodden into oblivion. 'It's what's on the other side.'

'Yes, Gary,' says Paolo, patiently. 'That's my own analysis. Now, all these pomped up guys are waiting for your words. Don't disappoint!'

'What do we expect?' Gary improvises. 'How shall we be? Who else will be there – shall we be alone? Amber, perhaps...'

'Oh no,' says Paolo, 'Amber has no class. But let's not rush – the meniscus – maybe like a tunnel, joining continents – then, a thin wall, a film, between us ... us, and us...'

'Perhaps a parchment?' Gary says. 'A drum – the stick on one side, on the other – air and sound. An ear – one side – the silent mind. The other – chaos, tumbling in, unasked, unwanted...'

'What shall we eat?' asks Paolo. 'Maybe it's an evolution. Remember – hippos in Heidelberg. Neanderthals assimilated, integrating, becoming Germans just like all of us...'

'I didn't think of that,' says Gary, quite confused. 'And if we're not alone, in the cave, or what it is – are the others live or dead? And we – alive? Dead? And the silence ... we shall still communicate – as if we spoke, the signs, the shrugs – contentless. How deep will silence be, Paolo? – after people all together, maybe people will be apart, free, brains only, cupping minds forever quivering, their orifices like fish-mouths in a dough... And, Paolo – careful! – no trickery with machines, or motors of some kind...'

'If you think so, Gary,' Paolo says, 'but that's our destiny as animals ... those brains, you can't do without them, even if you're mind – they make me think of lambs' brains ... sautéd, laid on half-skulls, drawn butter, maybe caviar somewhere.'

'No, Paolo,' Gary says. 'Let's keep our eyes on the leap, the break, the quality, the change...'

'The last transcendence,' Paolo says, 'is in my work. The city, Gary, and its government. That was when we became no longer animals – before, the hunt, the trek to find a breakfast, blundering into other bands, and running off – food, Gary! Seek! Find! We can't chum with them, those lookalikes.The larder! Remember our poor store! Nothing to go round.'

'Amber was strong on food,' says Gary. 'It's true – the city... S – gone under the volcano, into the rift, under the sea, into dust and under it, burnt, bombed, buried – the people all dispersed... I have no city, Paolo. That's why I remember it – I have no memory, it's true, but ... the city's where we grew. Stopped being wolves.'

'Oh Gary,' Paolo says, 'I've lots, of cities. Without them – yes, we'd be hyenas, dingo dogs.'

The thought's alarming, might it be so? Gary wonders, says, 'We should go together, Paolo. Through the barrier... Transcend once more.'

'Of course, Gary,' Paolo says. 'Tell me,' he asks shyly. 'How are you on capitalism? There's those who think that was transcendence too... invisible and clean, flies through the air – a flighty bird, made of blue glass and spit – how it transforms, though, builds tall nests...'

'It's dangerous, Paolo,' Gary says, carefully. 'There's criminals around, wherever...'

'Oh, Gary, I know all that,' says Paolo. 'But – we want to get away from what we were, from history, all the awful stuff; betrayals, paranoia, raids and persecutions ... Read a book of it, you'll puke... None of that, the past, the memories, none that we'd want to take with us... But – for sure, we'll need to take some cash, clean stuff. Something abstract that we can invest. Remember – in the world, there's fifteen million guys in goldmines. Dirty gold, Gary, massacres. Another crime upon the list – not one of those goldminers lives in any city I'm responsible for. Think, Gary – you'll have things you'll want to leave behind. It's best to start off clean. Your misogyny – that, you'll want to dump, for sure.'

'No, Paolo,' Gary says, offended. 'Women have been more than my equals, and I treat them so. As for crimes – Raoul was innocent, and yet...'

'Guys like that, Gary – they're our citizens too. Rust, obsolescence, motors running down ... that inventive road – it's not transcendence, Gary. Maybe it's a sport – those robots!' Paolo talks on, walking Gary up and down before the firemen in their shiny hats, tax farmers with their shabby gladstones...

'The other side, the other shore – it'll be clean, for sure,' says Paolo. 'The cyanide, the mercury – all that behind us. Maybe – Gary, you're not gay? Maybe we should take some ballerinas, balance it all out. Someone to carry all our bags – we might, no, we must, stay for a while. Then bring the others in...'

'No, Paolo,' Gary says. 'It's not I'm gay or not – I don't think the other shore – if we arrive – is interested in that sort of thing. You must prepare for something spiritual...'

'Oh no!' says Paolo. 'That's the word I didn't want to hear. Everything must change, change totally. Us, our bodies – yet more intense and more complete, and on an upward slope – not always drudging down, like life is here...'

'I don't know, Paolo, how it might be there, or even if it is a place...' says Gary.

'Don't dither, Gary,' Paolo says. '*Davai! Avanti Savoia! Aux armes! And ever upward!*'

They link arms. They move their feet. A curtain, or a celluloid, a shudder, a transparency, a wrapping – it's a struggle... Then, they're through.

*

Gary sees the walls – faintly pink, and distant sounds of tinkling, bells or bottles... A cave. There's Mae, on the wall, still dead and splayed. And all the other shades, 'If they were ghosts,' he thinks, 'they'd laugh or cry – but maybe they aren't ghosts. So what? What did ghosts do for me?'

There's Claude – he's moribund, but still alive and giving views on everything to all the world; the profs disputing Everything, Nadine – creeping towards power; and high up on the roof, between those ribs of stone, perhaps, all cobwebby, and clinging like a bat is Fancy, mouth agape, and shrieking silent and not loved enough... Amber is missing – for sure she's stopping motorists, climbing in beside them, working out some scam... Another who's not loved enough but doesn't care, she's marshal of the asphalt now...

'Paolo,' Gary says. 'What do you see?'

'Oh, nothing much,' says Paolo. 'To be honest – it looks like some vague plans I had, for making a new happy place, a pavilion, a divan for heavy talkers...'

'Well,' Gary says, 'we mustn't be surprised. If there's no transcendence: that just shows – we didn't make it. Maybe it's just us. Or it's the species. It's worth knowing, anyway. You and I – we'll never be the same – we made the steps, into the underground...'

'It didn't seem that way to me,' says Paolo. 'I was alone, and it was bright and pastel. Lit, and on a rise.'

'Nothing for me,' says Gary, 'was resolved. I only saw the past – a pond, where every creature lasts a day, and eats the others and gets ate...'

It wasn't so. Nothing got eaten. No one said anything of note, or different from what they'd said before.

'Purity and justice' – there was Annie mouthing it again. 'The spirit's in the bottle,' how she laughed, repetition was her forte...

'We could have taken Amber,' Paolo says. 'She would have danced for us.' He sounds disappointed. 'She was the best. The black swan, the Sacrifice. It's a reproach for me – her excellence: I should raise my game. The middling sort – it's not for me. You know, Gary, sometimes I feel a rage – you know what they say to me, "You're a *güter Mensch*, a good man – but you've no morals." Not true, but it ought to be. My rage is justified, of course. How do you manage, Gary?'

'I take it on the chin, Paolo, like they say. What else can you do? Making the best of things – isn't that the best?' says Gary. He wonders – was he on the wall, himself – what, young? Fresco? Unrecognisably old...

'Of course,' says Paolo, 'I have my people – not the clowns made up,' and he waves to his dressy court. 'Real people. Who know how to cheat at cards,' and he laughs... 'You need to structure your life inside each episode... When I was with Amber – the food ... the dance ... domestic, self-contained. It holds you back. Your ankles yield, your gut shoots out... The heights, Gary. How'd you get up there...?'

'The heights don't change, Paolo, there's no revelation, no better view. They stay heights, whether you are up on them, or if it's someone else – as it will be...' says Gary. 'Heights is nothing special.'

'Amber's to be watched,' says Paolo. 'She has no house, no dwelling, there's no interior that's hers, no context. We can't count that old DeSoto... She's an extravagant, a wanderer.'

'You did a stretch of road with her?' asks Gary.

'You start so,' Paolo says. 'Working a strip. Then it's to a village, and so, and so. Some are fixed on that first track, the banditry, the flow of people, rich, desperate, some with donkeys, some with bundles, others...'

'Yes,' Gary says, 'that's attractive. That tells you about the destinations, and the chance of getting there or – then, there's the fucking tunes they sing, that infest your ears. Songs of the fleas! Away, away!'

'It must have meaning,' Paolo says. 'If it doesn't, you must give it one. Then – it has meaning! Does it lie in Everything? Or in the epic? Not the cave you say you saw, but the penetration, piercing the wall, the surface... Some heroes making it, other not – is that the meaning? Trivial! Justice? Between us, Gary – who cares? You're not into that, perhaps, the epic. You need to start with something – as a toddler, even, if you want to end up universal. There's better, though. Through the walls, the curtains, the distances... Seeing the new, the lovely, people, on their couches, sending messages, burnishing their knives...' He laughs: some of this he doesn't mean. 'Well, Gary, we must find your S, your city. Are you sure it wasn't Stockholm?'

'Yes,' Gary says. 'I'm absolutely sure. Don't bother. I left, it went – it can't have been significant. There'll have been a market, selling camels, that's for sure. But once – they were all over everywhere. Sunfilled markets: the poor beasts. It doesn't matter, Paolo.'

'No,' Paolo says, 'it doesn't. Being killed, quite unexpectedly – that matters more.'

'I don't think about it much,' says Gary. 'Unexpectedly? What's the force in that?'

'I know,' says Paolo, 'I don't think about it at all. I think about it all the time. There's guys paid to think and act – they're everywhere. Acting – that's tough, as professions go – must be the worst. I don't intend to be a victim. That's the trick. There's guys paid to stop me being victim – I think about them all the time – but ... thinking, no, that's not quite it. You'd go crazy, if you thought. You'd reach conclusions, if you thought.'

'What's the trick, Paolo?' asks Gary, quite confused.

'I believe in religions, Gary,' Paolo says, 'and home and family, and rights. It's my job. If you want to leave my territory – then go. I'll be the sovereign – but if you think I've done you bad – then say! If that's not enough, then fight. But ... if it goes too far – I'll smash you. Play dirty – I'll be dirty too. You understand, I'm sure. Respect, Gary – it's the first, the necessary step, towards the justice that we want.'

*

How we laughed, in Rehab, in Dark City, Gary thinks. It's obligatory – everything, they say, has a funny side.

He meets with Amber, for a Viking meal. Porridge and oatcakes. 'It's synthetic stuff,' says Amber. 'Sets you up, and solid for a week – then we chip you out, and you can start again. Of course – those Vikings – a degenerate lot. Slavers. Farmers on their holidays, sacking other farmers' crops.'

'This Paolo,' Gary says. 'Small cheese, a poppy of the middling height... He doesn't seem cut out for visions and diasporas ... intuiting and holding on.'

'Oh no,' says Amber, fiercely. 'Love unrequited – I went through all that. He's the master. Did you see his dull black eyes?'

'You go through that with everyone, Amber,' says Gary. 'Try to be manipulative, and lie. You're happier so...'

'Oh Gary,' Amber says, hugging him. 'You creep. You pick up rocks, but rarely do you throw them, hit the gold... Paolo? – we'll push him up and suck him down and out. Make him one of us, or one of them. If he can't perform – we'll huff him – that way he'll find out what draughts is all about. He's not your kind, Gary. Snuggle in his thoughts, tell me if he has some – and leave the vengeance for us tougher guys.'

'Still,' says Gary, 'I hear you softening.'

'No,' says Amber. 'I cry easy. Especially kittens.'

Gary eats, reluctantly, from an iron pot. A long iron ladle: a black oak stool: – the black kitchen stacked with iron pots and ladles. A block. An iron spindle, iron griddles, spits.

'Now, iron man,' says Amber. 'You've eaten to your brim: you can't decay, just rust. You're ready now.'

By the road, there is a cistern. 'No, Amber,' Gary says. 'This is not a bath. You don't get clean in there.'

'You're wrong, Gary,' Amber says. 'And right. You've those two tedious myths – the pure, the just. Come, down in the water,' and she leads him down. 'You see,' she says, 'You're used to lilac, cyclamen, clinging to a wall, or blue powders, taken from the sea and frosting out – a paste, a dust, that slowly dries and – out comes what there was before. The blue before the water. You know what that can be, Gary, though now there's clouds – once: nothing. Nothing at all, for ever. Here – the water's green. Come on in, come down, open your eyes – it's bottle green, and you're a liquid, made of a hundred grasses, a *centerbe*, water of life, strong like you're made at the beginning – it makes you laugh and dance – and vomit too, and in the end, it kills – but ... this is where the beasts once came, your little camels, Gary, and you see what they could glimpse – the green before, the garden where they hoped to live eternally... Not being bright, clued up, like us – until the final day, they thought they would persist, amid the lush, the peonies, the hollyhocks... Maybe the thought will give you strength ... though when you're out and in the air again, you won't be clean; I shan't be just.'

'I see – I saw – something,' Gary says. 'I don't know what. Stagnant water, there for years, for centuries perhaps.'

'Perhaps – something will come to you,' says Amber. 'Not everyone has the chance, the offer.'

'It's a great gift, Amber,' Gary says. 'You tried to give. No one else tried, not like you. I do appreciate...'

'When you're asked to help us out with Paolo,' Amber says. 'No one would believe that ... something so repugnant to you – your cleanliness ... your judgment ... didn't have a sentimental undercoat. I could show you: I could dance for you.'

'It might make me, well, on edge,' says Gary. 'In return – might you ask me to do some harm to Paolo? – I don't admire him, true, but not like you, it's not he's not done what I want. He is, in principle – a person threatening, destructive...'

'My dance,' Amber persists. 'Is better far than love. Dance can't be unrequited. It's what you might be, Gary, your naked self, as I might see you.'

'Exactly so,' says Gary. 'Best kept covered up...'

But, of course, she has begun.

She's clumsy, and unshaven. Embarrassing. Without inhibition. Her show would need a great set of gestures in return.

*

Paolo is no more.

'I didn't want justice done to Paolo,' Gary says. 'Maybe justice doesn't enter in at all. If it isn't done all round, it doesn't count, they say. Paolo – the people's choice. What's involved in that? Who cares if he's been chosen? If he's corrupt...'

'Such drama!' Amber says. 'No one asked you to load the gun or heft the two-by-four. People are punished all the time, you know. Mostly you play a tiny part. If he's a crook, other crooks will take it out on him, and take his place. If he's just good or bad ... like if he's good *and* bad, getting rid of him – it's right and wrong. Whatever happens – it takes lots of guys, and any blame is spread around.'

'I don't feel bad,' says Gary. 'Just, another person, not me, can do everything I've done. And I could walk away.'

'It's deep stuff,' Amber says. 'I could put it clearer. You're one of us, all of us. But – my dance...'

'Oh yes,' says Gary. 'It binds us two, like nothing else.'

'And love?' Amber asks. 'You may not know it, but that's the closest you will get to what you want... Beyond the limits of the self.'

'And then it flies away,' says Gary. 'Turns from eagle into snake – like you and Paolo. Me – with Nadine: who remembers that? It ended in a morning's mystery...'

'Oh well,' says Amber, 'if you want that truth, about what really happens – there's murder too. That resolves, gives you a shove, and everything is bright, potential... Everyone is doing it – guys and gals, nephews of the Genghiz, grandsons of Agamemnon, daughters of Eve and Eva Braun... Yours is an academic quest, Gary. Are you satisfied you're not dissatisfied? If you don't like the palace I'll move into – build one yourself, hatch out the peacocks from these eggs...'

'Those, Amber,' Gary says, 'those are ostriches'.'

'You have to follow in processions,' Amber says, irritated, 'if you want your coronation.'

'There are limits,' Gary says. 'I've encountered all of them. If you read some books – we're all born Jewish. That prof – has a theory of Everything – and you don't need even to read.'

'I'm the first one to have helped you, Gary,' Amber says. 'You've not begun to experience dreadful things. You've no idea if you have principles, and if they would resist. You think you've been exploited – really, you've always been compliant so's you could end on top.'

'I could drop, I guess,' says Gary. 'Would I have learned more so? Gone to rescue some group interned, embottled in some disaster, public, photographed, eternal?'

'I've shown you everything,' says Amber. 'You've swallowed it.'

'Paolo went silently,' says Gary. 'I don't think he'd anything inside his belly.'

'I left nothing out,' says Amber, weeping now. 'If you could be instructed, civilised – I've done my best.'

'What's left, then, Amber?' Gary asks, despairing. 'Spaghetti? *Coratella?* Pluck?'

'You're lost, Gary,' Amber says, mocking a little. 'You've always been lost, but there was other people, mercenaries and holy monks, butchers, ambassadors – enthusiasm and sacrifice along with the destruction. Now, I can only lead you through the ruins... They don't even look like ruins – the lights, the colours...'

'I'm not a fighter, Amber,' Gary says. He sounds quite miserable.

'That's why you're still here,' says Amber. 'Eating the thorn bushes. And fighting's stupid. Creep up behind – it pays off, you go home at day's end.'

'I must go on,' says Gary. 'But I've been everywhere.'

'I'd send you up the line,' says Amber. 'There's guys who boss whole continents – clean hands, don't count the bodies, pay someone else to do what you must do...'

'Amber,' says Gary. 'You're lyrical – but it's all your gang...'

'Don't play the innocent, my dear,' says Amber. 'You've spun the wheel, like all the rest. Now – take the next step, with clean feet...'

*

These baths are in the modern style. Beneath, there is eternal flame.

'Those scraggy birds,' says Gary to the guy. 'Ostriches. Peacocks...'

'Don't be put off,' says the guy. 'They're black and bald, but – they aren't what you think. They boiled themselves...' and he shoos them off.

'There's a miasma here,' says Gary. 'The water's grey.'

'Oh,' says the guy. 'It's age. There's copper in those gold taps – it leeches out, and there's the oil below, that heats. It's old old leaves. The stones – you'd not believe – they're full of creeping things, the crap of snails, the eyes of toads...' He laughs. 'This was all hot sea. Salty as a cod. Then it was peaks. From drownings into avalanche: it's history – every day there's more. They say it's always different. But only Southerners like you come here to bathe. The nordics – they aren't pure, even when they sweat...'

'Are there drownings here, despite...?' Gary asks. 'I've always found a peace, a laugh or two, here in the water, with no uniform... The dust outside, the grit in your skin...'

Some birds flap off. There's circling overhead, a buzzing ... quite mechanical.

'I'm off to see a guy much higher up,' says Gary, swallowing some fear. 'I'm told I must be pure.'

'Oh, my dear,' the guy says. 'You're not ready for the end, not yet. Those skinny little legs of yours – they'll carry you along some tracks... And as for laughs – most gods relax a bit, and even like a game. *Go,* or darts. It's blasphemy to say – but most are multiple: they've personalities cloned, they can play with – or against – themselves, they've spirits inside...'

'Like bottled jinn,' says Gary. 'No, my friend. I'm not prepared for death – but to meet a guy who's at the top, a king of kings, shah of shahs, the big malk, maharajah, lord of the elephants... My lookalike, my brother...'

'That's the right attitude,' says the bath attendant, the guy. 'Prepare your questions. Defer to the answers. Don't speak of scaffolds, hookahs – you're in a no-smoke area. The revolution's done, it's onward, now, and upward. Don't look up – there is a buzzing in the sky, but ignore all that, or else it looks like there's a higher-up, above the guy you're talking to...'

'Maybe now, my friend,' says Gary. 'You could whip me with those thorny twigs...'

And so he does. It's the guy's job.

*

'Any tips?' Gary asks, leaving.

'Usually you give me one,' the guy says, irritated. 'When you see the big boss, say where you're from and why you have no family. Accept the task you're set.'

'I come from S,' says Gary.

'Sicily? It's a good story,' says the guy. 'It's in the middle.'

'A city,' Gary says. 'I'm sure it doesn't exist, but I must have parents, come from a place. I'm just beginning. I'm clean. I want to see scores settled – once and for all.' The guy nods, not grasping much.

'If you see justice,' Gary says. 'If you get justice – you'll have an explanation of it all. That is for sure.'

*

Here's the building. Where the boss is.

Gary goes up the steps.

ABOUT THE AUTHOR

John Fraser has lived in Rome since 1980. Previously, he worked in England and Canada.

www.ingramcontent.com/pod-product-compliance
Lightning Source LLC
Chambersburg PA
CBHW020422180626
46812CB00003B/1103